Praise for Maggie Knox

'An utterly adorable, pitch-perfect romance with
just the right amount of Christmas cheer . . . a
pure delight, I couldn't stop from smiling'
Taylor Jenkins Reid

'A fun and fabulous festive read'
Heidi Swain

'I thoroughly enjoyed this story of finding
yourself while being someone else'
Sue Moorcroft

'I devoured this delightful romantic comedy
in two nights . . . it's perfect'
Colleen Oakley

'Deliciously fun and wildly romantic . . . like *The
Great British Bake Off* meets *Gilmore Girls*'
Jennifer Robson

'A double dose of fun-loving, feel-good, Christmas cheer,
with a recipe for love that's deliciously irresistible'
Karen Schaler

ALSO BY MAGGIE KNOX

The Holiday Swap

TITLES BY KARMA BROWN

The 4% Fix: How One Hour Can Change Your Life
Recipe for a Perfect Wife
The Life Lucy Knew
In This Moment
The Choices We Make
Come Away with Me

TITLES BY MARISSA STAPLEY

Lucky
The Last Resort
Things to Do When It's Raining
Mating for Life

ALL I WANT FOR CHRISTMAS

Maggie Knox

HODDER

First published in Great Britain in 2022 by Hodder & Stoughton
An Hachette UK company

5

A CIP catalogue record for this title is available from the British Library

Paperback ISBN 978 1 529 35639 7
eBook ISBN 978 1 529 35640 3

Printed and bound in Great Britain by Clays Ltd, Elcograf S.p.A.

Hodder & Stoughton policy is to use papers that are natural, renewable
and recyclable products and made from wood grown in sustainable
forests. The logging and manufacturing processes are expected to
conform to the environmental regulations of the country of origin.

Hodder & Stoughton Ltd
Carmelite House
50 Victoria Embankment
London EC4Y 0DZ

www.hodder.co.uk

This book is dedicated to our agents and north stars,
Carolyn Forde and Samantha Haywood

Three chords and the truth—
that's what a country song is.

—WILLIE NELSON

Three chords and the truth—
that's what a country song is.

−WILLIE NELSON

All I Want for Christmas

Last

Christmas . . .

Max

Nashville, Tennessee
December 1

What am I doing?

The question had been nagging at Max Brody all day. Actually, ever since he'd agreed to join *Starmaker*'s country music reality show, making him one of twenty contestants vying for that coveted first place.

Most people would think Max didn't need any of what a *Starmaker* win could mean—not the money, nor the fame. He had grown up in the Nashville celebrity spotlight, thanks to his father, Holden Brody, who was an iconic country music singer. And yet, here Max was: on a soundstage, trying to decide between a rock-hard blueberry muffin or a days-old custard pastry from the craft-services table. He chose neither and turned back to watch the other contestants warming up on the stage.

The room was decked out in preparation for the upcoming

holiday-themed shows, and it did look festive. But everything was fake—from the plastic evergreen boughs, to the cotton swaths of "snow"—which left Max feeling less than merry.

He didn't want to be here but *Starmaker* was Max's last kick at the can to make music on his own terms, in his own way—something he had so far been unable to do. Sure, he had released an album (who hadn't, in his music-royalty boots?), but the record hadn't done well. There had been no real splash, low sales . . . certainly nothing to warrant a second album.

Since then, he had been knocking around Nashville, being featured in entertainment magazines ("Who Is Max Brody, Son of the Great Holden Brody, Dating Now?" and "How Does Max Brody Keep That Stunning Six-Pack Looking So Fine?") and waiting for his next great thing so he could prove he had "it," just like his dad. No . . . to prove he was *nothing* like his dad. To show everyone he could be a star, too, but not the way his dad had done it—which, in Max's view, had meant trading fame for his soul. Holden Brody was as well-known for his addictions and philandering as he was for his Hall of Fame country music songs.

So, Max knew it was nearly time—*past time*—to leave Nashville, with its suffocating expectations and musical heartbreaks, behind.

"We don't *need* this, that's for sure," he whispered to his dog (and best confidante), tucking her squirming body deeper under his arm.

Patsy Canine, Max's rescue pup, was a papillon mix and ten pounds (if that) soaking wet. Her tiny body had a light coverage of hair, but her ears, which were twice the size they should have been based on her body, had waterfalls of blond hair cascading from them. Patsy continued wiggling inside the lavender-hued cable-knit sweater she wore, trying to get closer to the sugary pastries.

"Hey there! No dogs near craft services." Max turned at the familiar voice.

"Why must you always be breaking some rule, Max Brody?" Tasha Munroe added, before pulling Max into a hug, making Patsy squeal at the sudden crush.

"Oh, sorry there, Patsy Canine," Tasha said, giving the dog a chin scratch. Max had known Tasha since they were kids, and she was one of his closest friends. Though she had started out singing in her church choir, Tasha Munroe had fallen in love with country music and the world had fallen in love with her. With multiple platinum albums under her rhinestone belt, and at only thirty-two, she was the artist that most up-and-coming musicians wished to emulate. A superstar now, Tasha was better at deflecting the negative aspects of celebrity than Max was. She never apologized for her ambition and knew precisely who she was.

Now she gave Max a once-over. "Damn, how are you always so *freaking* effortless?"

Max not only had the musical pedigree, he had also inherited his father's impossibly good looks: dark hair that settled back into perfect waves when he ran a hand through it; a five-o'clock shadow that worked so well on him you'd wonder why he'd ever shave; cheekbones for days, and long eyelashes that framed deep brown eyes.

"You're one to talk," Max replied, to which Tasha waved a hand, dismissing the compliment.

"Smoke and mirrors. You know show business."

Tasha took a muffin from the craft-services table and then grimaced at its obvious staleness.

"That's what you get for agreeing to be a judge on a B-level show," Max said, looking pointedly at the sad muffin.

Starmaker had once been the hottest ticket in Nashville, garnering millions of viewers. Tasha Munroe had been discovered in the first season—chosen by the great country music producer Cruz McNeil, who was one of the show's creators—and was now back as a guest judge. But recent seasons were lagging. Perhaps the show's predictable format was tiresome to viewers, especially in a sea of reality show options, but there had been much talk and anticipation that this year was going to get it back on top of the Nielsen ratings. And from the producers' perspective, Max Brody was a big part of the strategy.

"Now, come on," Tasha replied. "Didn't you hear we have *the* Max Brody joining this season?"

They both laughed, and Tasha broke off a piece of the stale muffin for Patsy.

"Tash!" Max twisted away, but not before Patsy got the treat. "You know she can't have gluten."

Tasha rolled her eyes, her fake eyelashes so long they hit above her eyebrows. "Max, *you know she can.* Look how happy she is. Aren't you, girl? Aren't you?" Tasha cooed, giving her another small bit of muffin despite Max's annoyed glare. "Nice sweater, by the way."

"Oh, thanks." Max ran his hand over Patsy's sweater and felt a wave of pride.

On the stage in front of them, a dozen or so of the other contestants were warming up. Max had no clue who the contestants were, or what their stories were, because he hadn't met any of them yet—he hadn't bothered to.

It was probably time to pay closer attention because these contestants were his competition. But the white noise of the mingling voices made it tough for anyone to rise above the rest.

Until one did.

The voice that reached him belonged to a woman at the edge of the stage, closest to where Max and Tasha stood. It wasn't just that she was closest to Max. It was that her voice had that rare quality to it you didn't often hear—even in Nashville.

Tasha heard it, too, and nodded at the woman—whose long dark hair was in a braid over her shoulder, a baggy sweatshirt worn over plain black tights.

"That's Sadie Hunter," Tasha said. "Sort of a Brandi Carlile thing going on, right?"

Max frowned, watching Sadie Hunter pace in a slow circle near the edge of the stage. Then she turned toward them, and Max got a complete picture: she wasn't just talented, she was gorgeous, too. A gentle pink hue to her cheeks, and *those eyes*. Blue as a bluebird.

Tasha nudged Max's shoulder with her own. "Pretty as a peach."

"In that vanilla popstar sort of way, I guess." Max shrugged. "Bit sweet for me."

"Hmm," Tasha replied, giving him a wry smile. "I don't know, she sort of seems just your type."

"Hush up." Max raised his eyebrow at his friend.

Just then Cruz McNeil sidled up to them, a young guy with movie-star hair and a huge smile following a step behind him.

"Tasha, love, I want you to meet someone," Cruz said, completely ignoring Max. His silver hair was immaculately styled, but he still ran a hand over it to ensure there were no strands out of place.

Max was more than familiar with Cruz McNeil. Not only was he the producer and top judge on *Starmaker*, Cruz was *the* starmaker in town. At only forty-five, he had produced some of the highest-earning albums in the world and now had his own record label. And despite some unpleasant rumors, anyone he chose to work with became a sensation—including Max's own father.

"This is Johnny King," Cruz said. Johnny stepped forward with a bold confidence that belied his young age.

"Ms. Munroe, I'm your biggest fan. 'Lightning and Cowboys' is my theme song," Johnny said, shaking Tasha's hand enthusiastically.

"Is it now?" Tasha said, smiling at him. Max tried not to chuckle. "Lightning and Cowboys" was Tasha's most well-known hit, so Johnny using it to try to impress Tasha had, in Max's opinion, the opposite effect.

"Have you met Max Brody, Johnny?" Tasha turned to Max, her expression suggesting he should engage in this social nicety, especially because Cruz was looking on.

"Hey, man, good to meet you," Max said, shifting Patsy so he could shake Johnny's hand. "Good luck out there."

"Oh, Johnny doesn't need luck, Max," Cruz said, finally acknowledging his presence.

"I think we all need a little luck, Cruz," Tasha said pointedly.

"We sure do!" Johnny replied, grinning like a kid who had just been given all-out access to a candy store.

Cruz gave an almost imperceptible sigh. "Time to go," he said, nudging Johnny back toward the stage with the others. "See you at the table, Tasha?"

"I'll be right there," she replied breezily. She waited a beat after Cruz left before saying, "Max, you'd better get out there, too. I know Cruz can be frustrating. But he's the head judge. Don't piss him off before it even begins, okay?"

Max took a deep breath. "Yeah, I know." Then he looked around for his assistant. His longtime manager, Bobbi Lovett, had insisted that the *Starmaker* deal included an on-set assistant, despite his protests that he needed no such thing. Max liked to do things his own way.

"Hey . . . ummm . . . hey," Max said, pointing to the guy he had met the day before.

"That's Landon," Tasha whispered.

"How do you always know everything?" Max retorted, keeping his voice low.

Tasha smiled and shrugged, before sashaying back to the judges' table.

"What can I do for you, Mr. Brody?" Landon said. He kept his eyes on Tasha two seconds too long.

Max gave his fingers a couple of snaps. "Hey, Landon? Over here, man."

Landon turned back to Max, looking slightly dazed, his reaction slower than a Sunday afternoon.

"First of all, please call me Max." He handed Patsy to Landon, who held her at arm's length like she was a wriggling snake.

"Don't you worry, Landon, she's all bark and no bite," Max said, clipping her leash onto her collar. "Just don't try to take off her sweater—she hates that. And keep her on leash, at all times."

Landon nodded, looking nervous. Patsy gave Max a look that suggested she felt betrayed to be left in the care of such a novice.

"See you soon, girl," Max said. "Have fun with Landon."

Neither the assistant nor the dog seemed to think this was possible, but Max couldn't worry about that. He had to shift gears; it was time to be *the* Max Brody people were expecting to show up. As he climbed the few stairs to the main stage, he noticed Sadie Hunter watching him. He offered her the Brody smile, which disarmed even the grumpiest of folks, but she narrowed her eyes, her mouth set in a tight line.

"Whatever," Max grumbled under his breath, holding her gaze. He didn't have the time or energy for drama. He wasn't going to let anyone, including Sadie Hunter, distract him.

2

Sadie

Nashville, Tennessee
December 1

Sadie Hunter closed the equipment locker door behind her and sank down to the dusty floor. She pulled out her phone and opened the meditation app she had recently downloaded, then popped in her earbuds. The soothing sound of a flowing river began. She closed her eyes and breathed in through her nose, as the velvet-voiced narrator instructed, then out through her mouth. But when the voice gently urged her to clear her mind, she ran into trouble. As usual, her mind became a chaotic vortex of worries. *What if I don't win? Am I going to have to go back to Wisconsin again? If I stay here, what am I going to do about money? How will I pay my rent?*

Sadie had quit her job waiting tables at a busy meat and three in the Gulch after earning a spot on *Starmaker*. Now she had a chance to vie for the five-hundred-thousand-dollar prize—including the opportunity to record an album with star producer Cruz McNeil, which for Sadie was perhaps the most alluring part—but that prize was only a long shot. She had now spent a solid seven years of her life working toward her big break—and on days like this, even though she was in the middle of taking one giant step forward, she could feel the yawning chasm behind her. If she didn't win, she'd have to go back to playing small gigs anywhere she could find them. Touring college venues and trying to convince herself that singing the national anthem to rowdy crowds waiting for a game buzzer was going to get her somewhere.

Or she'd have to give up.

Sadie increased her phone's volume, but it didn't do any good. The persistent voice in her head just got louder, asking how she was ever going to be happy if she gave up on her dream. Plus, the river was now loud enough to remind her of whitewater rapids. Sadie squeezed her eyes shut against the cacophony. *Clear your mind. Clear your mind.*

Instead, she found her mind filling with thoughts of Max Brody. She had seen him chatting casually with Tasha Munroe earlier. Tasha was one of Sadie's musical idols. That morning, Sadie had noticed Tasha standing nearby, listening to her practice—and now she imagined Tasha had been telling Max that Sadie was no competition for him, that he had nothing to worry about when it came to her.

What was Max Brody even doing on *Starmaker*? He couldn't possibly need money or to win a recording contract. He was Nashville royalty already. He was used to getting whatever he wanted—and treating people however he wanted. When their eyes had met as he passed by the soundstage earlier she hadn't seen a hint of recognition in his expression. But they had met, years earlier, the first time Sadie had tried to make a go of it in Nashville—before she had run out of money and been forced to temporarily move back home. Meeting Max Brody was a memory she tried to suppress, and one Max had clearly forgotten. Sadie wondered if she was the only person who knew that underneath his handsome, charming exterior, and despite the fact that he carried the most adorable dog around with him wherever he went, held doors, and minded his Southern manners, the truth was, Max was a jerk.

She slid her phone out of the pocket of her baggy sweatshirt and turned off the meditation app, then hit the FaceTime icon and held her breath. Soon, her gran's face would appear on-screen and she'd have a few moments of being reminded that she needed to believe in herself and her lifelong dream.

But it wasn't Gran who answered.

"Sadie! What's wrong? You look upset!"

"Mom." Sadie quickly wiped under her eyes, but knew she couldn't magically erase the stress-induced dark circles there. "I'm fine. I'm just . . ." But she knew if she told her mom how she was feeling, Lynn would insist that the solution was simple: come home. Forget about the dream that had done nothing but cause her years of disappointment. Forget, even, about the exciting long shot that was *Starmaker*. Lynn spent a lot of time worrying about her only child's well-being and had decided long ago that the music industry was a dangerous place for Sadie. A place where a person could easily get hurt.

"Is Gran there? I wanted to say a quick hi to her, that's all. See if she's recovered."

"She's here but she's just lying down," Lynn said, and for a moment Sadie thought she saw a flicker of sadness cross her mother's face. But then there was a commotion in the background and Sadie smiled as she heard her gran insisting she was perfectly fine. Seconds later, Gran's face appeared, first sideways, then upside down.

"Hello? Can you hear me? Is this thing on?"

"Loud and clear, Gran."

"This contraption you gave me so we could keep in touch when you moved back to Nashville actually works!"

"It's not a contraption," Sadie said, still smiling. "It's a smartphone."

"Well, it *is* that. Smart as a cookie." Gran squinted into the screen. "Where on earth are you right now, Sadie Jane? A closet?"

"We-elll—"

"Sadie Jane *Hunter!* Please tell me you aren't having one of your episodes. What happened with the meditating? It works for Lady Gaga."

"Doesn't work for me," Sadie muttered.

"Well, she probably doesn't do it in an equipment closet. Come on, stand up. Brush yourself off. Get back out there and do what *I know* you were put on this world to do."

Sadie could hear her mother in the background, telling Gran to ease up and not push Sadie so hard, that there were plenty of other things she could do with her life. But Sadie knew this wasn't true.

"Okay, okay, maybe I *am* having a small episode. Thanks for snapping me out of it, Gran."

"Tell me about the other contestants. Who do you need to look out for?"

Sadie decided not to mention Max Brody. She knew Gran was a big fan of his father, Holden Brody, and didn't want to hear her swoon about Sadie getting to be one degree from great-ness. "There's this one guy, Johnny King, who has a pretty good voice, but he's also got this *presence*. You just *want* to watch him. He's the one I'm worried about. And he's only twenty-one years old!"

"Are you going to start insisting that at twenty-eight years old you're a washed-up old lady again?! Remember who you're talking to."

"Twenty-eight isn't that young, not in the music world."

"Nonsense," Gran said. "Age is just a number. Your beauti-ful voice is going to be what people notice."

"My voice might not be enough."

Gran moved her face close to the screen, pinning her grand-daughter with a pointed gaze. "You're right. It isn't *just* your voice. It's you. *You* got yourself onto that show. Your poise, de-termination, *and* your voice. Do you hear me? Now, you go on out there and make me proud." *Make me proud* was what Gran always said to Sadie before she performed, and she had been do-ing so since Sadie was knee-high to a grasshopper. Sadie smiled and was about to say goodbye when all at once, her gran's screen blurred, as if she had dropped the phone. Sadie heard her gran coughing for a moment, then her mother's voice. Lynn appeared on-screen once more.

"She just . . . swallowed some water wrong." Her mother's expression was full of worry. "Good luck today, Sadie. And don't forget—if it doesn't work out, you can always come home." *Ah*. Sadie should have known the worry was about *her*. "I'll miss not having you home for Christmas this year," she continued.

"I'll check in later," was all Sadie said. "I should really get back."

Then she hung up and was alone with her thoughts once more, a ball of anxiety still pressing itself against her sternum.

You look *amazing*," said Hugo, the stylist assigned to Sadie—a lucky break, because he was one of the best, and had come from Tasha Munroe's tour crew. He had put Sadie in a red backless minidress, gauzy and trimmed all over with frills that should have been too much, but instead were just perfect because he had toned down the look with milk chocolate–brown cowboy boots. The dark circles under her eyes had been magicked away by a makeup artist, and her long dark hair hung loose and wavy down her exposed back. Hugo lifted up her locks and dusted on some body shimmer powder.

"Love the piercing," he said, referring to the tiny diamond stud Sadie had worn in her nose since she was seventeen. Her mom had been chagrined when she came home with it one day after school—but she had been feeling inspired by Pink, her favorite singer at the time. "It shows that you're adorable—but you have an edge. Now, go get 'em, gorgeous."

As Sadie walked toward the soundstage, she tried to calm herself. She was just going to have to breathe in her fear and breathe out powerful music. She wished there was an app for *that*.

She stepped out onto the stage and sat down at the piano. Her eyes adjusted to the bright lights, then roamed quickly over the ledge of the piano and across to the judges' table, where

Tasha, Cruz, and the other two judges—country music icons Monica Cleary and Darryl "D.J." Jones—sat, their faces arranged in neutral expressions. The other competitors sat in the front row—but perfectly coiffed Johnny King in a bright purple suit, no shirt underneath, washboard stomach on full display, was most noticeable. His posture was casual and relaxed, his long legs were crossed at the ankles, his socks were emblazoned with hot pink guitars.

She'd chosen to sing "Sweet Dreams," by Patsy Cline. It was a comforting old favorite, one of the first songs Gran had taught her to sing, and a great opportunity to show off the range of her voice. Sadie ran her fingers lightly across the keys, preparing herself. Now her gaze landed on Max Brody, who was as understatedly hip as Johnny King was garishly alluring. Max was staring off to the left of the stage, where Sadie knew a large clock was affixed to the wall. It appeared he was counting the seconds down until this tedium was over. Sadie felt frustrated just looking at him—but then, as she let her gaze linger on Max, she noticed there was a surprising benefit to having him in her line of vision. It was making her forget how nervous she was. So she kept her eyes on Max as she began to play the haunting opening bars of her song. As she sang those first lines about sweet dreams that could never come true, Max's gaze finally shifted to the stage and she saw it: surprise.

Max Brody, I have something to prove to you, she thought. It was a short tune, but powerful—and by the closing bars, she knew she'd nailed it. Johnny King even hopped up on his chair to give her a standing ovation—but really, Sadie knew, he was just using the opportunity to show off for the cameras.

The judges were in unanimous agreement. "I mean," Tasha was saying, "I just *knew* when I stumbled on this one practicing earlier today that she was someone to watch."

Sadie blushed as she sat beaming on the stage, letting the compliments wash over her, thinking about what her gran had said to her earlier about this being her life's purpose.

"Star quality, definitely," Cruz McNeil was now saying, looking Sadie over appraisingly and with interest, as if noticing her for the first time. Sadie was smiling so much it was starting to hurt her cheeks. And her smile got wider *still* when she saw the scowl on Max's face. Sadie had just proven he was going to need to stay on his toes to beat her, and that felt incredible.

Later, after all the performances were over, the day's rankings were announced: underdog Sadie had impressed the judges and come in first place—but Johnny King's showstopping rendition of Shania Twain's "Whose Bed Have Your Boots Been Under?" was nipping at her heels, a close second. Max Brody's version of Johnny Cash's "Folsom Prison Blues" had somehow earned him third place, even though Sadie could have put money on him choosing a song like that. So predictable.

"Your prize for winning today's competition—and as a nod to your name, Sadie"—Tasha winked as she said this—"is that *you* get first pick of a contestant to partner up with for the duet round of competition. Everyone else will have their partners randomly assigned."

Sadie was about to point to Johnny King—he was her stiffest competition, sure, but she'd get more attention if she sang with him—when someone called, "Cut!"

Wait. What was going on?

One of the directors, an energetic man named Chuck, approached. "Okay. So, this part is now scripted," Chuck said. All the contestants had been told there would be certain portions of the show that were predetermined, but Sadie still felt taken aback. "Pretty simple. You're supposed to pick Max Brody. Okay? So when the cameras roll, you just point to Brody, bat those baby blues, and say you choose him."

"You mean I don't really have a choice?"

Chuck just shrugged. "We need Brody in the spotlight as much as possible and if he keeps on trotting out tired old Johnny Cash covers, that ain't gonna happen. Ratings. It's that simple. Alright, so let's get rolling."

"But that's not fair," Sadie muttered.

"Whoever told you this business was fair?" Chuck said, dashing back to his position beside camera A as if he hadn't just totally ruined her big moment.

"And rolling!"

Tasha delivered her line again and Sadie mustered up an excited smile in response. "I choose . . ." She closed her eyes for a moment. *Damn it, I don't want to do this.* She opened her eyes and met Max's nonchalant gaze. "Max Brody. *Of course.* Who else would I pick? Thank you, everyone!"

The glare of the lights as Sadie made her way off the stage made it impossible for her to see Max's reaction. But she could just imagine his smug, entitled smirk—and it made her more determined than ever to win it all.

Out in the hallway, she felt a hand on her arm and turned around. Cruz McNeil, who she'd never spoken to, was standing behind her. "You're one of the top contenders already," he said in a just-between-us voice that gave Sadie a thrill. "All the judges think you're definitely something special. Myself included."

"Thank you so much, Mr. McNeil!" Sadie said, feeling her cheeks flush with happiness. He squeezed her upper arm again.

"Please. Call me Cruz. And, see you around."

As Cruz walked away, Sadie saw Max approaching her, his assistant, Landon, in tow. Max was the only contestant who had his own personal assistant, of course. But not even his arrogant expression as he passed her without a word could dampen her mood. She was going to have to figure out a way to work with Max, but that was a problem she could deal with another day. Today, Sadie sang all the way back to her dressing room.

3

Max

Nashville, Tennessee
December 8

"This is not a good idea." Sadie clenched and unclenched her hands, her freshly manicured nails leaving half-moon marks in her palms.

Max, standing beside her, let out a short laugh. "I don't have bad ideas." He had a good five inches on her, though less when she was in heels like she was right now. Still, he leaned down to whisper in her ear, "Don't you trust me?" His tone was playful.

"Obviously not," Sadie hissed in return.

Max wasn't sure precisely what he had done to piss Sadie Hunter off in the short time they'd known each other. He wasn't thrilled about being paired up with her, either. She seemed insecure, inexperienced, and had the energy of a buzzing bee when the first pollen of spring arrived. He wished she'd relax, because her nervousness was awakening the stage fright Max had suffered from since he was a kid.

Sadie shifted to put a wedge of space between them, absentmindedly tugging on the hem of her miniskirt, which was quite short and only hit mid-thigh.

"Stop fussing. You look beautiful," Max said. He stared straight ahead as he said it, but out of the corner of his eye he saw Sadie turn to look at him. His heart may have been beating like hummingbird wings, but he was skilled at hiding it behind his charming smile, which he now put on.

Max's good looks were his suit of armor, and he reminded himself that's what people would notice. He worked to slow his racing heart, picturing himself doing the thing that had been an antidote to his stage fright and anxiety for years—knitting. *Cast on, stitch, stitch, stitch . . .*

He imagined the needles, cool and smooth, clicking softly in his hands as he finished a row, the feel of the yarn as he held it against the needles so as not to lose his stitch. His mom had taught him after the time he froze onstage at age eight, forgetting his lines as one of the critical players (Pig #3) in the elementary school's production of *The Three Little Pigs*. She had said it helped her back when she was performing, and sure enough, it had become his go-to stress reducer over the years. He kept it a closely guarded secret, because he didn't really want to be known as "Max Brody, Nashville prince and knitting aficionado."

Max glanced at Sadie again, distracted by her tugging on her skirt. Wardrobe had spiffed her up, but they had also given her half an outfit: the miniskirt that showcased her long, toned legs and the sheer tank top that skimmed her curves. She wore it well, but Max wasn't sure she could pull it off—she couldn't stop fidgeting from one foot to the next, practically toppling over in her mile-high heels. He raised an eyebrow and avoided saying what he was really thinking.

"What?" Sadie asked, turning her blue eyes on him. He hadn't been feeding her a line when he said she looked beautiful. But she was also so high-strung that he was relieved today was a "one and done" for the two of them, and then he would be free to go solo for the rest of the show.

"What's the matter?" Sadie asked again. A slight sheen of sweat covered her forehead.

Man, she looks as nervous as a long-tailed cat in a room full of rocking chairs. "Not a thing, sweetheart."

Sadie looked like she had more to say, but then Cruz McNeil came up behind them. Max watched as Cruz brushed Sadie's long brown hair off her bare, fake-tanned shoulder, his fingers lingering on the spaghetti strap of her sequined tank top, but didn't say anything. It was none of his business, really, if something *extra* was happening between Sadie and Cruz.

It was against the show's rules, of course, but that hadn't stopped past judges and show contestants from getting cozy. Besides, this was Nashville. Anything could happen here in the pursuit of "making it" in the business. However, he hoped Sadie would keep her wits about her. One of them blowing it could mean the end of the road for the other as well.

"How are we feeling?" Cruz asked, coming to stand in front of them.

"Feeling fine." Max gave Cruz a confident smile and tucked

his hands into his jean pockets. "We're all set. Thanks to your coaching yesterday."

Max may not have been Cruz's biggest fan, but thanks to Tasha's recent reminder about the starmaking producer, he knew he had to play his part and suck up as needed.

"Glad to hear it. You guys nailed that last take, and if you do it *just like that*, you have a great shot—both of you—for making it through as individuals," Cruz said.

Cruz turned to Sadie. "You okay, darlin'?"

She nodded, and Max watched as Sadie set her shoulders back a hair. She was talented, there was no question. But it took more than that to make it in this business.

Max was well-versed in the backstories of musicians like Sadie Hunter, having met many over the years. She had probably ended up here after hundreds of small gigs in bars, likely putting everything else in her life on hold—and being willing to do almost anything—while she chased this tantalizing dream.

Max understood deep down that he wasn't in a position to be so callous about chasing dreams. He had waltzed onto the show because of name recognition—a draw to pull in viewers, as his father's fans were still heartbroken at his retirement. The show's producers wanted to boost ratings, and they felt Max Brody could be their golden ticket.

"Okay, Max, Sadie, you're up," Cruz said to the pair. "*Remember*. This could be the most important song you're ever going to sing. Stick to the plan, and make us believe you're already the stars I know you are."

As soon as Cruz left backstage, with go-time only moments

away, Max reached for Sadie's hand. "What the hell do you think you're doing?" she asked, pulling away.

She had a high flush to her cheeks, and gave him a look that suggested he take a step back, *now*.

"Giving them what they want. Which is a good show." Then he reached for her hand again, but this time he did it more gently, allowing his fingers to slowly intertwine with hers. They walked onstage, hand in hand, to where Max's guitar and two mics waited for them. The Christmas decorations had been moved offstage for their performance, leaving only sheets of hanging twinkle lights behind them.

"Can we get a stool out here?" Max asked, shielding his eyes against the spotlights. The song Max and Sadie had been assigned was probably the most covered duet of all time—"Islands in the Stream." The arrangement Cruz had suggested was only a hair above a cheesy karaoke version of the song, which was precisely why Max had told Sadie he had a *new idea* for the song only minutes before they were scheduled to perform.

A stool appeared onstage, and Max set it behind one of the mics. Then he shortened the microphone stand so it was at Sadie's height when she was seated.

"Kick off your shoes," he said, covering her mic with his hand. "And smile, okay?"

"Don't tell me what to do," Sadie whispered. But she slid off her heels, her toenails polished a baby pink to match her fingernails, and sat on the stool.

"All set?" Cruz asked, the other judges looking on somewhat impatiently.

Sadie nodded, and Max picked up his guitar. "We've made a bit of a change," he said into the mic. Then he started strumming the guitar strings, softly, giving his fingers time to warm up and his heartbeat time to slow. Picking the guitar strings felt similar to having knitting needles in hand, and taking a moment before starting the song helped him relax. *You've got this, Max.*

Cruz looked at Max curiously, then shrugged as the other judges glanced over at him, eyebrows raised.

The first bars of the song came over the speakers and Sadie waved a hand. Then she leaned into her microphone and said, "No music, thanks. We're doing this acoustic." She smiled at Max, and it didn't reach her eyes even though he was the only one who would see that.

Max strummed the guitar, the familiar chords filling the soundstage, which were soon matched by his voice—deep and smooth as he delivered the first line of the song, keeping his eyes on Sadie. He may have suffered from stage fright, but he was no slouch when it came to performing.

Sadie casually tapped her hand against her thigh as she swayed slightly on the stool to the rhythm of the song, smiling right back at Max.

They sang the song slowly to one another, the guitar chords the only accompaniment to their voices, which were perfectly matched. The effect was magical—their chemistry undeniable. Even Cruz seemed enchanted by the performance when Max glanced at him. The three other judges sat up a little straighter in their chairs and Max knew they had them precisely where they needed them.

At one point Sadie got off the stool and took her mic off the stand while Max sang his part. Then she walked slowly, barefoot, over to where Max stood and ran a hand down his arm while she sang to him. Max was, despite himself, mesmerized by Sadie—and he leaned toward her, their voices rising as they reached the crescendo.

The judges were blown away. The grizzled D.J., who had been in the business first as a musician and later as a producer, said it was the most original version of the song he'd ever seen performed, and that they were meant for one another. *Maybe even off the stage, too*, Monica, the willow-thin bottle-blond judge (who had won *Starmaker* three years prior), added, with a wicked grin. Of course, it would ultimately be up to the viewers to decide Max and Sadie's fate. The following week, when this performance aired, viewers could vote for their favorites by texting the number that had been assigned to each duet.

Sadie smiled shyly, and then without hesitation reached out to hold Max's hand again. He was surprised, but didn't show it. Instead, he grinned at her, then kissed her hand. Sadie managed to make it seem like it was a welcome gesture.

But as they walked backstage, away from the microphones and judges, she said, "You were a bit pitchy at the end there. I hope that doesn't get me eliminated." They were on their way to the greenroom for their postshow interviews, to be aired alongside the performance for the viewers next week, so they were alone.

"I was *not* pitchy. I am never pitchy." Max frowned, running a hand through his dark wavy hair. He knew the performance, including his part, had been flawless. Thanks to *his* idea to strip everything back to just their voices and his guitar. The least she could do was thank him for his brilliant idea.

Sadie reached for the greenroom's door handle, gave Max a withering look, and said, "I guess we'll see, won't we?"

Max Brody and Sadie Hunter . . .
Their "Islands in the Stream" cover
BROKE THE INTERNET last week!

Up until last night, the last thing anyone needed was another season of *Starmaker*, even with Max Brody and Tasha Munroe on board . . . but that was before #Saxie. If you don't know what we're talking about, crawl out from under the rock you've been living under for the past 24hrs and scroll down for a video of the most sizzling performance in the show's history.

In keeping with the *Starmaker* been-there-done-that vibe of late, Max Brody—yes, *that* Brody, son of the legendary Holden, whose voice can cause panties to drop from coast to coast—and Sadie Hunter took the stage for Duet Week to do a cover of "Islands in the Stream."

But y'all, this was no karaoke performance. Max and Sadie were pure electricity. With Max strumming away on his guitar (can we be jealous of a guitar?), and Sadie's voice—that VOICE!—purring out of the speakers, it was clear something special was going on. Even if these two didn't have talent to spare, it would have been a white-hot performance because of the way he looked at her (like she was a rare steak and he was a hungry cowboy) and the way she looked at him (like he was the sexiest man alive, which, let's face it, might be true).

Needless to say, in our opinion they smashed Duet Week, but more importantly, they won the hearts (and more than a few libidos) of the country, and a fan base who want only one thing: **more #Saxie!**

If *Starmaker* is smart, they'll give us a repeat performance. Now, for the big question: Are they really crushing on each other, or is it all for show? Is romance blossoming, right before our very eyes? Either way, we reckon most of North America would now pay to watch #Saxie read an Applebee's menu together . . .

4

Sadie

Nashville, Tennessee
December 8

As Sadie packed up for the day in her dressing room, she had to pick off bits of red and green glitter that had been dusted over the set by an enthusiastic intern tasked with making everything look "festive." She was almost finished when her phone rang. It was Amalia Zuckerman, her manager.

"Have you looked at Twitter? I swear to Goddess, you two broke the internet when the duet aired. *Brilliant*. It's a holiday season *miracle!*"

Sadie put Amalia on speaker and opened her Twitter account. "Holy bananas," was all she could say.

"The Saxie hashtag is trending! This is amazing. And I believe the words you were looking for were, 'Holy shit,' Miss Vanilla Twist."

Sadie smiled. When Amalia had first signed Sadie she had

told her it was because she was adorable, as widely appealing as vanilla soft serve ice cream—but with a twist: a voice like the richest dark chocolate. Amalia only used the nickname when things were going well.

Sadie opened the Twitter app on her phone and stared down at it:

> Christmas is coming up! Can Max and Sadie please do a Christmas song duet next, *Starmaker*!!??
> #AllIWantForChristmas #SaxieForever

> I want to come back reincarnated as Max's guitar at the moment Sadie reached out and casually strummed it. Who knew "Islands in the Stream" could be so sexy? #Saxie #Hereforit

The *Starmaker* account had tweeted a video of Max and Sadie singing their song, and it had been retweeted one hundred thousand times in the past hour. The number rose as she watched.

"Sweetie? You there?"

"Yeah. I'm here, Amalia."

"Listen, I'm on my way. The producers called and they want a meeting. With us, the show execs, and judges." Sadie's heart lifted. "And Max and his reps, too." And then, sank. "See you soon, okay, Vanilla?"

"Vanilla *Twist*," Sadie answered her. "Don't forget the 'Twist.'"

Sadie read a few more excited tweets before logging out of the application. Her gran had texted her a whole bunch of dynamite emojis, but even the fact that Gran had figured out emojis wasn't enough to shake her out of the darkness of the premonition she was having. Everyone thought she and Max had this magical fairy dust thing going. Was she the only one who felt they weren't heading anywhere good?

The meeting took place in one of the boardrooms on the other side of the studio—far away from the prying eyes of the main stage cameras. Even though she could take a break from having to worry about how her hair looked or if her skirt was riding up, her heart was barreling away from her like a Greyhound bus heading out of town. She and Amalia were across the rectangular table from Max and his manager, Bobbi, the studio execs at one end of the table, and the judges—Cruz, Tasha, Monica, and D.J.—at the other.

"Shall we dive right in?" Penny Washington, the network's director of unscripted programming, said, leaning forward and smiling first at Max, then Sadie.

Sadie pasted on a return smile and kept her sweaty hands clasped in front of her, hoping she wasn't about to dive into shark-infested waters. She looked down and noticed a nail was chipped. She looked up and saw Max watching her, eyebrows raised as if to say, *We're in an important meeting with the* Starmaker *execs and* you're *thinking about nail polish?* She resisted the urge to make a face at him and turned her full attention to what Penny was saying.

"The online sensation you two caused with your duet is unprecedented, even for *Starmaker*—and we've made our share of splashes in the world."

Sadie could feel a "but" coming on. She held her breath for it.

"But, as you both know, we are coming up to our double elimination round. On the next episode we shoot, contestants will be expected to engage in a *Starmaker* Showstoppers Battle—and two people will be sent home, rather than just one."

It hung in the air, the idea of being sent home. Sadie didn't know what to do, so she smiled.

"We know all this," Amalia said, in her customary brusque tone.

"Exactly," Bobbi added. "So why have you called us in here to discuss it?"

"We'd like to offer Max and Sadie both immunity during double elimination," Penny said. Sadie waited to feel better, but didn't. Because there was another "but." She just knew it.

"But . . ." *There it was.* "You'd have to agree to pair up. To continue the competition as a duo. As Saxie."

Sadie felt a wave of nausea almost overtake her. She looked away from Penny, directly into Max's eyes. He looked just as disgusted as she felt.

Sadie braced herself for one more "but."

"*But*, you have to understand . . . What's being offered to you is unheard of. And, some might say, not exactly fair. The rules are being changed for you two, and the consequence is—"

Consequence? Now when Sadie's eyes met Max's they shared a twin look of alarm. They hadn't done anything wrong, so why were they getting a consequence?

"—that if you don't agree to stay on as"—Penny cleared her throat, as if she realized how ridiculous it was—"as *Saxie* . . . one of you has to leave."

"What? So soon?" Sadie's voice sounded strangled. These weren't the rules!

"Now, hey," Cruz drawled. "This seems a bit arbitrary. Sadie is a talent in her own right—"

"As is Max," Bobbi chimed in, her voice tight.

"Right, right, they both are. None of this seems quite fair, really."

"Cruz," Penny said. "You of all people know we have some work to do when it comes to ratings. And surely you've seen the online furor. Saxie is what our viewers want."

Cruz shot Sadie a helpless look. "Yes, ma'am. I understand. Sometimes you just have to give the people what they want."

While Sadie was disappointed there didn't seem to be anything anyone could do about this pairing she was facing with Max, she was grateful to Cruz for at least trying to go to bat for her—and for saying she was talented. She watched as Cruz rubbed his hand across his eyes for a moment, like he was very tired—and recalled he was having issues with his chain of restaurants, Cruz's Catfish. It was nice of him to be concerned about her, when he clearly had problems of his own.

"We do realize this is an unusual arrangement," Penny went on. "But we have a separate contract with Max Brody. And it stipulates that he is not to be eliminated until the final round." She glanced at Sadie. "This is the kind of privileged information you signed an NDA not to reveal, don't forget," she said. Sadie couldn't do anything but nod as Penny continued, her intense gaze holding Sadie's. "The reality is that if you don't agree to continue on together, it is very likely *you'll* be the one sent home, Sadie."

Sadie had gone through so many emotions in the past

minute she felt like she had whiplash—and the place her heart settled on was frustration. The odds were stacked against her. She was not a Brody, and didn't have some magical contract. So all she could do was sit here and do what she was told.

But it was all just so unfair.

She felt a tear making its way down her cheek. Sadie had vowed that if she ever got voted off *Starmaker* she was not going to cry—but this was before she had realized she had less of a chance of winning than some of the other contestants, simply because of who she was. *Life's not fair, Sadie. You already know this.* She lifted her chin, squared her shoulders—and saw that Max was watching her closely.

She had expected to see him looking self-satisfied—but he didn't. He looked into her eyes for a long moment and it felt like time stopped, like they were the only people in the room. It felt the way it did when they sang together. Her heart was still racing, but for a different reason now.

"Fine," Max said, breaking her gaze and standing up from the table. "We'll perform together as"—he swallowed repeatedly, trying to get it out—"as Saxie. Is that all you wanted to talk about?"

Before anyone could answer, Max strode out of the boardroom, and Bobbi followed in his path. Out in the hall, Sadie could hear Landon's voice, asking Max if he needed anything.

"Thank you," Sadie said to no one in particular, feeling out of her depth.

"You're welcome, doll," Cruz replied, with another one of those kind, concerned smiles. But Sadie couldn't bring herself to return it as Amalia led her from the room. Her mood sank even further when she saw Max and Bobbi waiting for them in the hallway. Bobbi had her arm linked through Max's and was holding tight, as if he might take off running down the hall otherwise. And Max's scowl was even deeper than usual.

"Come on, you two," Bobbi said to Sadie and Amalia. "Let's go find somewhere to have that chat we discussed." She shot Amalia a meaningful look, then led the way further down the hall.

Once they found an empty meeting room, Amalia closed the door behind them and stood by Sadie's side.

"Okay, here goes," Bobbi began. "We feel that if you two really lean into this pair-up—as in, convince the world you're in love, act like a couple on set *and* in public—you'll be America's sweethearts in no time."

Sadie glanced at Max and saw his brow furrow.

"How are we supposed to do that, we don't even—" She had been about to conclude with *like each other* but was halted mid-sentence by Amalia's not-so-subtle elbow nudge.

"It just makes sense," Amalia added. "The rumor on the set is you're sleeping together anyway. Why fight it? Owning it means you will win this competition hands down through viewers' votes alone."

Sadie looked at Max again to see how he was reacting to this—but he was staring down at his cowboy boots like they somehow contained the meaning of life in their curlicued etchings. Sadie's throat had gone dry. She opened her mouth to protest—but found she couldn't do it.

Sadie wanted to win.

Finally, Max returned her gaze. And she saw it in his eyes. *He* wanted to win, too. "What do you think, Sadie?" he said, his tone flat.

"I'm not sure. I mean, we don't really know each other."

"Max, you know this sort of thing happens all the time," Bobbi said. "That show business is full of fake relationships." She turned to Sadie. "It's really no big deal. It's make-believe. And the payoff would be astronomical."

Sadie closed her eyes for a moment, then opened them again. Max was frowning at his toes again—but he was her shot. *This* was her shot. She'd be a fool to say anything but yes. So, "I'll do it," she answered.

Max scowled. "So will I," he seconded. "Now, are we done here? I have someplace I need to be."

"Wait!" Bobbi said, pulling out her phone. "Max, take Sadie in your arms. Come on, just do it."

Max sighed, then stepped close and put his hands on her hips—but rolled his eyes as he did it, while Sadie gritted her teeth. Her heart was fluttering, though, probably because standing this close to Max reminded her of being onstage.

"Sadie, look up at him like you're about to kiss him. Lean close. Come on, make it look like you don't know I'm here, and—" As soon as she snapped a photo Max released Sadie like she was a hot potato. "Perfect. Now to go 'leak' this to the press!"

Max ran a hand through his hair and turned to Sadie, a grimace on his handsome face. It was the day after their meeting and they were in a rehearsal room planning their duet—or, more accurately, arguing about it.

"Absolutely no way. I am not singing that song with you."

"Come on, Max—"

"No. They may be forcing us together, but I hate that song, I won't."

"'Forcing us'? That's not quite how I remember it. *We* agreed to this, Max. Can you at least make an effort?"

"Thanks to that photo, the Saxie hashtag is trending. What more do you want from me?"

Sadie sighed and forced herself to take a few calming breaths. "Let's just settle on a song, okay? And please, not 'Silent Night,' performed in the tired style of Johnny Cash, with you staring moodily into the middle distance while I gaze at you and hum along."

"Johnny Cash's style is never, ever *tired*," Max said tersely. He put his head down and strummed his guitar, and even the notes sounded defensive. There were plenty of rumors about who the guitar had belonged to, including his own music legend father, but Max was tight-lipped about its origins. However, he treated it almost as well as he treated Patsy—who was currently being walked around the parking lot by Landon—so Sadie suspected the guitar carried as much pedigree as Max himself did. He stopped strumming and ran a hand through his dark hair again. Somehow, it managed to fall perfectly back into place—whereas every time Sadie left Hair and Makeup she had to force herself not to touch her long, thick waves even once, or she'd wreck the artfully contrived, over-hair-sprayed style.

She watched as Max, his full lips set in a perma-scowl, paced the small room. How was it possible that she had such great onstage chemistry with this man? She supposed it was because chemistry was just that: mix A with B and watch C happen. But just because you could mix baking soda with vinegar and watch it erupt into a volcano did not mean that baking soda was in love with vinegar. In fact, it could mean the opposite.

"Okay, fine, what about 'The Angels Cried'?" Max said.

Sadie laughed at him, she couldn't help it. "There is absolutely nothing sexy about angels crying!"

He stopped pacing and spun around. "Why does everything have to be sexy? Can you not be serious about music for one second?"

Her eyes widened. "I am very serious about music!"

He maintained the I-am-a-true-artist-and-you-are-just-wasting-my-time expression she was beginning to seriously loathe, and took a long look at her, letting his eyes sweep up and down her body and the revealing outfit Wardrobe had put her in, again. "Coulda fooled me, sweetheart."

Sadie felt suddenly off-kilter. It was the fact that he wore too much cologne, she decided. "Max, please just listen to me for one second." She looked up at him and sang the opening lines of "Christmas Without You," the Kenny and Dolly duet she was advocating for.

His expression changed almost immediately. He started to sing along with her, almost as if he couldn't help himself. At first he refused to look at her, but that was almost better. She closed her eyes and focused on the way their voices blended together and complemented one another perfectly—then opened her eyes to find him watching her, an inscrutable expression on his face. She felt like she was caught in an electrical current. Instead of fighting it, she allowed the now-powerful connection between them into her voice. It turned the sweet song about two lovers longing to be together over Christmas into something seriously sexy.

She could still smell his cologne, an earthy, spicy scent she didn't exactly hate at that moment, as well as his cinnamon-gum-scented breath. She was grateful she had rubbed her skin with vanilla oil earlier and doubled up on the mouthwash. She sang a line about laughing until they fell out of bed, and he bent his head toward hers to sing his line, as if drawn toward her by a magnet. Then . . .

There was a knock at the door and Johnny King swaggered in, wearing a Christmas-themed tie covered in flashing lights. He was followed closely by Cruz, who took in Max and Sadie standing so close with what Sadie thought for a moment might have been a disappointed look. To her surprise, Max pulled her closer. It made sense, she supposed—they were meant to be pretending to be a couple. But she had to work to make it look as natural as it had felt a moment before. "Hi there!" she chirped.

"Hey, Miss Sadie." Cruz tipped an imaginary hat. "Max."

"Hey, lovebirds!" Johnny crooned. "I signed up for this room, and you're officially"—he tapped his oversized gold watch—"taking up my time."

Max scowled. And even though Sadie knew the judges took turns with contestants and it wasn't their week with Cruz, she felt a surge of jealousy. Johnny was their biggest competition, and was breathing down their neck in viewer votes. He was as close to winning this thing as they were. Closer, because it now seemed Cruz was dedicating himself to mentoring him.

"We're all done here," Sadie said, pasting on a smile.

Johnny clapped his hands together as he sat down on a couch in the corner of the room and said, "Alright, Cruz, let's rock!"

Just then Cruz caught Sadie's gaze. It was almost imperceptible, but he rolled his eyes, and Sadie had to force down a chuckle.

Now she clocked the expression on Max's face as he watched Johnny and Cruz settle in on the couch, clearly about to have a serious tête-à-tête about whatever Johnny's next winning move should be. The only way to describe Max's facial expression now was one of pure envy. And all this gave Sadie pause. He really did want this, for reasons she could not figure out. Max Brody, son of the great Holden Brody, seemed as intent on winning *Starmaker* as she was. And while everyone else seemed to roll out an imaginary red carpet anytime Max came anywhere near, Cruz—arguably the most influential member of the *Starmaker* team—barely gave him the time of day.

Sadie tugged the sleeve of Max's denim jacket and murmured, "Let's go," but she could tell what Max wanted most was to be sitting where Johnny King was.

5

Max

Nashville, Tennessee
December 15

M ax? Are you in there?" Two short raps on the trailer's metal door followed, and Max jumped up from the small couch where he'd been sitting.

The show had set up trailers in the soundstage's parking lot for when contestants needed a moment of privacy, to call family or shed a few tears after receiving biting criticism from the judges. Max had told Landon he'd be in trailer #2 going over "contract negotiations" with Bobbi. There were no contract negotiations, however. He simply needed to get away from the prying eyes of the other contestants, and the hushed gossip that followed him, for a spell.

He was about to say, "Just a minute!" when the door to the trailer door swung open. Sadie poked her head inside.

She took in the scene, her eyes moving from his face to his hands, which were in front of him . . . and holding knitting needles. A ball of pink yarn had fallen from his lap when he stood, and rested near his feet, one long string connecting the ball to the half-knit dog sweater he had been working on.

"Don't you knock?" he grumbled, quickly setting the knitting needles and sweater behind him on the couch and then shifting to block Sadie's view. He cleared his throat and shoved his hands in his pockets, wondering what the chances were that Sadie would mind her own business. *Not freakin' likely.*

"Why are you never where you're supposed to be?" Sadie retorted. That was fair enough. Max followed his own schedule and rules, only bending to those of the show when he absolutely had to. He got away with it, but while he benefitted from the privilege his last name provided, what he longed for most was freedom from it.

"Besides, I did knock. *Twice.*" Sadie tugged on the sleeves of her sweater, tucking the ends over her hands and then crossing her arms over her chest, a sure sign she was annoyed. Max was starting to recognize her tells. "So, you knit, huh?"

"Yes, *I knit,*" Max replied. "But it's not . . . something I advertise, okay?" Then he pointed at the door, which still stood open. "Could you close that before Patsy bolts?"

Sadie obliged, then glanced at Patsy. The dog was fast asleep on a fur-covered pillow, lying on her back in a heather-grey sweater with her stumpy legs sticking up in the air. "Does she always sleep like that?"

Max chuckled. "Yeah, she's one of a kind."

"Look, I would love to take a deep dive into the whole 'Max Brody, Incognito Knitter' thing," Sadie said, absentmindedly tugging on the hem of her short skirt. Her long forest green cardigan hung just about an inch above the skirt. "But Cruz is in a mood, he has a meeting he said can't be changed, so we need to do the rehearsal now."

"Well, Cruz can wait another dang minute. And why are you all made up like that?" Max asked, noting Sadie's stage-ready makeup and sleek side ponytail.

"It's a dress rehearsal, remember? Full costume and makeup and these ridiculously uncomfortable shoes." She stuck one long leg out in front of her, showing off the golden-hued heels before losing her balance and pitching into Max. As he steadied her, the warm scent of vanilla wafted into his nose and he suddenly wished he didn't have to let her go. Which confused the hell out of him, because 97 percent of the time Sadie Hunter was a thorn in his side.

"You really aren't a stiletto gal, are you?" He set her back on her feet, but the vanilla scent lingered, as did the unwelcome desire to take her in his arms again.

"Says the guy who never has to wear anything uncomfortable."

Max looked down at his outfit—jeans slung low, held up by a leather belt with a wide buckle, cowboy boots, a white T-shirt over which he would throw a leather jacket. This was his everyday outfit, but also his onstage one. He knew it wasn't fair.

"Anyway, we'd better head inside. Need me to carry

anything?" Sadie looked pointedly to the couch, where Max had tried to hide his knitting supplies, a lilt of amusement on her face.

"All good, thanks." He shoved the yarn and needles into the black leather messenger bag he was rarely without. This was going to be a *whole thing* now. Sadie was what his mom used to call the "niggling" sort—unable to mind her own business, even when it was clear she should. Plus, the last thing he wanted to do was have to explain why he was knitting a dog sweater in a *Starmaker* trailer, because it all linked back to his mom, and he didn't want to talk about her.

Patsy got up and stretched when Max called out to her. Sadie reached into her cardigan pocket and pulled out a jerky treat, holding it between her fingers. Max was about to protest but then Sadie said, "It's organic chicken, no wheat."

He shrugged, annoyed Sadie was feeding Patsy—who was on a strict diet, because gluten made her skin itch—but also pleased at her thoughtfulness.

"You're really good," Sadie said, crouching down to smooth the flyaways on Patsy's ears, running her hand along the soft sweater. "My gran knits, and this pattern is not easy."

Max was about to say, "Thanks, but let's change the subject" when the door flew open again. This time there was no knock, no warning at all. And in a split second Patsy had bolted out the open door.

Landon looked stunned as Patsy ran past him. Max was mere seconds behind Patsy, but Sadie beat him to it, racing out the trailer after the dog. However, she forgot about her shoes, jumping out the door and skipping the stairs altogether.

At first Sadie landed on her feet, heels and all, which impressed the hell out of Max. But then she fell sideways, hard, and was a moment later sitting on the ground holding her left ankle with a pained expression on her face.

"Sadie, shit!" Max pushed around Landon and jumped from the trailer as well, landing easily in his boots. He crouched beside her, concerned. "Are you okay?"

"Don't worry about me," Sadie said between clenched teeth. She looked pale even under her makeup, and Max knew she had to be in a lot of pain. "Get Patsy."

The dog, bored by the parking lot, trotted back toward Sadie and Max, then plopped herself down and rested her head on Sadie's thigh.

"Good girl," Sadie murmured, her voice catching with the pain. Then she pulled another piece of jerky out of her sweater's pocket and gave it to Patsy.

"You shouldn't reward her, you know," Max said, fastening Patsy's harness so she couldn't escape again.

Landon was now beside them, apologizing and sweating profusely, despite the fact that it was December in Nashville and so not at all warm. "Ms. Hunter, Mr. Brody, I am so sorry. Mr. McNeil told me to get out here and find the two of you, and then I came to the trailer, and I should have knocked."

"Landon, it's fine, man." Max didn't have time to be angry with his assistant right now. "Can you take Patsy back inside and tell Cruz we need a minute?"

The assistant, wide eyed as he glanced at Sadie's rapidly swelling ankle, took Patsy in his arms. "What should I tell Mr. McNeil?"

"Tell him we need a goddamn minute!" Max's exasperation

boiled over. Twenty minutes earlier he had been happily knitting in the trailer, humming one of his favorite Christmas tunes, John Denver's "Christmas for Cowboys," which had also been one of his mom's favorites. It was the song they used to sing on repeat while decorating the tree every holiday. He had been feeling relaxed and nostalgic just before Sadie had shown up, but now he was back to being irritated.

Sadie put a hand on Max's arm. "Landon, tell Cruz we are going through one of the verses together and we'll be right there." Max had to admit Sadie ran circles around him when it came to tact and good manners.

"Go on, before he storms out here and we're all in trouble," she added. Landon nodded, and headed back inside the soundstage's building.

Max returned his focus to Sadie. He ran gentle fingers over her ankle, which had nearly doubled in size. Sadie pulled her leg back slightly at his touch. "That bad, huh?"

"I'm fine. I've sprained my ankle before."

"Your ankle looks like it swallowed a golf ball. It might be broken." He carefully pressed on the swollen area again, and she cringed. "You should probably get an X-ray."

"No way," Sadie said, shaking her head. "We need to get inside. Like I said, Cruz was in a *mood*. I overheard him on the phone. Something about his restaurants."

Max had never eaten at Cruz's Catfish—the seafood restaurant chain the producer had started with a partner—but he'd heard rumors that not only was the catfish terrible, the chain was in financial trouble thanks to recent food poisoning outbreaks.

"Can you help me up?"

Max came behind Sadie and crouched so he could slide his arms under hers. "Ready?"

She nodded.

"Okay, one, two . . . three." Max stood, hoisting Sadie up as he did. She leaned back against his chest for a moment, and he held tight. "You okay? Can you put weight on it?"

Still holding Sadie under her arms, he peered around to see her face when she didn't answer him. She did not look good. "You going to pass out on me here, Sadie?"

She shook her head, then determinedly set her bad foot on the ground, gingerly shifting her weight. She drew in a sharp breath, and Max took her weight back into his arms as she stood again on one leg.

"I can't walk. How am I going to perform?" She sounded close to tears, and Max felt beyond guilty. Sure, he didn't ask her to jump out of the trailer in three-inch heels, but she *had* done it to try to catch his dog.

"Well, lucky for you, I do a hundred push-ups a day," Max said, shifting beside her without letting her go.

"You know, you mention that a lot."

He laughed, then picked her up in his arms, careful to make sure her skirt was tucked in so she wouldn't flash anyone on their way back in.

"What's the plan here?" Sadie asked. "Are you going to carry me around all day?"

"If I have to." Max gave her a smile. Not the Brody one, a *real one* this time. "Besides, I didn't get my workout in today, and I'd say you have enough weight to you that I probably won't need to."

She batted at his arm, rolling her eyes—but it was good-natured, Max noted. *Progress.*

As he walked back to the soundstage, easily carrying Sadie in his arms, he said, "You know, I don't just knit dog sweaters."

"No?" Sadie replied, her eyes meeting his.

"I also knit blankets for the preemies at the hospital. And I've been known to whip up the odd hat or mittens for friends." He wasn't sure why he blurted those personal details out, and he felt somewhat embarrassed by it. But then she gave him a warm smile, which made him glad he had.

"Well, look at you, Max Brody. Surprising me yet again," Sadie said. "Who taught you how to knit?"

"My mom," he replied, breaking eye contact.

Before Sadie could ask any other questions about his mom, Max said, "Can you reach the handle?" They were now at the building's door. Sadie stretched an arm out, clasping the handle.

"Easy does it," he said, maneuvering carefully to avoid any part of Sadie hitting the edges of the doorway.

"What do we say?" Sadie asked. "I don't want them to make me go to the hospital."

"We'll just say you turned your ankle, because of those ridiculous shoes. And that if they don't start putting you in more appropriate footwear, well, you'll sue."

"I can't sue over shoes!" Sadie laughed.

"Sweetheart, this is America. You can sue over *anything.*"

"Fine," Sadie said, her arms tight around Max's neck. "I shall demand flats from now on, or I sue their asses."

"That's my girl," Max murmured with a grin.

He was instantly self-conscious, as if only then remembering Sadie was barely his friend, let alone his "girl." He wasn't used to this off-kilter feeling, and he didn't love it.

Just then Cruz came around the corner, speeding up when he saw Max carrying Sadie. He was pushing a wheelchair, which was on set for any injuries or if a contestant got woozy during a performance.

"Landon filled me in. How bad is it?" he asked, setting a hand on Sadie's knee. Max glanced at Cruz's hand on Sadie's bare leg, and had the urge to push it off.

"Not the best, not the worst," Sadie replied, giving Cruz a warm smile, to Max's chagrin.

"Max, let me take Sadie. You need to go back and get your jacket. Dress rehearsal is starting in ten minutes."

"Uh, that's okay. I can grab it after Sadie's settled. She needs some ice for that ankle."

"Already done. Landon is getting it ready as we speak. Come on now." Cruz gestured for Max to set Sadie down in the wheelchair. He lowered her to the seat as gently as he could, and Cruz set one of the footrests in the highest position to support her injured leg.

"Thanks, Max," Sadie said. But then she turned to Cruz, thanking him for getting the wheelchair, and Max felt like a third wheel. Another feeling he did not love.

"Our poor songbird has a broken wing," Cruz said, crouching beside the wheelchair, his forehead creased in concern. "Think you can perform from the chair?"

"My voice isn't sprained," Sadie replied.

"That's my girl," Cruz said. Max hated the proprietary way Cruz addressed Sadie, all the while chastising himself for saying precisely the same to her only moments before.

As Cruz pushed Sadie down the hall, Max stood by the door, watching them until they'd turned the corner.

6

Sadie

S adie limped from wilted houseplant to wilted houseplant in her apartment, a watering can held aloft. She lived in SoBro, a neighborhood in Nashville known for its trendy shops and restaurants. Sadie had taken the apartment because she could see the edge of the Music City Center from her tiny terrace. When she had moved back to Nashville months earlier, after raising enough money to make a go of it again—*Starmaker* was just a long shot on the horizon—she had decided that this time around, she needed to try to put down roots and convince the universe she really did belong here. Houseplants seemed like a good way to do that—they literally *had* roots. So she had visited a local greenhouse and loaded up on them. But all her plants—the croton, the dracaena, especially the orchid, and even the bamboo, which she had believed was impossible to kill—were now dried-out husks. The only plant that was still alive was the Christmas cactus. But it was stubbornly refusing to release its festive bloom, and its leaves were starting to brown around the edges. She resolutely watered all the plants anyway, hoping for a miracle.

When that was done, she sat down on her couch and picked up the Tasha Munroe autobiography she had been planning to read for ages. It was rare to have one and a half days off from the rigorous *Starmaker* taping schedule, and Sadie had been looking forward to it. But now that she was alone, she found she missed the bustle and the excitement of the set.

And, if she was being honest with herself, she missed Max, too. He had been very kind to her after she hurt her ankle the day before. Truth was, she hadn't exactly hated being fussed over all day by Max Brody. And he had stood by her side while she explained to the producers that wearing heels was clearly a health hazard and she would still be wearing stylish but more practical footwear from now on, *thankyouverymuch*. All things considered, it had not been her worst day. She had seen a new side of Max. A side of him that was kind and caring underneath the swagger. A side of him that knit dog sweaters, and blankets for newborn babies. Maybe, she was actually starting to enjoy being around Max. What did that mean?

A loud buzzing snapped her out of her reverie. For a moment she had no idea what she was hearing. *Right*. Her apartment buzzer. She stood and hobbled to the receiver.

"Hello?"

"Sweets! It's Gran!"

"*What?!* Gran!?"

"Surprise! Merry Early Christmas! I've come to stay with you for a few days!"

"Hang on, I'll come downstairs and help you upstairs with your bags! Stay right where you are!"

An elated Sadie limped down the hallway to the elevator, hoping her gran wouldn't notice she was injured—but, of course, it was the first thing she commented on when Sadie entered the wood-paneled lobby downstairs.

"What in the world?" Gran exclaimed. "*Are you hurt?* I didn't think singing was a contact sport!"

"I'm fine," Sadie said, trying not to grimace as she lifted her gran's small suitcase and headed for the elevator bank. "What's important is that you're *here*. How did you get here?"

"Put down that bag and give me a proper hug. And then, let *me* carry it. I may be old but I am certainly not too old to carry a tiny bag—especially with you in rough shape! I'm glad I came. You need me! And to answer your question, I flew here, obviously."

"But why?"

For just a second, sadness crept into her eyes—but then it was gone and Sadie wondered if she had imagined it. "Because I miss you terribly and the idea of not seeing you this Christmas because of your taping schedule broke my heart a little. Now, how about that hug?"

Sadie threw her arms around her gran. She seemed smaller since the last time Sadie had seen her, during her last trip home to Milwaukee months before, to sing the anthem at a Panthers basketball game. As she gently squeezed her gran's birdlike shoulder blades, she felt a tingle of alarm but pushed it away.

"Let me get a good look at you." Gran pulled back and gazed up at her granddaughter with eyes the same bright blue as Sadie's. "Ah, there's my girl. How I've missed you."

Sadie breathed in her gran's familiar scent: L'Air du Temps and Yardley powder. "I've missed you, too."

They made their way toward the elevator bank, Sadie limping along and Gran peering about at the lobby, nodding her head approvingly all the while. "I like this place. Not at all as seedy as I pictured it."

Sadie laughed. "You pictured me living somewhere seedy?"

"Well, the Nashville music scene used to be a bit more rough around the edges than it is now. Or so I heard. *My* career saw me playing in some different locales than Nashville, as you know."

It was Gran who had first sparked a love of singing in Sadie. Before Sadie had been born, she—then Elsie McKay, not Elsie Hunter—had been part of an all-female jazz ensemble reminiscent of the Andrews Sisters, who traveled the Midwest singing to war veterans. By the time Sadie came along, Elsie mostly only sang in the choir at church, but she had made sure her granddaughter's life was full of music.

Upstairs, Sadie gave Gran a tour of her small but cozy apartment—galley kitchen, terrace overlooking SoBro's cafés and shops and the Music City Center, living room, bedroom, tiny bathroom. Then Gran opened her suitcase and took out a hand-knit blanket, which she spread across the couch. "There we go, that warms the place up a little, doesn't it?" She glanced up at Sadie and raised an eyebrow. "Takes some of the attention away from those dead plants. You should probably stick with singing and stay away from horticulture, my dear."

Sadie laughed. "You're probably right, Gran. And thank you for the blanket."

"I have something else for you." She sat down on the newly livened up couch and pulled a little gift-wrapped package out of her purse. The deep green paper was covered in tiny silver snowflakes. Gran's eyes danced. "I came all the way here to give you your Christmas gift in person, and I can't wait another minute for you to open it!"

"I don't have anything for you," Sadie said, limping over to the couch. "I had been planning to ship some gifts home . . ."

"Nonsense! I do not need a single thing in the world except time with you. Now, go on, open it."

Sadie carefully eased the paper off the gift to reveal a little blue velvet box. She popped open the lid and saw a golden stud in the shape of a tiny shamrock. "Thank you, Gran," Sadie said. "It's perfect."

"I know it," Gran said with a grin. "Your mom and granddad have always hated that nose stud of yours. In my day, it was a big deal for women to wear pants, for heaven's sake. You should be able to express yourself in any way you see fit." Her expression changed again for a moment, and Sadie thought she saw that shadow of sadness pass over it once more. "Plus, I like the idea of you having something special from me to keep close. A good luck charm for when I can't be by your side." Her voice seemed to break. "I'll always be with you, you know."

"You'll just be in Milwaukee," Sadie said, her throat suddenly tight, too. "I'll come home to visit again soon. Once the show's over."

"Once you've *won*," Gran said. "And you're the big star I've always known you were going to be." She reached for her granddaughter's hand and squeezed it, and Sadie had to resist the urge to throw herself into her gran's arms and have a good, pointless cry.

"Gran, what's wrong with us?" Sadie said, smiling through the tears she felt dampening the corners of her eyes. "We don't see each other for a few months and we get like this?"

"I know, I know," Gran said. "Not really the Hunter family style to emote quite this much, but it has been too long since we've seen one another. That's all." She squeezed Sadie's hand again. "Now, catch me up. I'm seeing your face in all the newspapers, and you're always on the evening news. You and that Max Brody." She cocked her head and raised an eyebrow, inquisitive. "You tend to brush me off when I ask about him on the phone."

"Right. Me and Max. Gran, the thing about that is—"

But Sadie's gran spoke over her, her brow now furrowed with concern. "The thing is, I'm worried about you, Sadie. It looks like you two are having a marvelous time—but I'd hate to see anything derail you. I always thought you'd get your career sorted first before you worried too much about romance. I don't mean to meddle, but the women in this family don't have the best luck when it comes to love, you know that."

This *was* true. Midway through her second Midwestern tour with her singing group, Elsie Munro had fallen in love at first sight with Herbert Hunter, Sadie's grandfather, while playing for a group of soldiers who had just returned from Vietnam. When Elsie talked about it—which was rare now, after all that had happened—she said he was simply the handsomest man she had ever seen in a uniform. *But*, she would add as the years went by, that was not a good reason to marry a man. She even once said she couldn't think of *any* good reason to marry at all. Sadie's Grandpa Herb was ultimately a good man—but staid, set in his ways, difficult to know.

Elsie and Herb had a whirlwind wedding—hastened, Sadie understood, although it was never openly discussed, by an unplanned pregnancy. Then they settled in Milwaukee and Herb made it clear the only sort of singing acceptable for a wife of his to do was at church, or while doing housework. This was not something Elsie had realized about Herb when she had fallen for him in his uniform. Sadie's Uncle Blair was born, her mom, Lynn, came along shortly thereafter, and Elsie set about the task of being a mother and a wife. But she never stopped missing her singing days. She once told Sadie her longing to sing was something she kept waiting to get over, only she never did. So, once Lynn and Blair were both finished with school, Elsie dropped a bombshell: she planned to move out and pay the rent on her own apartment by teaching singing lessons to youngsters. Perhaps most scandalous of all—to Herb, at least—she supplemented her income performing jazz standards once a week at a local supper club. She still returned to the family home a few times a week, to put meals in the fridge for the man who was still her husband in name alone. Not exactly a romantic story for the books.

Then Sadie's mother had her own wrong turn when it came to romance. At nineteen, shortly after Elsie and Herb's swept-under-the-rug split, Lynn married her high school sweetheart. Sadie only knew her father had been a charming football star named Jamie. He was probably still charming, wherever he was. She had never met him. There was a photo of him in her high school hallway, rakish and grinning, hoisting a trophy— but Sadie had always avoided looking at that photo. What she knew of her parents' love story was that Jamie had swept then-cheerleader Lynn off her feet. Then he had taken off when Sadie was two, leaving nothing but a note behind saying marriage and fatherhood just weren't for him, and he was thinking of becoming a pilot. They never heard from him again. Sadie had no clue whether he became a pilot or not. She told herself she didn't care about him. But his absence did sting. And these two marital disappointments had tarnished her view of true love. She scoffed at romantic movies and didn't read love stories. She thought she was more practical than that. She wasn't going to rule out love and marriage, she just wasn't going to make it a priority. So, of course, Elsie would be concerned to see her veering off course like this.

But a love affair was *not* in the cards for Sadie and Max.

"Gran, you don't have to worry about me. I'm not going to let romance get in the way of my dreams." She was about to tell her gran the truth, something she had been too nervous to do on the phone or by text lest someone overhear her secret. She had signed a nondisclosure agreement, but she knew Gran was a vault.

Sadie opened her mouth to explain everything—but was interrupted by the trilling of her door buzzer. "Hang on, Gran."

"Sadie? Hey . . . it's Max here." He sounded uncharacteristically shy. "Patsy's favorite freeze-dried raw kibble comes from a store in SoBro, meaning I was in the neighborhood, so I thought I'd check in and see how your ankle is."

Sadie was surprised by this—and felt a pleasant flush rise to her cheeks. "Come on up, Max," she said, then went to let in her second guest of the day. She opened the door to Max standing in the hall, holding a small box.

"Hey," he said, chewing his lip for a second.

"Hey, yourself."

"So, I noticed you like to drink tea on set for your voice—and we both know the stuff they serve is garbage," he said, holding his gift out to her. It was a box of A Cup of Christmas tea, from Nashville Tea Co. "This is so much better."

"Thank you, Max," she said, touched by his thoughtfulness. She offered to hang up his leather jacket, and felt the warmth of his skin as their hands touched.

"Well, I thought an emergency tea delivery was in order, since you're injured and all. This was my mom's favorite. How's the ankle?"

"Hell-oo-oo?" Gran called out from the living room.

Max stopped talking and looked at her quizzically.

"You have another visitor. I'm interrupting."

"It's my gran. She just arrived for a surprise visit." Sadie leaned in and lowered her voice to a whisper. "She has no idea. She thinks we're . . ."

"Right." He ducked his head and whispered, too. "We pretend all the time, so what's the harm in doing it now?"

Sadie looked up at him for a long moment, confused about what she was feeling. Seconds before, she had been ready to tell her gran the truth. But now, she wasn't sure what the truth was. "My ankle is starting to feel a lot better," was all she said, before she turned away and led him into her apartment to make introductions.

"I'm Elsie Hunter, lovely to meet you," Gran said with a smile. "But Sadie just calls me Gran, of course."

"Pleasure to meet you, ma'am," Max said. "Please, don't stand up. You look so cozy there." He approached the couch and reached out his hand to shake hers. "I love that blanket. You didn't knit that yourself, did you? That hurdle stitch is *not* easy to pull off."

"I sure did, young man," Gran replied, surprised. Sadie went into the kitchen to turn on the kettle and found herself smiling as she listened to the sound of Gran and Max chattering on about the complexity of hurdle stitches.

Then Max called out, "Now, Sadie, you're injured! You let me make that tea."

"This is not the smug, entitled, self-important young man I expected to meet," Gran whispered when Sadie was back beside her on the couch.

"Shhh!" Sadie glanced through the galley kitchen door to see if Max had overheard.

"Do you have any milk?" he called.

"I do," Sadie called back.

"Max, I am just such a big old fan of your father," Gran said as Max served the tea.

"Oh yeah?" Sadie noticed his smile dim a watt or two when his dad came up.

"What was it like, being raised by the great Holden Brody?" Gran's fandom was making her sound positively girlish.

"It was . . . well, *never boring*," Max said. "We got to travel a lot. I met a ton of musical greats."

"Gran, you should tell Max about *your* singing career," Sadie suggested, and caught a grateful look from Max at the topic change.

"Oh, please," Gran said dismissively. "I'd hardly call what I had a career."

"Not true," Sadie said. "Gran's got the most amazing voice."

"Well, that must mean you come by your incredible voice honestly," Max said, while Gran beamed at him, clearly charmed. Sadie loved seeing her gran so happy, as Max peppered her with questions about her short singing career. They refilled their tea several times as they chatted—and soon it was getting dark outside. Sadie's stomach growled and she hoped no one noticed. But no such luck.

"Uh-oh," Max said with a laugh, glancing over at Sadie. "She's hungry. You know what that means, right?"

Gran shared his laughter. "I sure do! She's been like this since birth. You need to keep her blood sugar at a certain level or she melts down."

"Gran! Max! That is *not* true."

"It is *so true*," they both said in unison—and Sadie found herself laughing along with them.

"I took the bus here," Max said. "But— well, I have access to a driver." He looked embarrassed when he said this. Sadie was coming to realize Max didn't exactly enjoy all the trappings that came along with being a Brody. "Elsie, have you ever been to Nashville before?"

"I can't say I have."

"Well, we can't let the inside of this apartment be the only thing you see. Let me take you two out on the town."

"I don't know, you looked pretty tired out from the travel, Gran. We could always just order in."

"Up to you, of course," Max said. "But I've got a regular table at a gastro-pub called Ernie's. It's not fancy, but it's got the most comfortable booths, and is my favorite spot for down-home cooking. A good meal might be just what Elsie needs to feel restored."

"Young man, I can't argue with you there," Gran said, pushing herself up off the couch. "I have reached the age where I will never say no to a good time, or a good meal, when it's offered."

"But, Max . . ." Sadie began.

Max looked at her—and Sadie saw realization dawn on him. "Right. Elsie, you should know, when Sadie and I are out in public together, things can get a little crazy with the media. Maybe you're not up for that."

Sadie hoped Gran would say she *wasn't* up for it. Pretending to be in love was going to feel even more disingenuous with her gran there to witness the deception—all the while not having a clue that her granddaughter was lying.

"We'll be fine," Gran said decisively. She turned to Sadie. "Come on, dear. Let's the two of us go freshen ourselves up for a night out. We'll want to look nice for all those photographers."

Sadie smiled wanly and followed along. When they were in the bedroom, Gran took Sadie's hands in hers. "Now, *that* is a nice boy," she said. "Maybe our family's streak of bad luck in love is over."

I have an idea," Max said, once they were all in the back of his town car together, cruising through the streets of Nashville. Almost every corner was decked out with a lit-up tree, and most of the building exteriors were strung with lights and hung with wreaths. The sidewalks were still bustling with holiday shoppers and seasonal visitors.

Max leaned forward and tapped on the glass divider. "Hey,

Debra, can you take us to Party City?" Debra, who had apparently been working for Max's family for years, was wearing sequined reindeer antlers that shook and sparkled as she nodded her head and said, "Sure thing!"

It was a weekday evening nowhere near Halloween, so the costume store was fairly empty. The cashier did a double take when they walked in and took out her phone to snap a quick photo when she thought they were unaware—but that was about it. No one else was around to witness Saxie at a costume shop.

"What's your plan here, Max?" Gran asked, puzzled.

"We're going to go out," Max explained. "But in disguise. Wigs, glasses, the whole bit. No one will know who we are!"

He picked up a deep brown wig that was styled into thick victory rolls at the nape. When he put it on Gran's head she hooted with laughter and shooed him away. "But it looks perfect on you," Max drawled. "Very LaVerne Andrews, just your style."

"I'm not the one who needs to go incognito," Gran replied.

"No reason you can't join in the fun, though." He grabbed an opera-length string of pearls and handed them to Gran, then turned to Sadie. "What about you? I'm thinking . . . Chewbacca mask?"

She swatted at him. "Do you really think this is going to work?"

"Why wouldn't it? Nashville is full of eccentrics. We'll blend right in."

He grabbed a cowboy hat with bright red curls attached and stuck it on his head, then added some dark-rimmed nerd glasses. "What do you think?"

Sadie couldn't help but laugh as he waggled his eyebrows at her in the absurd getup.

In the end, Gran agreed to the wig and the pearls, while Sadie decided on a blunt, black Cleopatra-esque bob paired with thick-rimmed cat's-eye tortoiseshell glasses. She hardly recognized herself when she looked in the mirror. Meanwhile, Max bought an ash-blond mullet and a pair of blue-tinted John Lennon–style glasses that concealed his deep brown eyes.

"You two truly do look ridiculous," Gran said with a chuckle as they headed back to the waiting car. "And, I'll admit—this is *fun*."

The disguises worked. At the restaurant, they got a few odd looks as they waited for their table, but no one recognized them. They were left in peace at a table laden with hot chicken dip, crab cakes, chicken and biscuits, crispy Brussels sprouts—and the restaurant's signature goat cheese board.

Sadie was ravenous but couldn't help but notice her gran didn't eat much. She just picked at the food on her plate and asked for hot water with lemon a few times. She also took a pill halfway through the meal and brushed Sadie off when she tried to ask what the pill was for. "I'm in my eighties, not my twenties. I could not possibly eat the way you two are without a little pill for my digestion—but that doesn't mean I'm not having a ball! Quit your worrying, Sadie."

Once their leftovers were packaged up and the bill was paid—Sadie had insisted they go Dutch—Max turned to Sadie and Elsie, his eyes lit up with another idea. "Want me to get us a table at the Song Sparrow?"

At the mention of the Song Sparrow, Sadie's heart skipped a beat. She looked down at the table, then back up at Max. They had met there years before—and Max hadn't been all that nice to her. But the guy she had been getting to know these past few days—and especially tonight—seemed like a different person. Was it really possible he'd changed? How could she know for sure?

"Watching live music at the Song Sparrow would be a delight—everyone has played there, from Cash to Cline," Gran said, her expression turning dreamy for a moment. But then she came back down to Earth. "I know my limits, though. I must call it a night. However, I *insist* you two go on without me, especially when you're both dressed to kill. I'm a grown woman and can get myself back to Sadie's place if she gives me the key or code or what have you. I have my cell phone here if I get into any trouble."

No matter how much they protested, Gran wouldn't hear of Max and Sadie accompanying her back to the apartment—but she did allow Max to send her back with his driver, while they went on to the Song Sparrow in a taxi.

Soon, the curlicued Song Sparrow sign came into view, even more noticeable than usual because it was strung with bright red Christmas lights and a giant wreath was pegged to the "o." The taxi drew to a halt and Max paid before Sadie could, then opened the door for her. "I will say one thing," he drawled. "That gran of yours is right that we can't let these getups go to waste." He adjusted his mullet and Sadie laughed. He looked truly absurd. She had laughed more tonight than she had in ages—and felt grateful to Max for that

It was crowded and loud inside the Song Sparrow, even at the out-of-the-way table Max was able to secure for them by talking to the manager. The band on the stage was an upbeat bluegrass trio. While Max went up to the bar, Sadie's phone lit up. She quickly answered, thinking it might be her gran calling to say she was having trouble getting into her apartment.

"Sadie? Hey, this is Cruz calling. Cruz McNeil."

As if there could be any other. "Hey, Cruz," she said with a surprised smile just as Max returned to the table with their drinks. She stood and walked further into the bar so she could hear him better.

"I was just calling to see how you're doing. How's your ankle? Sounds like you're out and about?"

"Max and I are at the Song Sparrow. I'm getting around just fine. It's nice of you to check in, though." She felt elated. Maybe Cruz wasn't entirely focused on Johnny after all and was interested in mentoring her, too.

"Well, that's good to hear, Sadie. I was feeling awfully guilty, after you had to come to us producers and ask for a wardrobe concept change. And you were absolutely right—high heels are a hazard. I'm just glad to hear one of the top contenders is back on her feet, though."

One of the top contenders. Sadie's smile grew a few sizes as she thanked Cruz for checking in and he told her to go have a good time; he'd see her tomorrow.

Back at their table, Max had a sour expression on his face. "Cruz McNeil is calling you personally?" he said, his voice tight. He was jealous, Sadie realized. He wanted that kind of attention from Cruz for himself—but Cruz was one of the rare people in Nashville who didn't fall all over himself around Max.

"He was checking to see how my ankle was," she said.

"I'm sure he was," Max muttered.

"Excuse me? What's that supposed to mean?"

He toyed with his still full beer bottle, ripping the label to tiny shreds—and Sadie couldn't help but be reminded of something she had been avoiding thinking about, because she hadn't wanted it to ruin the nice evening she and Max were having: the time they had met, years before, in this very place. Max looked up at her again. "Cruz has a reputation."

"I know it. A reputation for being the best in the business, the kind of person who can help someone get ahead."

"You could say that, I suppose."

"I don't think I like what you're implying."

"Oh yeah? What exactly am I implying?"

They sat facing each other, fire rather than warmth in their eyes now. "That Cruz could not possibly be interested in me for my talent."

"Here we go again. The real Sadie Hunter is back. Insecure. Always ready to pitch a fit."

"The *real* Sadie Hunter?" Sadie's voice was so loud, even over the music, that the couple at the next table looked over. "How about you? *Your* true colors? You've been so charming tonight, but that's not the real you, is it? That's just the Max Brody you like the world to see, so everyone will fall in love with you and treat you like royalty!"

"What the hell is that supposed to mean?" he growled. Sadie swept her eyes around the room, then back to Max. Moments before, it had seemed like water under the bridge, a chance meeting years before when they were both a lot younger. But now, seeing this side of Max come out in full force so easily, she knew she had to get it off her chest.

"We met before, you know. Six years ago."

Max's expression darkened further. "Six years? That wasn't exactly the best time in my life."

"It was the first time I came to Nashville. I was just out of school and I had scraped together enough money—with Gran's help—to stay for a month. I managed to get a slot to sing here for New Talent Night. I was incredibly nervous. You were there."

"You must have looked different. I would have remembered you."

When someone shows you who they are, believe them, was something Gran often said to Sadie. And hadn't Max shown her who he was, six years before? Sadie needed to remember to protect her heart.

"I went outside, around the back of the tavern—and you were leaning against a wall, having a cigarette, looking like James Dean."

"Your voice," he said, realization dawning. "I knew I'd heard it before. But I thought it was just because it was—"

"Common," Sadie interrupted. "Right?"

"Don't put words in my mouth," he snapped. "You know your voice is anything but common!"

"It sure is easy to get you to drop your charming veneer!"

"Know what? I should go. And you should get home, too. Go see how your gran is feeling." He took out his phone. "I'll see if my driver is on her way back here yet. She'll take you home."

"I can get myself home. I don't need *you*. But don't you want to hear the rest of the story of how we met? Or are you too afraid it's going to make you look bad?"

Max rubbed a hand across the stubble on his chin. "Go ahead, then," he said reluctantly.

"Well, you dragged on your cigarette and told me that you were no stranger to stage fright. I couldn't believe my luck, getting to meet *the great* Holden Brody's son on the night I also got to sing at the Song Sparrow. Then you gave me a tip: you said the best way to deal with fear was to look out at your audience, find a friendly face, and sing to that person and that person alone. You promised you'd be out there in the crowd. That when I looked for you I'd find you. That you'd be my friendly face. And you told me to wait for you after the show. You said you'd make a few introductions to some industry people who were here that night." Sadie stopped talking and looked down at the table, embarrassed now to think about how starstruck she had been. She had thought meeting Max Brody was going to lead to her big break. She looked back up at him. "Is any of this ringing a bell?"

Max nodded, unaffected. "Yeah. That was advice my mom gave me, back in my school pageant days: look for a friendly face. So?"

"When I went out there to sing I looked for you—but you were ducking out the back door with a blonde. We never talked. You never did make those introductions. I guess I was pretty naïve back then, right, Max? You had no intention of sticking around at all."

"Right," Max said, his voice now as cold as the beer bottle in her hand. "Sounds like something I would have done back then."

Sadie stared at him, waiting to feel relieved that she had told him this. But she didn't feel better at all. She'd been hanging on to something for six years that he either had no memory of or didn't care about. She felt foolish. Still, she couldn't resist pressing on the bruise one more time. "Why did you even bother telling me that story about your mom's advice then, or making me feel like you actually understood how I was feeling, if you were just going to leave?"

Something flickered across Max's expression that looked a lot like guilt and remorse. For a moment Sadie thought he was actually going to answer her properly—and somehow make it better between them again. But by the time he opened his mouth his expression was defensive again. "You need to move on," he said as he got up to leave. "This is a long time to be holding a grudge, even for someone as dramatic as you."

He walked out before she could respond. But the truth was, she had nothing more to say.

7

Max

Nashville, Tennessee
December 22

At the three rapid knocks on the door, Max's fingers immediately paused on his guitar strings, and a scowl took over his face. He felt like he was endlessly being disturbed—whether during rehearsals or while he was trying to chill out with some yarn and John Denver.

"What?" Max replied, with more irritation than necessary. Sadie, seated on the piano's bench, shot him a familiar look—the one she sported when she disapproved of what he was doing, or saying. He shook his head at her as if to say, *Do not start with me*. Sadie murmured that he was "impossible," and his scowl deepened.

"Uh, can I come in?" It was Landon. Max was still mildly

annoyed with his assistant. If Landon had been more careful, Patsy wouldn't have escaped the trailer the week before, Sadie wouldn't have jumped in her ridiculous heels to go after the little dog, she wouldn't have sprained her ankle, and Max would never have gone to her apartment to check up on her that night. Which meant he wouldn't have met her gran or had so much fun getting costumes and going out for dinner. But he also wouldn't have ended up at the Song Sparrow with Sadie, where everything unraveled as quickly as a sharp yarn pull on a half-knit sweater.

He *did* remember that night at the Song Sparrow now, but until Sadie had brought it up, he hadn't remembered meeting her there because of what else had happened that evening. Max should have just explained himself, but being back at the Sparrow had ignited a barrage of unpleasant feelings he'd worked hard to lock up. She also hadn't given him a chance to explain, being so committed to her own version about why he'd taken off that night (that he was a jackass, and that's what jackasses do). He wasn't proud that he'd left her there, twice now, but she had made him madder than a stinging hornet with her accusations.

So, yeah. The unfortunate chain of events wasn't exactly Landon's fault, but none of it would have happened without his carelessness, either. Sadie's ankle seemed to be better, even though it remained an alarming mash-up of green-and-yellow bruising. But she was clearly still *not* happy with Max, and holding her own grudge.

Well, the feeling is mutual, Sadie.

Just before Landon had interrupted, they had been working

on their next duet—a cover of "All I Want for Christmas"—for the upcoming Christmas-themed episode of *Starmaker*. The tension was thick in the rehearsal room. He and Sadie had been at each other's throats, disagreeing on everything from the arrangement to the temperature of their rehearsal room. Max liked it warm, so he could play in only a T-shirt, but Sadie's preferred rehearsal outfit was tights and long, bulky sweaters.

"Look, if you had to wear what I do every time you stepped onstage, which is basically nothing, you'd be reaching for big sweaters, too," she had quipped when he'd suggested she simply take off a layer if she was too hot. It was the most she'd said to him in days.

"Hello?" Landon knocked again—gently, rapidly, like a baby woodpecker testing its first tree—as he slowly opened the door, peeking his head in. It was then Max realized why his assistant was being so cautious: it was this fake relationship. Landon probably didn't want to disturb them in case things were hot and heavy behind closed doors. *Ha!* The reality could not be further from the truth.

"To what do we owe this great pleasure, Landon?" Max could practically feel Sadie shooting him that look again. He wasn't interested in seeing it, so he kept his eyes downcast and on the strings, as he plucked-plucked-plucked.

"You have a visitor," Landon said.

Now Max glanced up. Then looked at Sadie, who shrugged, as surprised as he was.

"Who has a visitor?" Max asked.

"Well, he didn't want me to—"

"Maximillian, my boy!" Holden Brody stepped through

the rehearsal room's doorway, and Landon beamed at the musical legend while Sadie stared in shock, mouthing, *"Maximillian?"* Max scowled at the use of his full name (which he never went by), and felt a flurry of emotions, none of them good.

Holden Brody was approaching sixty, but he looked much younger. Max shared his dad's chiseled jawline, his dark hair (though Holden had twice-monthly coloring appointments to keep his that way) and deep brown eyes. Holden had on one of the cowboy hats he was rarely without.

"And you must be Sadie Hunter," Holden said, taking his hat off with one hand and bowing slightly toward her. "What a pleasure it is to meet you."

"It's an honor to meet you, Mr. Brody." She smiled under his gaze, and Max's irritation ratcheted up. Though he was used to his father's effect on people—everyone responded the same way to Holden Brody, as though he were a god (and he was, at least in Nashville)—seeing Sadie fall under his spell made his stomach twist.

"Please, call me Holden," Max's dad said. Then he turned to Max, lowering his voice almost to a whisper. "Well done, Maxy. She's delightful."

Sadie looked tickled to hear Max's childhood nickname. "I didn't 'do' anything, Dad." Max's tone made it clear Holden's visit was not a welcome surprise. "Why are you here?"

For one moment Max saw his dad's perfect veneer wobble, but he soon recovered and turned to Landon. "Would you mind, young man? It's leaning against the wall, just outside the door."

"What is?" Max asked as Landon practically ran through

the doorway to retrieve whatever it was Holden had brought with him. He was back a moment later, lumbering slightly with the awkwardly shaped, gift-wrapped box.

"Happy Birthday, Max." Holden gestured for Landon to give Max the gift.

"'Happy Birthday'?" Sadie slowly turned toward Max. "Today's your birthday? Why didn't you say anything?"

"Should I get a cake?" Landon asked.

"No, Landon, you should not get a cake," Max replied at the same time Holden and Sadie said, "Good idea!" and "Yes, and candles, too!"

Landon was gone in a flash and Max put a hand to his forehead, rubbing the bridge of his nose. He suddenly had a pounding headache, and his fingers itched for the yarn and needles in his bag. The meditative clicking sounds and predictable rhythm of knitting calmed him better than anything else could. But obviously now was not the time for that.

"Go on, open it up," Holden said, sitting on the arm of the small sofa in the room.

"Being a Christmas baby can be tough, so Max's mom always wanted to make sure he got a proper birthday celebration, too," he said to Sadie. "And even though she's gone, I've continued the tradition."

What Max wanted to say was that Holden had only started remembering his birthday in the past couple of years. Before that, Holden Brody was far too self-centered, unavailable, and often drunk to keep something so mundane as his only son's birthday top of mind.

"Look, Dad, thanks for dropping by, but Sadie and I have to

rehearse. Maybe we can do this later?" He set the wrapped gift, unopened, against the rehearsal room's back wall.

"Aren't you going to open it?" Sadie glanced between Max and the gift. "Your dad went to all the trouble . . ."

Holden put a hand up. "It's fine, Sadie. Max is a workaholic— like his dad." He winked then. "You can bring it to Christmas dinner, Maxy." Then Holden turned to Sadie. "And that just gave me a great idea! Sadie, why don't you join us? For Christmas dinner? Max's sister, Becca, is in England and won't make it home this year, and if you don't come it will just be the two of us at the huge dining room table."

Sadie was momentarily speechless, and she gave Max a searching look.

"Dad, I'm sure Sadie has her own plans," Max said.

"Well, I don't, actually. I'm from Milwaukee, so I can't get there and get back in time for the next show." Sadie gave Max another glance, trying to gauge his reaction, but he kept his face blank. He was confused about why Sadie would agree to spend Christmas dinner with him when she could barely seem to stand being in his presence. Just another example of how he would never really understand Sadie Hunter.

"It's settled, then." Holden clapped his hands on his denim-clad thighs. "Well, it isn't every day I get to have Christmas dinner with 'hashtag' Saxie. I'm looking forward to it."

"Me, too," Sadie said, grinning at Holden. "My gran is possibly your biggest fan. She'll be beside herself to know how I'm spending Christmas this year."

Max stayed silent, his grip on the neck of his guitar tight enough the strings pressed painfully into his palm. He wondered if this was why Sadie agreed to dinner—a feather in her cap, to say she'd spent Christmas with "the great Holden Brody." That was one way to make it in this town—exploiting your networks however you could.

"If you don't mind, close the door on the way out," Max said to his dad, the edge still in his voice.

Holden nodded. "Bye, son. And Happy Birthday."

Max looked down at his guitar, waiting to hear the door latch click. The room went quiet, Max now alone with Sadie.

"You two could not look more alike," Sadie said, breaking the silence. "And he really knows how to fill a room, doesn't he? He has unbelievable stage presence even when he's not onstage."

When Max didn't respond, Sadie walked over to the box leaning against the wall, limping slightly because of her ankle.

"It looks like a guitar, maybe?"

"It is a guitar." Max wished he could ignore the gift. "But I already have a guitar. See?" He treasured the instrument in his hands because of the person who had gifted it to him. Max wondered if his father even remembered where this guitar had come from, and why trying to replace it was like a slap in the face for his son.

"Aren't you curious?" she asked, touching the wrapping paper.

"Leave it alone, Sadie," Max said, his voice sharp. He knew he shouldn't take his frustrations out on her, but his dad always had this effect on him. He hated the truth of that as much as how it felt. "Just for once, can you leave it alone?"

Sadie crossed her arms tightly over her chest, the wrapping paper forgotten. "What's that supposed to mean?"

He sighed wearily. The last thing he needed was another fight with Sadie. "It means we have work to do. If we don't get this nailed down we won't win, and then we both go home. Is that what you want?"

"Of course not." She stood there for a moment longer and then limped back over to the piano and sat down, placing her fingers on the keys. Max could only imagine what she was thinking, and rightfully so—that he was spoiled and entitled. What sort of son didn't open his father's birthday gift?

But that wasn't his whole story, and he didn't know how to explain it to Sadie. So he decided to focus on the music, because that was the only thing he could control, especially now that Holden had invited Sadie over for Christmas dinner. He was not prepared for his worlds to collide like that.

Max strummed the opening sequence for the cover song, and with one last glance at his father's gift, he turned his attention to Sadie. Her fingers were gentle yet confident on the keys, and when she began singing goosebumps ran up and down Max's arms. *Damn, could she sing.* It was pure talent—the sort of raw voice that came along so rarely you couldn't help but be mesmerized by it. If she could shake her insecurities and harness that nervous energy, she would take over Nashville.

He joined her in the second verse, their voices melding flawlessly. They had slowed the song way down, as they'd done with "Islands in the Stream," and Max knew even Johnny

King, also a fan favorite, couldn't beat this thing he and Sadie had going. It was magical, just like the judges said. They may not have been a good match without the music (*understatement of the century, Max*), but when they sang together, there was nowhere else Max would rather be.

8

Sadie

Nashville, Tennessee
December 24

The *Starmaker All I Want for Christmas Holiday Extrava-ganza* had been broadcast live-to-air the night before, so the atmosphere on set was less intense than usual. Everyone was tired, and ready for Christmas. The day was spent shooting B-roll and short interviews with the contestants where they were asked to share their favorite holiday traditions, and what they were going to miss most about not being home for the holidays.

Sadie couldn't wait to get back to her apartment and enjoy the care package her gran had left before heading to the airport to return to Wisconsin that morning. Sadie knew it was filled with familiar holiday goodies from home like seven-layer bars and stollen, a fruitcake-like bread she liked to spread thickly with cream cheese. It always took her right back to her childhood when Lynn, Elsie, and Sadie would cover their kitchen counters at home with candied citrus peel, marzipan, spices, and powdered sugar.

She was packing up to leave when her cell phone rang. It was Amalia.

"We need to have a meeting. Now."

Sadie's heart sank. "Is something wrong?"

"No, nothing's wrong. But it's urgent. I'm outside the studio waiting to pick you up."

Once outside, Sadie made her way across the parking lot to where her manager waited, ushering Sadie to her car.

"No questions now," Amalia said. "We need to meet in a neutral location and sort this out. And then you and Max can decide what you think."

"Where is this neutral location?"

"Love Point."

"Doesn't sound very *neutral* to me."

As Amalia piloted her gleaming white Audi through Nashville's streets, all the storefronts and buildings glimmered with holiday lights. They left the city behind and kept going, eventually pulling into the circular parking lot that surrounded the hill they were about to climb. There weren't many cars left at the popular tourist spot. Everyone was home for Christmas Eve.

"I feel like I'm being kidnapped," Sadie admitted as they sat, waiting—for what, Sadie wasn't sure, but she presumed it had to do with Bobbi and Max.

"Don't be silly!" Amalia laughed her crow-caw of a laugh, then darted a glance out the slightly open window. "Ah. Here they come. Okay, let's go. Here." She handed Sadie a flashlight and turned on a small lantern she held.

"Amalia, this is just—"

"Trust me, okay? Have I ever steered you wrong before?" Amalia led her toward the base of the hill, where Max and Bobbi waited, holding flashlights, too. Max seemed equally mystified—and mildly alarmed. "Hey," he said to Sadie, nodding his head. Things hadn't exactly been great with them lately. The only time they got along was when they were singing together. But still, she widened her eyes at him, as if to say, *What the hell is this?* Max shrugged in response. At least they could agree on one thing: this was odd.

"Come on, you two," Bobbi called out. Rather than one of her customary sleek pantsuits, she had on an expensive-looking jogging suit and running shoes. "It's a steep climb, but short."

Sadie was glad she'd sworn off high heels for good as she climbed the dark embankment. She was acutely aware of Max right behind her. At the top of the point, she surveyed the scene. *"Wow."*

The entirety of Nashville was spread out before them, holiday lights glittering like rubies, emeralds, and diamonds. She felt a pang of nostalgia for home, which would be blanketed in a cozy and festive layer of snow on Christmas Eve. But she also understood, seeing Nashville from this height, why astronauts who went to space said it changed them forever: because it gave you a new perspective. As she looked down at the city she had been trying to conquer for such a long time, Sadie realized it wasn't that big after all. She could see it from end to end. It had less power over her, from this viewpoint. She also felt a wave of affection for it, and wondered if that was why the spot they were at was called Love Point. How could you *not* love Nashville, seeing it like this?

"Over here!" Bobbi called. She'd found a picnic table close by and was waving them over. Bobbi and Max set their flashlights on the table, then Amalia pulled a bottle of champagne from her bag.

Max frowned. "What are we celebrating?"

"The two of you. That gorgeous duet you sang last night—you're at the height of your popularity with viewers right now." Amalia popped the cork while Bobbi produced paper cups and passed them around.

"We have a proposal," Amalia began. At this, Bobbi chuckled—and Sadie frowned. What was going on here?

"Yes," Bobbi chimed in. "Exactly. A *proposal*. I think we can all agree that 'hashtag' Saxie, this incredible persona you've created, has immense potential."

"But," Amalia interjected, as Sadie found herself wondering if they'd practiced this little routine in advance. "You are only as good as the last news cycle. Right now, you are shiny, you are new, you are *riveting*. But that is all going to change, because in this industry change is constant. In order to launch you two into the stratosphere, we think that once this little charade is over—" At the word *charade* she waved her hand around as if shooing away a bug, and Bobbi took over. They had *definitely* practiced.

"—we need to make your breakup spectacular. Which means raising the stakes."

Sadie could feel Max's body growing tense beside her. They had spent so much time together she understood the nuances of his body language. She felt nervous, too.

"What exactly are you talking about?" she said.

"We think Max needs to propose," Bobbi answered.

"What?!" Max exploded.

For her part, Sadie was unable to utter a single word—or to quite catch her breath.

"Hear us out," Amalia said. "And wipe those horrified expressions off your faces. You don't have to actually get married!" She laughed so hard her eyes teared up. "But what we need is for the public to *think* you're getting married. We need them to get completely invested in your upcoming wedding. The dress! The venue! The wedding party! The rumored musical guests! You'll be on the covers of all the tabs every damn week. Bobbi and I did some calculations, and if you win both 'fan favorite' segments of the *Starmaker* competition, you win the whole damn thing. Guaranteed. And you're a shoo-in for that."

"But," Bobbi said, her voice now dead serious. "Once the show ends, there will be nothing new for the news cycle. I mean, you'll have a few weeks, maybe a month if you're lucky, of people still being interested. Max, you always get press, but it's not for the reasons you want. It's never about your music, and if we can keep attention on you two, we can get your music more attention, too. But you have to give them something new to chew on. Get engaged."

"But," Max sputtered.

Bobbi talked over him. "The night you win the show, you cement your place in people's hearts when Max, overcome by his emotions, drops down to one knee and asks for Sadie's hand in front of an audience of millions. Then, following a one-year engagement, just after you return to *Starmaker* to sing your song on the holiday extravaganza, you'll break up in dazzling, public fashion."

"Absolutely not," Max said.

Sadie was silent, though. She gazed down at the picnic table, where in the flickering lantern light she could see that someone had carved "Raf + Suze 4-ever and ever." Who knew where these two people were now? Still together? Probably not. All it took was one look at what had happened with Sadie's parents, or her grandparents, to understand that true love was just a fantasy.

Going all in on faking it, however, could potentially have its career benefits. Sadie turned to Max slowly.

"Why not? If we're just pretending, what does it matter?"

"Are you serious, Sadie?" His expression was intense— maybe even scared. "You would actually want to pretend to be . . . engaged to be married?"

The way he said "engaged to be married" made it sound quite serious indeed. And, Sadie had to admit, it made her heart skip a beat and her body do something that could technically be referred to as a swooning, if anyone had noticed. But no one did. And that was the point. The chemistry between Sadie and Max had nothing to do with the real world. It only existed in the musical world—and this was a world in which Max and Sadie both wanted to make a lasting name for themselves.

"They're right," Sadie said, leveling her eyes at Max. "This is a sure shot at our mutual goals. It means all this"—she waved her hand, attempting to be as blasé about it as Amalia had been—"will be worth something. It won't just be a one-and-done moment, forgotten about as soon as someone more interesting comes along."

Max just stared at her, long and hard, as if seeing her for the first time—and not especially liking what he saw. She could see him gritting his teeth, and there it was: that familiar way his jaw got very tense.

"Max, you understand fame," Bobbi said, and Max began to look annoyed. He *did* understand. He was *famous*. He wanted more, though. Max wanted his own kind of notoriety—Sadie knew that by now. And he didn't need her to get it. Not as much as she needed him.

Bobbi gave Max a pointed look before continuing. "There are flashes in the pan, and then there are those chosen ones who become beloved, outside of any advantages they might have. You will get where you want to be—but only if you do what we say. Trust me."

Max did trust Bobbi, Sadie knew this. But he was still extremely skeptical. "Do we have to get *engaged*?" he said. "Can't we just pretend to be together until that final performance next Christmas, and then break up? Won't that be enough for everyone?"

"It won't," Amalia said. "People will get bored. But if there's one thing people never get bored of, it's a royal wedding. And, Max, *you* are Nashville royalty. And, Sadie, you are Cinderella—" Now it was Sadie's turn to grit her teeth. "We just need to take you one step further. *This* is the step. The step that will help make all your dreams come true. And all you have to do . . ."

"Is propose," Bobbi concluded, as if it were the simplest thing in the world.

Max sighed as if someone had suggested that all he had to do to achieve his goal was agree to pluck out every single hair on his head with tweezers. Sadie glowered at him, hating how hopeful she felt, how squarely her dreams rested in his hands.

"Fine," he finally said.

Sadie swallowed her surprise. She echoed her own, "Fine," then extended her hand so they could shake on it. She looked into his eyes as they continued to hold onto each other's hands—and again she had that sensation of falling. It passed, though. This was a business agreement, nothing more. "We have a deal, then," Sadie said, releasing his hand.

Amalia and Bobbi lifted their paper cups, full of champagne, and proposed a toast. But Max just shook his head. "I'm not a real champagne drinker. See you tomorrow, Sadie. Dinner is at seven, but Holden likes a long cocktail hour, so come early."

He looked solemn when he said this, and despite her frustration with him, Sadie also felt a pang of something. He was clearly dreading dinner with his dad—when, meanwhile, Sadie would have given anything to be going home and having dinner with her gran and mom. They always ate early—turkey *and* ham, mashed potatoes *and* roasted—and went for a long walk to look at Christmas lights. Then a few friends and family members stopped by for an open house, which was never really planned but somehow always happened, and out came the cheese board and old-fashioneds. Elsie and Sadie would sit at the piano together, playing their favorite holiday songs. Sadie had the sense Max's mom had given him the kind of safe harbor she felt she had when she went home. Now all he had was Holden.

As Sadie watched Max walk away she decided something. If she was going to be a part of his life for one full year, maybe she could at least find a way to help him not look so miserable all the time—because a man who was supposed to be crazy in love and engaged to be married was supposed to look *happy*.

Sadie had an idea. Finding the perfect Christmas gift. It would be a good test for pretending to be engaged to him. If she could nail the perfect gift for Max Brody, if she could actually make him smile, she knew she would also be able to make everyone in the world believe, for one full year, that she was madly in love with him. That she wanted nothing more than to spend the rest of her life by his side.

"Amalia, could you please take me to Opry Mills?" It was a massive shopping center that would probably be a zoo on Christmas Eve—but Sadie knew what she had to do. "I need to find the perfect gift."

9

Max

Nashville, Tennessee
December 25

Max sat on the gargantuan white L-shaped couch in the opulent living room of his childhood home, where he had been staying for the past few weeks. The floors in his condo in the Gulch were being replaced, and moving home had seemed easier than temporarily relocating somewhere else for the month. Plus, with *Starmaker*'s demanding schedule he'd figured he would barely be home.

He tried to focus on anything but his now-opened birthday gift, its glossy surface mirroring the twinkle lights from the Christmas tree. It was over the top, even for Holden Brody—a blond Gibson SJ-200, vintage but in pristine condition and supposedly played by one of the Everly Brothers at a concert in the late 1950s.

"He couldn't have bought me, like, a book? A pair of socks?" Max said to Patsy, straightening her sweater, a bright red knit with rows of white-and-gold Christmas ornaments that he had finished only yesterday. In truth, Max had no idea what other families bought for birthdays. Everything had always been over the top in the Brody Mansion.

Patsy nuzzled her nose into the crook of Max's neck and gave a long sigh.

"Exactly my point. I don't need this guitar. *I have a guitar.*" Sure, it wasn't an SJ-200. It didn't hold the same pedigree, the patina was worn, and the sound could be finicky, depending on the humidity and temperature. But it had belonged to his mom. She'd played it the one and only time she'd been onstage at the Grand Ole Opry.

"Go chart your own course, my love," his mom had told him when she gave it to him, just over six years earlier. Maren's once-melodic voice had been weak from the grueling treatments, and she had numbness in her fingers, so couldn't play anymore. Though she'd had cancer, it was a bout of pneumonia that had resulted in her death only eight months after her diagnosis. Max hadn't had nearly enough time with her.

So yes, his guitar was sentimental, but it was also a damn fine instrument and it didn't need replacing.

Max glanced at his watch, his anxiety ratcheting up. Sadie was due to arrive in about ten minutes. He was supposed to propose in a couple of days, after the finale. If being onstage playing a well-rehearsed song still caused him to break out in a nervous sweat, how would he manage getting down on one knee to propose to Sadie? That was a performance he wasn't sure he could pull off.

And then there was the even bigger issue: Max had complicated feelings toward Sadie. There, yeah, he admitted it. He couldn't shake the sense that this plan—even if executed perfectly—was going to backfire . . . big time.

S o, I had just sung this line . . . You may know it, Sadie." Holden leaned back against the overstuffed easy chair with his cocktail glass—three fingers of scotch—in hand and sang, *"In my whiskey dreams, I like you best with just your T-shirt on . . ."*

"I think I may have heard it once or twice," Sadie said. It was one of Holden's most famous songs, and was now a permanent fixture on the country music charts.

"So, this young woman is holding up a bottle of whiskey. She was right near the front, but I couldn't see much. You know how bright those spotlights are." Holden sipped his scotch. He no longer drank the way he had when Max was younger—like a fish, whatever was within reach though he preferred an expensive red wine or a fine whiskey—but he had never committed to total sobriety.

"Anyway, I already had my bottle ready—I always did a shot of whiskey at that part of the song, and people loved it. Showbiz," Holden said with a shrug. Max stared into his beer glass, having heard this story a hundred times.

"But I stopped singing and said, 'Honey, why don't you come up and join me?'"

One of the household staff poked her head into the

great room. "Mr. Brody, I'm heading out now," she said. "Everything is in the refrigerator, and I've made up the guest room."

"Thank you, sweetheart," Holden said. Sadie glanced at Max—she was not a fan of the term "sweetheart"—and he gave her a weak smile, because now she knew he had picked it up from his dad.

"So, security helped this young lady up onstage and it was then that I saw the problem." He laughed, caught up in the memory.

"What was it?" Sadie asked, taking a small sip of her own drink—a glass of red wine that she had been nursing for a while.

"She was only wearing a T-shirt!" Holden exploded with more laughter, delighted by his own storytelling. "I hadn't been able to see her legs, so had no idea she had half stripped before coming up on the stage."

Sadie gave an appropriately placed gasp and said, "No, she didn't!"

"She sure did, darlin'." He took a gulp of his scotch. Max set his half-finished beer down, the only drink he'd had all night, because the alcohol was making his stomach turn.

"I assure you I would not have invited her up if I'd known she was half naked. I am a father to a daughter after all," Holden said. "But it was an honest mistake, and, well, the show must go on."

Max didn't love the way Sadie seemed so enamored with his dad and his stories. He wasn't jealous—he was merely annoyed by the spotlight that followed his dad everywhere. The backdrop of Max's life.

"What do you think, son? Should we open the lovely gifts

Sadie brought for us?" Holden turned to their guest. "You being here is a gift for both of us, isn't that right, Maxy?"

"Hmm-hmm," Max replied quietly. "The gift that keeps on givin'."

Sadie, who was close enough to hear his quip, cleared her throat and tightened her ponytail. But her smile never faltered. *Why did you say that?* Max silently berated himself. Why did he turn into such a jerk when she was around?

She went to the Christmas tree—dripping in silver and gold decorations that sparkled with hundreds of miniature white lights—and pulled a couple of presents out from underneath its lowest branches.

"This is for you," she said, handing a large, square package wrapped in festive paper with a shiny white bow on its top to Holden. Then she handed two wrapped gifts to Max, one that was in a rectangular box (again with a large white bow), and one that was somewhat awkwardly shaped. Sadie pointed at that one. "That's for Patsy Canine."

Hearing her name, Patsy got up from her pillow and sauntered over the cushions to Sadie, where she turned around exactly three times and then settled with a little grunt right up against her leg.

"Well, what do we have here?" Holden asked, pulling the wrapping paper off. Inside the box was a pastry, in the shape of an elongated letter "O" and covered in a layer of white icing. "Did Max tell you about my sweet tooth?"

Sadie just smiled (Max hadn't told her a thing about Holden, because his father was his least favorite topic) and said, "It's called Kringle—very traditional in Wisconsin. This one has cherries, cranberries, and cream cheese. It's from my favorite bakery back home. We always have one at Christmastime."

Max saw a wistful look pass over Sadie's face, and he felt badly she was spending Christmas with him and his dad instead of her own family. He wasn't Holden's biggest fan, but there were still plenty of good memories for Max in this house, especially during the holidays, which had been his mom's favorite time of year.

Max knew Sadie must have had the Kringle shipped and he was impressed she'd gone to the trouble. He smiled at her, then pointed to the two packages on his lap.

"Which one first?"

"Patsy's," she replied.

Max opened the gift—a bag of organic chicken jerky treats—and shook it. Patsy's head snapped up. "Look what Sadie got for you, girl." He took one out and handed it to Sadie, who then gave it to Patsy.

"You're her best friend now," Max said, and sure enough, Patsy crawled up on Sadie's lap and leaned against her chest, staring at her adoringly.

Sadie scratched under Patsy's chin. "Okay, now you, Max."

With a few rips, Max had his gift open. His hands paused for a moment when he realized what it was. "Oh, wow." He looked over at her, again surprised by her thoughtfulness. "Thank you, Sadie."

It was a small, beige linen bag, all one piece with a wide fabric handle.

"What is it?" Holden asked.

"It's a project bag," Sadie replied, turning to Holden. "For yarn." For a moment she looked uncomfortable, as though she had given away one of Max's secrets.

"It's for my knitting stuff, Dad," Max explained.

"Ah. Well, isn't that thoughtful, Maxy?"

"It is," Max replied quietly.

Max got up from the couch and pulled a small, gold-paper-wrapped gift from under the tree. He handed it to Sadie.

"You didn't have to get me anything," she said, looking surprised as she took it from him. Their fingers touched briefly, and a spark traveled between them. Max had an almost overwhelming urge to keep holding her hand. When she pulled away, he felt a crush of disappointment.

"Oh," she said, her voice low. She stared at the gift in her hands, and for a moment Max thought she hated it. He felt incredibly stupid—it had been a last-minute idea. What sort of boyfriend didn't give his girlfriend a Christmas gift?

But then she jumped up and threw her arms around his neck, giving him a kiss on the cheek. "Thank you," she said. "I love them."

"I'm, uh, glad," Max said, taken slightly aback. This was a version of Sadie he wasn't really familiar with—open and effusive. She was now trying on the pair of fingerless gloves he'd knit, the marshmallow-colored yarn soft and fine, while still being warm.

"It's so your hands don't get cold when we're rehearsing," Max said, turning a bit red.

"They're perfect." Sadie held out her hands, admiring the gloves.

"Now, come on, you two lovebirds. I think you can do better than a peck on the cheek," Holden said. "Go on now. Don't hold back on my account."

For a moment the two of them stood statue still, facing one another. Then Sadie put her arms back around Max's neck, the gloves soft against his skin, and he wondered if her heart was beating as quickly as his. She leaned into him, going up on her toes. They were mere inches apart when Sadie paused. Max paused, too, and whispered, "Okay?"

When Sadie gave an almost imperceptible nod, he closed the distance between them. Her lips were warm and tasted of vanilla and red wine. Max's knees almost gave out. Apparently, their voices weren't the only things that fit together perfectly. He closed his eyes, the pressure of her lips and her body tight against him making him unsteady. A long (but not long enough) moment later she pulled away and whispered, "Merry Christmas, Max."

"Merry Christmas, Sadie," he replied. He felt feverish from the kiss, and noticed a deep pink hue to Sadie's cheeks that hadn't been there earlier. He wished they could do that again.

Max had almost forgotten they weren't alone, until Holden said, "How about you take Sadie out for some fresh air, to see the stars, Maxy?"

Sadie, seeming flustered, glanced at her watch. "I should probably get going."

"Why on earth would you do that?" Holden said. "We have a guest room all ready for you. Unless you'd rather share with Max?"

"Dad!" Max exclaimed. He didn't know what else to say

because, of course, if he and Sadie were the couple they said they were, they would *want* to share a bed. They were grown adults after all.

"The guest room is great, thank you. Max snores," Sadie quickly replied.

Holden chuckled, and Max frowned. He did *not* snore.

"I had Martha set out some toiletries and a pair of pajamas," Holden said.

"It's decided, then." Holden capped the crystal whiskey decanter after refilling his glass, grinning at the happy couple.

I'm sorry about my dad. The whole sharing a room thing. And that story . . ." Max paused, drawing in a deep breath. The two sat in comfortable lounge chairs under the backyard pergola, which was lit up with red, green, and white twinkle lights—festive and bright against the dark night sky.

"Nothing to apologize for," Sadie replied. "Thanks for inviting me, Max. If I wasn't here I would be . . . I don't know. Eating frozen pizza for dinner?"

"Well, technically I didn't invite you." Max looked up at the black sky, noting the stars were putting on quite the show. And now that he was out in the cool air he felt better—like he could take a full breath, finally.

"Why do you always have to do that?" The irritation in her voice was hard to miss.

"Do what?"

She turned to him. Her face lit up by the Christmas lights

that lined the pergola's open-air roof, Max couldn't ignore how beautiful Sadie looked tonight. In moments like this he felt confused about how he was supposed to act toward her. They spent a lot of their time convincing everyone around them that they were more than just duet partners. It wasn't real, of course. Sure, some days he *did* experience more than a comfortable camaraderie with Sadie. Yet, other days he wished he didn't have to listen to her tell him all the ways he was a jackass, like right now.

"It's like you go out of your way to be nasty. To make sure people don't like you or get to know you," Sadie said.

Max leaned back in the chair, let out a sigh. "What you see is what you get."

"That's bullshit, and you know it," she retorted.

He noted her mouth held in a tight line, her arms crossed over her chest, her hands still cozy inside the fingerless gloves. *God, if she wasn't as gorgeous when she was mad at him as when she wasn't.* He thought back to the kiss, only ten minutes before. Max knew it didn't mean anything, and yet . . . he couldn't stop thinking about it. Which *had* to mean something.

"Why are you always fixin' to start a fight? Can we just have five minutes of peace, Sadie?" Max asked, trying to shift his focus away from her full lips and how they had felt against his own. "It is Christmas after all."

"Fine," Sadie replied with a huff. "Whatever *you* want, Max."

Max had been on edge much of the evening, especially when he thought about his birthday gift, or the fact that he had agreed to propose to Sadie in a couple of days. But none of that was Sadie's fault. And even though she could start an argument in an empty house, she didn't deserve to be on the receiving end of his frustrations. He was about to apologize for being "nasty" when he noticed Sadie shivering.

"Are you cold?"

"No." Her body shook with a strong shiver.

Max went to the pool house and grabbed two thick blankets, soft and warm. "Scooch forward." He wrapped the woolen plaid blanket around her shoulders.

"Better?" Max asked.

They both looked out across the darkened, expansive lawn that in the light of day boasted mature fruit trees, elaborate gardens, and marble statues.

"This place is really something else. I can't imagine what it was like growing up here." Sadie's tone had softened.

Max took a moment before responding. "Things often look better from the outside," he finally said. "It wasn't always so . . . glamorous."

"Oh, I didn't mean it like that," Sadie said. "Sure, it's impressive as hell. You have two kitchens. And six bathrooms!"

"Actually, there are ten bathrooms."

"Oh, only ten bathrooms? You poor thing." Sadie turned the corners of her mouth down into an exaggerated frown, which made Max laugh.

"I know it's ridiculous. I can only imagine how this all looks to you."

"It looks a little like my greatest dreams coming true," Sadie replied. "But what I meant is that I think it would have been a bit lonely to grow up like this. My family isn't exactly huge, but our kitchen was small enough that even when it was only me, my mom, Gran and Grandpa for Christmas dinner, it felt like we filled the space right up. Our dining table was pretty tiny, especially compared to that boat-sized thing you have in there." Sadie pointed back over her shoulder, and Max laughed again. Their dining table could comfortably fit twenty guests.

"There were a lot of touching elbows and getting your sleeves in the mashed potatoes when you tried to serve them," Sadie added nostalgically.

"That sounds pretty great to me." Max smiled as he pictured a younger Sadie with her long sleeves dragging through a bowl of potatoes. "Y'all cozied up like that for dinner."

"It was," she replied. "I know you were probably surrounded by a lot of people all the time, but they worked for your parents, right? No one was here simply because they wanted to be."

Max sat quietly, his heart beating quickly again. Sadie stated the thing he had spent much of his adult life so far trying to reconcile. How you could feel so lonely when you were never alone.

All people saw was the extravagance of the Brody lifestyle. The majestic gates, the curated home full of expensive items, the number of staff necessary to keep the household running, the random people who popped in and out, taking all his father's attention—including at times when Max had needed it most, like after his mom had died. It was partly why Max believed his sister, Becca—who had no interest in the music business—had gone to boarding school in England, and then never came back. It was also why he missed his mom more than ever. Maren had brought life and warmth to the house in a way no one else had since.

"Sorry, I didn't mean to upset you." Sadie reached out from under her blanket and laid a hand on Max's arm. "You know, I should probably go. I never planned to stay over, and we have to rehearse tomorrow."

"First, you didn't upset me, Sadie. You just pretty much nailed it," Max replied. "And I want you to stay. It's late. We can head to the studio together in the morning."

There was a moment of silence between them, and then Sadie said, "I am pretty excited by the pajamas."

Max let out a huge laugh, leaning his head back.

"Who has brand-new sets of silk pajamas, in multiple sizes, just lying around?"

"You don't know the half of it," Max replied.

Sadie chuckled, but then suddenly went quiet. Max turned toward her. "You okay over there?"

"Max . . . do you think we're going to win?" she asked. The carefree Sadie from a moment ago was gone.

Max paused, then nodded. "Yeah, I think so."

"Really? Or are you just saying that to make me feel better, because I . . ." She shook her head, her voice shaky.

"Hey now, what's going on?"

"This is it for me, Max. I'm done in Nashville if this doesn't work out."

Max took that in, realizing that despite their many differences, *Starmaker* represented the end of the line for both of them. It was the most vulnerable he had ever seen her. Suddenly, he wanted to fix everything.

He reached out to hold her gloved hand, and then gave it a little shake until she looked at him. *"We're going to win, Sadie Hunter. You won't be able to leave Nashville, even if you want to. I promise."*

It was then he knew that regardless of how they came to be duet partners, or how much Sadie could get under his skin, or how frustrated he was with his own life, he would do whatever it took to keep this promise to her. He would find a way to pull off the proposal.

Sadie squeezed his hand in response. "Thank you for saying that."

"It's the truth, Sadie."

"It's the truth," Sadie repeated, smiling at him. "Well, we should probably turn in. Early start tomorrow."

"Yep, we have to keep our 'instruments' rested," Max said, clearing his throat and giving her a wink. He set his hands on his knees, readying to get up. "Speaking of instruments, do you want a guitar?"

Sadie laughed. "You really are a spoiled Nashville prince."

Max shrugged. "I already have a guitar. So if you want it, it's yours. I'm serious."

"Max, I can't take your vintage Gibson SJ-200, which was played by one of the Everly Brothers!"

"How did you know that?" They hadn't talked about the gift, which he had tucked under the Christmas tree before Sadie arrived.

"Your dad told me all about it while you took Patsy out after dinner."

"Of course he did." Max sighed. "Well, fine. You don't have to take it, but I'm never playing it."

Sadie was quiet, and he couldn't quite read her expression when he glanced over at her. "You have to work your crap out, Max Brody."

He inhaled deeply. "Yeah, I know."

10

Sadie

Sadie hit the FaceTime icon again, and *again* received the message that Gran was "unavailable." This was odd. No matter where she went, Gran brought her phone. She tried to swallow her disappointment—but she had been counting on seeing her gran's face before singing with Max in the *Starmaker* finale. This was *it*. And she was nervous. Amalia kept insisting they were "guaranteed" to win, but Amalia didn't have a crystal ball. Anything could happen. Johnny King was still a fan favorite, especially after killing it with an unexpected cover of Tammy Wynette's "My Elusive Dreams." He had ended the song by staring into the camera for a long moment before wiping away a tear. The internet had buzzed about this new, emotional side of Johnny—and how maybe he had what it took to go all the way. Some had even started tweeting that Johnny deserved it more than #Saxie. He didn't have a partner to lean on after all. That wasn't true, though. More and more lately, Johnny and Cruz appeared joined at the hip. Sadie had been hopeful that Cruz was starting to see her as a true contender. But it seemed that the closer she appeared to get to Max, the less friendly Cruz was.

It had been a while since she'd felt this nervous about performing. Max had gone off somewhere—to prepare for the bogus proposal if they won, she assumed. But, just in case, Bobbi and Amalia had come up with an alternate plan: if Max and Sadie's sultry rendition of Taylor Swift's "'tis the damn season" was not enough, and Johnny pulled ahead in viewers' votes and prevailed, Max was to steal the spotlight by dropping down on one knee and proposing anyway.

To be honest, the whole thing just felt weird. If he were to propose in real life, Sadie knew Max well enough by now to know he would never do it in such a public, sensational way. He took music seriously, and he took life seriously. He'd agreed to do something that was completely contrived, and totally out of character—but, still, Sadie knew he was not a sellout.

Am I, though?

It was a good question. The last month had been such a blur that Sadie had rarely stopped to consider how she felt about all this—and when she did stop to think, it was mostly just to give herself an internal pep talk. *Keep going. This is your dream. This is your last chance.* Now, if things went according to plan, Sadie was about to embark on a yearlong, public engagement to someone she had complicated feelings for. They had experienced so much together—highs, lows, and in between. And family time, too, because not only had she gotten a few glimpses into Max's life, but he had seen into her personal life, too. She could not compartmentalize her feelings for Max into an easy-to-explain category. When she sang with him it felt like they really were in love. It was fleeting, but it was there. And, when they had kissed at the Brody Mansion, that had felt real, too. Just thinking about it again made her skin tingle. She could still feel the intensity of his lips on hers—and, if she was being honest, she wanted to feel that again.

A voice on her phone startled Sadie. "Gran!"

But it wasn't Gran. It was Lynn. "Sadie?"

"Hi! Mom!" Sadie tried not to look disappointed to see her mother on the screen, her face almost a mirror image of her own, but with her dark hair cut into a bob and a few extra worry lines between her dark brows. "I was just trying to reach Gran before the finale," Sadie said.

Sadie noticed her mom looked pale and tired. "Is everything okay, Mom?"

"Yes! Of course! Everything is fine! It's—it's the silliest thing. Your poor gran overdid it with the singing lessons and lost her voice. She can't even croak out one word, and she refuses to get on a call with you where she can't say anything, so she told me she was going to text you." Sadie couldn't be sure, but thought her mother's eyes were shining with tears. She wasn't at home; there was an unfamiliar dismal blue wall behind her. What was going on? "So, I'm going to hang up and let her—and you—get to it, okay?" Before Sadie could say anything to that, or get a closer look, Lynn hung up and Sadie's text notification chimed.

Hello, my dear, this is your Gran. I'm so sorry I can't talk to you tonight. What a silly thing, to lose my voice!

Sadie frowned and typed, But I thought you were taking a lesson break?

Decided not to. Needed a bit of pin money. Now, I don't think you have too much longer before you have to start preparing to go onstage, and if I know you, you're probably feeling pretty nervous right about now. Sweaty palms? Racing heart? Mind filled with thoughts about how maybe you just aren't cut out for this and should come back to Wisconsin and make your mother happy, even if you know you're going to be miserable?

Sadie chuckled. Her gran sure did know her better than anyone. She was starting to feel calmer already. Gran was still typing, and Sadie waited for more words to replace the moving dots.

Ever since you were a little girl, we all knew you had a special gift. Your mom knew it, too, even if it worried her—because chasing a dream that might break your heart is a hard way to live, and mothers only want their kids to be happy. But something that has become very clear as we all watch you on this show is how purely happy singing makes you. It's a beautiful thing to witness. You have an incredible talent. Your voice is special, but it's not just that—YOU are special, because you have been so determined. You have never once wavered from your ultimate goal, and I know it is not going to be tonight that you start wavering. I believe in you with all my heart. Now go on out there and make me proud.

Sadie's eyes were now blurring with tears as she read her gran's words, then typed back: Thank you so much, Gran. I love you. I needed this.

I love you, too. And so did I. Break a leg, my darling.

There were no more words after that. But all of Sadie's nervous misgivings had disappeared. She *could* do this. She *would* do this. The next hour of her life was not going to be about Max, her complicated feelings for him, and whatever came next. It was going to be about her dreams, her goals, and her unwavering determination to make it all happen. She put her phone away and went to her dressing room door. It was time.

She opened the door and Max was standing there waiting for her, an inscrutable expression on his face. An expression that made her heart start to run away from her again.

"Sadie, we need to talk."

Max stood in the center of Sadie's dressing room, running his hands through his perfectly coiffed hair so many times that Sadie began to get even more nervous than she already was. Finally, he stopped and turned to her. "You look perfect," he began, taking in her lavender peasant-style crop blouse and flowy matching skirt, which Hugo had paired with white cowboy boots.

"So do you." He was wearing soft grey dress pants and a matching jacket, no tie, his white shirt unbuttoned a little extra to reveal the top of his chest. "Max, I—"

He shook his head. "Wait. I need to tell you something. About that night we first met. I *do* remember, okay?"

"Max, just forget it. I made way too big a deal over that. It's fine. Water under the bridge. Now is not the time—"

"No. Please, listen. Talking about this doesn't come easily to me. But you need to know. It was one of the hardest nights of my life, okay? But *of course* I remember meeting you, and I remember your voice." He stepped closer to her. "I remember you coming outside and huddling against that wall, looking beautiful and hopeful. I remember how much I wanted to help you."

Her body was starting to tingle all over, the way it had when they kissed. "Why are you telling me this now?"

"Because I have to. You need to know this. The blond woman you saw me leaving with, that was my sister, Becca." He closed his eyes, and she could tell he was in pain.

She put her hand on his arm. "Max. It's okay."

He opened his eyes. "The reason Becca came to the Sparrow to find me is because she knew I liked to go there on New Talent Night." He looked sheepish for a moment. "Well, because sometimes Monday nights at the Sparrow are the only thing that feels real in Nashville. All these people with their dreams not broken yet, with their passion for music just so raw, you know? It always helped me remember why I wanted to make music, too."

The clock on the wall was showing that the time they were expected onstage was drawing perilously near. "Max, we don't need to do this now," Sadie said gently.

Max shook his head again, refocused himself. "I don't think I can go on unless I get this out. Unless you know the truth." He took a deep breath. "My sister came to get me because I wasn't answering my phone, and it was urgent. My mother had—" His voice broke. "She'd collapsed, and was in the hospital about to have emergency surgery. It was the night everything changed. One minute my mother was perfectly healthy and the next she was fighting a losing battle for her life. And that moment we met outside? It was the last cigarette I ever had, for one thing. I was such a dumbass back then. But sometimes I think it was the last moment I was ever really happy. So, I didn't forget it, Sadie. I just blocked it out. And tried to shut *you* out."

"Oh, Max." She looked up into his mournful eyes, wishing desperately she could ease his pain. "I'm so sorry. I wasn't fair to you. I always seem to think the worst of you."

"I'm sorry, too, Sadie. I don't blame you for thinking I'm a huge asshole, that I fed you some line about looking for a friendly face, made you promises I had no intention of keeping, and then took off on you. I just needed you to know, tonight especially, that that's not what happened. Not at all. Everything changed for me that night. And—" He looked away. "I can't believe you were there. It feels like—"

He didn't finish that sentence. Didn't seem to be able to. But she knew the word he was looking for. *Fate*. She touched his arm and waited until he could look at her again. "It's okay. Really, it is. You can let this go now. And we can go out there and just sing together. Okay?"

He was still staring down at her, his expression intense. "All this, what we're in, it's supposed to be all fake. But it is real, isn't it? All this is really happening. We're real people. With real feelings." He let that last sentence hang in the air. Sadie didn't know what to do with it. Her sudden impulse was to pull him closer—and then what, exactly? *All this is really happening*, he had just said. But what exactly *was* happening here?

There was a tap at the dressing room door. "Sadie?" It was Joni, one of the production assistants, and she sounded panicked. "You're due on soon, and no one can find Max."

Sadie stepped away from Max and opened the door. "Max is in here with me," she said. "We're all good."

"Ah. I see." Joni smiled knowingly, as if what had been happening in Sadie's dressing room was something that could be understood by anyone at all. "You two are such a perfect couple. I'm pulling for you. But you really should get out there. It's time."

The moment was over. As Joni headed back down the hall, Sadie turned to Max. "We'll talk about this again, okay? But I'm glad you told me."

"I just don't want there to be any bad feelings between us when we sing tonight. I want it to be real."

There was that word again. "Real."

"It does feel real, doesn't it?" Sadie's heartbeat was fast, like moth wings inside her chest.

Max nodded his head. "Yes."

And she knew it was true. Come hell or high water, come

win or come lose, what was going on between them was real—
and she knew it now.

"Let's go out there and win this together," she whispered.

He reached for her and they walked out the dressing room
door hand in hand.

As they passed under the doorframe, Max looked up. A
slow smile spread across his face.

She looked up, too. The halls of the studio were still decked
out with holiday decorations. Someone had affixed a sprig of
mistletoe to the top of her dressing room door.

It happened so fast she was barely sure it happened at all.
He ducked his head and brushed his lips across hers, then
pulled back and whispered, "I'm not going to break a promise—
not this time. Let's go win this thing. And then . . ."

She smiled and walked with him down the hallway, her
mind awash in all the possibilities the words "and then" could
contain.

Sadie and Max took the stage hand in hand, the closeness
they had been feeling in the dressing room still lingering.
Sadie could almost believe they were the only two people in the
auditorium. She sat down at her piano and Max sat beside her
on the bench. They locked eyes for a moment before Sadie
turned and began the opening bars of "'tis the damn season."
She sang the first few bars and then Max joined in, and they
alternated throughout the song, their voices weaving in and
out, looking at each other intensely. Sadie heard her voice genuinely break when she sang the line about how he was the only
one who could tell which smiles she was faking. He squeezed

her hand when that happened, and she was sure she heard the studio audience sigh rapturously.

Sadie knew, without having to look out at the crowd, or at the faces of the judges, or at the screen that measured viewer reactions to the live broadcast with a series of hearts and stars, that they had done it. There was no contest. This competition was *theirs*.

After so many years of working and hoping, failing and failing again, it didn't feel real.

The music ended. They looked at each other, until Max grinned and mouthed, *We did it* (a moment that would later play over and over again in viral videos and eventually become a long-standing meme). They left the stage to gasps and applause, and sat together hand in hand, as nervous as Olympic athletes waiting to receive their score, while the judges conferred.

Tasha, back for the finale as a guest judge again, spoke first. She said they were incredibly authentic as a duo—and Sadie couldn't help but squeeze Max's hand as she said this. She leaned her head against Max's shoulder, breathlessly happy, as the dream continued to unfold: D.J. talked about the technical aspects of what they pulled off—the way they arranged the song to make it their own, turned it into a duet, and a successful one at that. "You should contact Taylor and see what she has to say about you two recording this one and making it legendary," he said with a smile. "I honestly don't think there's anything you two *can't* do together."

And Cruz? He was silent for a long, agonizing moment—then threw up his hands, jumped onto his chair, and gave them a standing ovation—much to Johnny King's obvious chagrin. "What can I say? That was freaking great. It was perfect. You are the next big thing, Sadie Hunter. And Max Brody." For just a second, Sadie felt Max stiffen, and knew he felt Cruz had added his name as an afterthought. But otherwise, there was no ruining this perfect moment. "No question about it. You've stolen the show—and everyone's hearts."

The viewers' votes started to roll in and Max and Sadie's were the highest in the history of the show—as were the show's ratings that night: more than double the already high ratings they had commanded after their second duet. Max jumped up, grabbed Sadie, hugged her, and swung her around. "We did it, Sadie! *We* did this!"

Sadie laughed with delight as it all started to sink in. They *had* done this. Later, when Johnny performed, he appeared shaken and deflated, with not even a fraction of his normally swaggering confidence. It was #Saxie by a landslide.

"Off you two go," Joni, the production assistant, said, hustling them toward the stage to claim their prize. "Congratulations!"

The judges crowded around, golden confetti flew everywhere, and Max lifted Sadie off her feet and swung her in a circle. After that Tasha put crowns on their heads and handed them star-shaped trophies. Someone brought out a novelty check—although Sadie knew her contract by heart. She knew she wasn't going to get that money until they performed their original holiday song at next year's *Starmaker All I Want for Christmas Holiday Extravaganza*. Cruz approached, brandishing a recording contract on a clipboard. They signed it and as he walked away, he whispered in Sadie's ear, "Let's chat at the after-party, yeah? You have a bright future, Sadie, and I'd love to be a part of it." Max was talking to Tasha and didn't see this exchange, so Sadie shared her own private smile. It was all starting to happen!

And then it was time. They were to take their final bow and Max was going to drop to one knee and secure their place in the hearts of their fans for the next year. Sadie's heart fluttered, but in a different way now.

She turned to face the small audience and could see Bobbi and Amalia in the front row, waiting, as expectant as Sadie was. But Max kept hold of her hand, kept facing the crowd. He did not kneel and pull out a ring. Sadie waited, but still, Max didn't turn to her. He just bowed to their adoring crowd over and over. Eventually, she did the same, her hand now clammy in his grasp.

Then it was over. The cameras turned off and they were alone on the stage, facing each other now. Max's expression was serious, filled with resolve.

"You didn't propose," Sadie found herself whispering.

"I'm sorry, Sadie. I just couldn't do it. I don't know what to say—except, it didn't feel right."

Sadie didn't know what to say, either. She didn't know how to explain how, all at once, she wanted to cry. She had everything she wanted, the very thing she had been working toward: a recording contract, fame. And yet, all she could think about was that Max Brody had somehow managed to break her heart.

By the time Sadie had composed herself, the after-party was in full swing. Hugo had come to her door with a glittering blue evening gown which he suggested she pair with the white cowboy boots she had worn during the performance. "Sadie

Hunter is going to need a signature style—and I think edgy-beautiful is it," he said, taking the white headband out of her hair and arranging her locks so they hung loose and natural around her shoulders. It was something Sadie had noticed that evening—more than a few people had spoken of her in the third person, and she was starting to feel like she was floating above herself. "There," Hugo had said when he was done. "Perfect. Effortless. You're going to be all anyone can look at."

She still had the sensation of being set adrift in a new world as she entered the soundstage, which had been transformed into a glamorous gala, complete with ice sculptures in Sadie's and Max's likenesses. There were champagne fountains, glittering strings of lights crisscrossing the ceiling, towering floral arrangements, and crowds of people—all of whom turned when she entered the room. Hugo was right. No one could take their eyes off of her. Except Max Brody, who couldn't quite meet her gaze when she saw him. She felt her cheeks start to burn. The whole thing had been a ridiculous idea—but it had been a ridiculous idea they had both agreed to. It wasn't fair that he had made the unilateral decision to ditch their grand plan.

Aside from Amalia and Bobbi, no one else knew about the fake proposal that hadn't happened. Everyone believed they were perfectly in love. So, she smiled brilliantly and walked across the room toward the supposed love of her life. The crowd parted like a sea. Johnny stepped forward to congratulate them, attempting to share some of the spotlight, but he now seemed dull in comparison to them, quickly receding into the background as flashbulbs erupted all around them. When Max murmured, "I'm sorry about that," in her ear and, "But you understand, don't you?" she just kept right on smiling.

Sadie felt her phone vibrating. It stopped, then started up again. She turned away from the cameras. She had five missed calls from her mom.

She headed toward the restrooms, hoping to find somewhere quiet to return her mom's call—and feeling guilty because this huge thing had happened to her, and she had been too caught up in her complicated feelings about Max to remember to call home and celebrate with the people who loved her most. But she could only inch her way across the room. Everyone wanted to talk to her or take a photo with her or congratulate her. She was just a few feet away from the restroom door, finally, when she felt a warm hand on her arm. "Well done, gorgeous," came Cruz's voice. She turned.

"Thanks, Cruz," she said. "It's pretty thrilling. But I have to—"

"Thrilling is right," Cruz said, keeping hold of her arm and pulling her into a quiet corner hidden by a tall urn filled with spruce fronds, holly berries, and snowy white orchids. "I can't tell you how pleased I am to have your name on my roster of artists I work with at my studio." He lowered his voice, "But I have to be honest with you: I think you'd be better off alone."

"Excuse me?" But Sadie's phone was ringing again and she couldn't focus. "Cruz, I really—"

"Whatever's going on between you and Max—pardon me for being blunt—it's not real, is it? It's a publicity stunt, yes?"

Sadie's voicemail notification sounded, and then a text message from her mom arrived. She was barely listening to Cruz as she read it. **Sadie, please call.**

Cruz nodded knowingly. "It was a smart move, at least as far as winning the competition went—but it's not going to work.

I've seen a lot of talent come and go in this business, and Brody may have a famous name, but he doesn't have staying power. He doesn't have his daddy's charisma, is the thing. He's soft. Knits sweaters for dogs, for God's sake."

Another message from her mom arrived. **You need to come home. Right away. It's Gran.** Adrenaline started to course through her veins. She looked up. "Listen, Cruz, I really need to—"

"What you need to do is listen to what I'm about to say to you." He gripped her arm a little too tightly and she realized with a sinking feeling that moments before, Cruz had asked her if her relationship with Max was fake—and she hadn't denied it.

"Wait," she said. "Max and I are together!"

Cruz just laughed. "Yeah, yeah, save it for the tabloids, Sadie. The truth is written all over your face. But Max doesn't matter. What matters is that I want to work with *you*, Sadie Hunter. I can deal with Max this year, we can record an album, since we're obligated to do so—but once the dust settles from this big win of yours, I want us to have a meeting, just the two of us. Okay? I want to be the one to record the solo Sadie Hunter album—because I have a feeling that's where the real action is going to be. And my gut"—he pointed to the slight paunch above his huge belt buckle in the shape of Tennessee—"is never, ever wrong."

Sadie agreed, wanting nothing more than to end this conversation.

"Max doesn't have half of the talent you do, doesn't want it like you do—can't be counted on to do what needs to be done to take his career to the next level. Know what I mean?"

Another message popped up on her screen. **Sadie. Please.**

Tell me you're getting these. Gran isn't well. I hate to tell you this way, but she doesn't have much time left.

She couldn't focus on what Cruz was saying now. "So, what do you think?" he asked her, a big grin on his face.

Sadie shook her head and started to back away. "Sounds great. I'll call you, I promise," she said. "We can set something up. But I really have to go now."

Then she spun around and rushed out of the room, pushing through the crowd and ignoring Max when he called out her name.

11

Max

Nashville, Tennessee
December 30

Where in the hell is she going?

"Sadie!" Max caught up to her in a few quick strides, her five-foot-seven frame no match for his six-foot one.

It was quieter away from the stage, but the hum of the partygoers stretched into the hallway, creating a celebratory feel in the air. There was a loud cacophony of cheering voices, and both Sadie and Max glanced back toward the stage, but neither of them said anything.

Sadie was clearly upset, Max could see that. As tears streamed down her cheeks, he felt like someone had punched him in the stomach.

"Sadie. What's wrong?" He touched her elbow and she turned to fully face him. Max ducked to look into her eyes, but she wouldn't meet his gaze. Then he thought about Cruz—he had seen them in the corner, tête-à-tête, only moments before she'd bolted.

"What did Cruz do? What did he say to you?" Max's jaw tightened.

"Nothing. I have to go, Max," was all Sadie said, the tears continuing to fall.

If this wasn't about Cruz, then what was going on? They had just won the whole dang thing. So why did Sadie look like she'd lost everything?

"Is this about the proposal?" He lowered his voice at the end, glancing around before he said it to make sure they were truly alone.

Sadie shook her head, looking more distraught. "Max, I really have to go. I can't talk now."

"Look, I'm sorry. Let me explain, okay?" he said, stepping a foot closer to her so they were only inches apart. Without even thinking about what he was doing, he reached up to wipe away her tears. "I know we agreed and I promise you I had every—"

She caught his hand, holding it firmly. "I can't do this. I have to go."

Max took a step back and let go of her hand. He was frustrated and confused about how upset she was. All he wanted to do was to take her in his arms.

"I'm lost here, Sadie. What's going on?"

She gave him a look—he couldn't read her face, *Is that sadness, disappointment, regret?*—and then turned toward the exit door, moving at a good clip in her white cowboy boots, despite the fabric and weight of the ball gown that encased her.

"Sadie! Goddamn it." Max let out a frustrated groan and

jogged after her again. "Let me help you. Whatever it is. I'm sorry about the proposal, I didn't think—"

But then she turned and held a hand out, stopping him in his tracks. Her face was pale.

"That's just it. You *don't* think, you do precisely what you want, Max. What's best for you," she said, her hands shaking.

"Please, listen to me. I know I let you down, but I had my reasons, okay?" He was about to explain, to tell her he'd fix everything, but she wasn't giving him the chance.

"You talk about wanting to be different. To avoid getting 'lost' in this town that takes so much more than it gives. But I'd say Nashville suits you, Max." Sadie's words hit him like a transport truck into a brick wall, and he couldn't catch his breath. "I don't need your help anymore." Her voice broke, but she held her head high. "Please let me go."

Max had believed things had changed between them. That at this point they were far more than simply duet partners. But seeing how she now looked at him—like she wanted to be anywhere else—he suddenly realized that nothing had changed.

Max held up his hands, took a purposeful step back. "Fine, Sadie. Go."

His tone held no warmth, because now he understood—and he was embarrassed to have so badly misread the situation. Max Brody was *not* naïve, and yet . . . Damn, he had let himself fall for her. Sadie Hunter had her own agenda, and had fooled him—she'd never seen the *real* Max. No, clearly, she only saw the version of him that the paparazzi liked to play up—the spoiled Nashville prince who cared more about himself than anything, or anyone. And if that's who she thought he was, well, he could play that role with his eyes closed.

Sadie wasted no time turning around and leaving him without another word.

He stood in the hallway for a time, hands shoved deeply into his pockets, staring into the empty space where she had just been, wondering how everything had so swiftly, epically, fallen apart.

M ax walked back onto the soundstage, the celebrations in full swing, and spotted his manager by the champagne fountain. He strode toward her and said, "Bobbi, we need to talk."

She excused herself from the conversation she'd been in and followed him over to a quiet corner. "We certainly do. What happened with our plan, Max? We had an agreement. Amalia's ticked off. Me, too." Then she looked around. "Where's Sadie?"

"It doesn't matter," Max said, shaking his head. "I'm heading out of town."

"Now? What for?" Bobbi looked surprised.

"I, uh, need to go check on one of our properties."

Bobbi narrowed her eyes. "I have known you a long time, and so I know when you're telling me a fib."

He ran a hand through his hair, frustration buzzing inside him. "I need to clear my head, okay? Just for a week. Two tops."

"You will clear your head *here*, in Nashville. Max, this is the worst time for you to be away! We currently have that precious gift of *positive momentum*. It's fleeting, as you know, and we need to take advantage of it. Get you and Sadie out on the town as much as we can! Make it splashy and sexy, okay? We'll deal with what didn't happen onstage later. Maybe we can figure out an even better time for you to propose."

"Hmm-hmm," Max replied, distracted again by Cruz, who was talking with Tasha at the bar. They shook hands—like they had just made a deal. Then Cruz pointed at Max and Tasha turned around, giving him a wave and a thumbs-up. He wondered what that was all about, but then Bobbi pulled his attention back.

"There's a lot on the line, Max. For everyone, not just you. You have two weeks before you have to start the album with Cruz. So whatever you have going on here . . ." Bobbi drew circles in the air in front of Max's chest. "You'd better figure it out. And fast."

Nearly twenty-four hours later Max stepped out of his rented pickup truck and into snow up past his ankles. After his early-morning flight from Nashville to Calgary, followed by a slow and somewhat treacherous drive—thanks to the recent snowfall—up the mountain toward Banff, Max was more than ready to relax.

A touch of the white stuff ended up inside his winter hiking boots, the painfully cold feel of it tingling against his skin. With Patsy tucked under his arm—her little body toasty in a hand-knit merino wool sweater—he filled his lungs with the mountain air, taking in the landscape. Snowcapped mountains surrounded him, the sky a shade of grey that let him know the bloated clouds would soon be dumping snowflakes faster than he'd be able to shovel them away.

It was dusk, New Year's Eve, and it had taken Max most of

the day to get here. He had debated calling Sadie a hundred times, but each time had remembered the look on her face just before she'd walked away from him for good.

He couldn't believe how only a day ago they were getting ready for the finale, and were only hours away from winning *Starmaker*. How he had been nervously trying to sort out how to tell her how he felt about her, and why he couldn't propose onstage in front of all those people who didn't care about either of them. Max felt badly about breaking his promise to Sadie, to their managers, but in the end, he simply hadn't been able to go through with it. *At least I dodged that heartbreak bullet*, he thought, now grateful that he hadn't fakeproposed. But in reality, he hadn't dodged anything. His heart still felt like it had been stomped on by a pair of newly heeled cowboy boots.

But that was all in the past now. Max had to think about his future, which is why he'd left the party after talking with Bobbi, had booked a morning flight to Calgary, and now stood in a foot of snow, having traded his cowboy boots for winter ones. And with every mile he had put between Nashville and these mountains, he had felt incrementally better.

Climbing a few steps to the cabin's front door, he nudged a wedge of snow away from its base. Max turned the key in the lock, fumbling slightly with his gloved hand, and pushed the door open. It was chilly inside—it was *freezing* outside, the sort of cold that made the tip of your nose go numb in seconds—but he'd get a fire going soon enough.

Max set Patsy down and she shook head to toe, like she had been for a swim. When he tugged the drop sheets off the couch and chairs, a puff of dust filled the air. He coughed once, waving the air in front of him, and then patted the chair's seat cushion.

"Up you get, Patsy Canine. I'll get us a fire going soon, okay?"

She jumped to the chair—an impressive feat for a dog her size—and settled into the cushion with a happy little groan.

Max looked around the small room, the sense of nostalgia moving through him so strongly he almost felt like he had to sit down beside Patsy lest his legs give out from under him. The last time he'd been here, his mom had still been alive. It had been the Christmas before she got sick, and if he'd had any idea how little time he had left with her . . .

A sharp pain clawed at his chest, and this time he sat down. Patsy rested her head in his lap.

"Home sweet home," he said quietly.

This
Christmas . . .

Max Brody and Sadie Hunter . . .
Long-Distance Love, or a Nashville Sham?

With Sadie Hunter on the European leg of the Tasha Munroe tour she's opening for, and Max Brody working on a solo album somewhere in the Canadian wilderness, we are suffering serious #Saxie withdrawal . . . It has been 263 days since we've seen the lovebirds together—but hey, who's counting? (HotStarGossip is counting! And we didn't count those blurry Majorca beach photos!)

So, WHEN will these American sweethearts get back into each other's arms (and back into the studio to record that highly anticipated Cruz McNeil produced album)? HotStarGossip reached out to the power couple's people, but the only comment was, "We don't comment on our clients' private lives." We did find someone willing to talk—a source who prefers to stay anonymous, but who we can confirm is legit—who gave a statement sure to distress #Saxie fans. "They were never a 'couple' in the romantic sense," the source said. "They fooled everyone, including the *Starmaker* judges and especially their loyal fans."

While we can't confirm or deny this, we do have to wonder . . . Is #Saxie magic, or make-believe? And . . . do we care when they are so dang entertaining?

Either way, the countdown is on to when we can get our #Saxie fix! Word is our Christmas wishes will come true soon enough. The dreamy duo is slated to sing an original holiday love song at the Grand Ole Opry at the holiday extravaganza, one year after winning *Starmaker* and millions of hearts in the process. Rein up, cowgirls and cowboys, because charade or not, this performance is sure to melt away that December chill!

12

Sadie

Nashville, Tennessee
December 13

Okay, shoulders back, stand up straight. If you don't want to pop out of this thing during that final dance number, we're going to need to lace you in *tight*. Deep breath, Sadie."

Sadie obeyed, but it still felt like the wind had been knocked out of her when Hugo—now the head of her wardrobe team on the road and a welcome familiar face every day—started yanking the laces on the black-and-gold corset she was wearing. "I can't believe this is the last night of Tasha's Rhinestone Cowgirl Tour," she managed.

Hugo's exertions punctuated his words: "On the bright side"—*yank*—"you"—*pull*—"won't"—*tug*—"have to do *this*"—*yank yank*—"for a while."

When Sadie could breathe again she said, "I know, but I'm

going to miss you. And everyone else. *Ouch*. How can it be over already?"

Hugo smiled, a little sadly. "I'm going to miss you, too. But I bet you're excited to finally get to spend some time with Max." His eyes lit up the way everyone's did when they talked about #Saxie. Somehow, even though Sadie had ended up going on tour with Tasha Munroe—something she had enthusiastically agreed to when Tasha called her up and pitched the idea— and Max had gone off the grid, hiding away to write music at his family's cabin in the Canadian Rockies, they had managed to convince the world they were still a couple—a couple who supported each other's separate career dreams, but would be back together soon. "I cannot wait to hear the song you wrote for the holiday extravaganza. You're being so secretive about it! Did you work on it when you managed to sneak away to see him last month during our break?"

Sadie forced a knowing smile and nodded. But the truth was, she hadn't spoken to Max in the past year—not since the night of their *Starmaker* win, which had started out as the best night of her life and turned into her worst nightmare, because she had lost her beloved gran, and it had been too late for her to say goodbye. She had tried to contact Max, after the dust had settled in her personal life—settled into a sludge of heartache she could hardly see her way through and tried to dull by constantly working—but he hadn't returned her calls or answered her texts. And she certainly hadn't sneaked off to visit him in his Canadian hideaway. They only communicated through Bobbi, who mostly passed along her regrets that no, Max wasn't ready to come back to Nashville and work on their album or on their Christmas song for *Starmaker* yet, and yes, she would keep trying to convince him. Meanwhile, Bobbi and Amalia fed the media a steady stream of "leaked" fake stories—photoshopped images of "Saxie" spotted on a private beach in Majorca, rumors about the supposed secret trip Sadie had taken to visit him at his cabin.

"Well, I'm just so excited for you, Sadie," Hugo said, making some final adjustments on the corset. "Next year is going to be huge. Two albums! Your own, and one with Max."

After Sadie had signed on to join Tasha's tour, she had also accepted Cruz McNeil's offer to lay down some tracks for her own solo album in his studio. At the time, she had been sure Max would be arriving back in Nashville soon, and that they'd get their album out of the way. She had never imagined he'd stay away so long—but in darker moments, when she relived the last time she saw him, she realized it just made sense. She couldn't count on Max and was going to need to forge her own path—even if their contractual obligations to *Starmaker* hung over her head like an axe waiting to drop.

"This tour has made you a star," Hugo continued. "Anything you record is going to be a smash hit."

It had all gone by so quickly. If Sadie closed her eyes she could see the highlights reel: a jumble of stadium stages, private jets, meet-and-greets, an endless parade of complicated outfits just like this one. Some incredible moments, like the nights when the crowds were receptive to her and shouted her name. And hard nights, too, like when someone in the crowd would shout, "Get off the stage! We want Tasha!" and Sadie would have to struggle not to cry, not to whip off her headset and shout, "I'm an actual human being up here! *And I can read lips!*"

Then there was what came after the shows. Sadie alone in one hotel room after another, trying her best not to fall apart. Running away from her grief by hopping on plane after plane, stage after stage—when nothing could change the fact that Gran was gone.

Sadie had to use every ounce of strength she had not to fall apart.

There had been good moments, too. Those were what she had to focus on. Like the first time Tasha asked her to come onstage with her for the show's finale, and Sadie sang with her while a full stadium cheered. In these moments, she felt like she was right where she belonged, *finally*. Tasha always reminded her that she had chosen her for a reason—it wasn't a fluke. She thought Sadie was talented and her good taste in opening acts was legendary. Tasha had gone from being an idol to a generous, wise mentor. In addition to giving Sadie the break of a lifetime—and saving her when she needed it most—she had given her a master class in a fickle and complex industry.

Sadie hummed a bar of "Don't Call." This was Tasha's most recent number one hit. *Baby, I know you've got my number, but don't you come callin'* . . . She felt her now-corset-constricted heart drop in anticipation of the final show. She didn't want the tour to be over—in part because it meant she was going to have to face the realities she had been avoiding. Her family life being one of them. Max Brody's absence in her life being another.

There was a knock on the door. "Hell-oooo?"

Sadie squeezed her eyes shut even tighter, wishing she could transport herself somewhere else.

But it was no use. She opened her eyes, and she was still where she was—and Cruz McNeil was still standing in front of her, a proprietary look on his face. He often looked at her as if he owned her, which it sometimes felt like he did. And lately, it felt like he was everywhere, taking full advantage of the standing invitation and backstage access he had to every show in town, including this one.

Cruz whistled as he took in her outfit. "Hugo, can we have the room?"

"Cruz, we don't have a ton of time here," Sadie said. "Maybe after the show?"

Cruz kept his friendly smile plastered on. "Oh, it'll just be a minute."

"No worries," Hugo said. "We're done here anyway." He patted her on the shoulder and paused in front of her, saying in a low voice, "I sewed a rose quartz crystal into the material just above your heart. Love you, babe. You're a natural."

"She is indeed," Cruz said, his tone suggesting he had played some role in this. There had been a time all Sadie had wanted was for Cruz to take a special interest in her. Now she longed to go back to a time when she could have been more careful what she wished for.

When they were alone, she crossed the room to put some distance between them and stood in front of the lit mirror, where she pretended to adjust her mic wire. "What's up, Cruz?"

"Just wondering if young Brody has gotten back to you yet. Didn't think that was something that could be asked in front of anyone else, considering you two are supposed to be *madly in love*." His voice became singsongy when he said that, and Sadie couldn't help but wince.

"No, no word," she said, hating the feeling she got when she talked about this with Cruz. She was hurt by Max's ghosting of her—but they had had an agreement, and that was to tell no one they were only pretending to be a couple. Sadie was not the kind of person who went back on her word—even if it had turned out Max was.

She turned away from the mirror and looked at Cruz. It was time to be direct. Time to end all this. Surely, Cruz would be supportive. He didn't seem to like Max very much anyway. "What are the chances I could just perform solo at the *Starmaker* holiday extravaganza? Max doesn't seem to want to have anything to do with it anyway. I'm sure Amalia and Bobbi could come up with some palatable way to spin it."

Cruz barked out a staccato, "Ha!" Then he stepped closer to her. "I know you two are faking, but no one *else* knows it. And there is *a lot* riding on the first public appearance of Saxie in an entire year being on that holiday special. A lot of advertising dollars riding on that, too."

Sadie knew he was right—and also that, as a producer and an investor, Cruz had a personal interest tied up in the *Starmaker* special doing well. And word on the street was he needed the money, because one lawsuit against Cruz's Catfish, his now-defunct chain of restaurants, had morphed into many. Apparently, the restaurant's signature Catfish 'n' Spaghetti dish had sickened multiple patrons.

"Max isn't responding to me, Cruz. He doesn't seem to

care. So if he's just not coming, I think we need an alternate plan."

"You're right," Cruz said thoughtfully. "We do need an alternate plan. And I think the alternate plan involves you flying out to that cabin of his and dragging that boy back here by the scruff of his neck. Do what you have to do. Bat those pretty baby blues of yours. Use your feminine wiles. If Max truly is Holden Brody's son, he'll follow you anywhere if you offer him a little honey."

"Cruz."

He held up his hands in supplication. "Sorry, sorry. You're a *fake* couple, right, right." He started to laugh, but stopped when he registered Sadie's stricken expression. "Oh, princess. I hate to see you looking so down. I'm here for you, you know that, right? We still have all those incredible tracks you laid down earlier this year just waiting in my studio, for when you're past all this kindergarten playtime stuff with Max and are ready to hang with the grown-ups. I promised you I would make you a star, and I'm going to. But first, you've gotta give *me* some honey. Write a hit song, and perform that song at the Grand Ole Opry with Max Brody for the Holiday Extravaganza. Record said song at my studio beforehand, so we have it ready to stream the night the show airs. Most wannabe stars would jump at the chance to do any of that." *Wannabe star.* She gritted her teeth as he put his finger on her chin and turned her face up toward his. She could smell onions on his breath and she had to force herself not to turn away in disgust. "Once you do this, you'll be free. I can arrange for you to use my private jet to get to Max, if you'd like."

"Cruz, I can't just go and get him."

Cruz stepped back. "Well, maybe I just can't release your tracks to you until you do."

"What?"

Cruz laughed again. "I was just funning with you, sweets. It was just a joke, don't look so upset."

Sadie stood still, staring at Cruz, trying to read his expression. He hadn't been joking—and she knew it. The master tapes for the tracks she had worked so hard to record were in his hands. She couldn't risk not doing what he was asking her to do.

"Okay, Cruz," Sadie said. "I'm on it."

"I know you are, doll. See you out there. Knock 'em dead tonight. Can't wait for the after-party, should be a barn burner. And let me know if you need my jet."

But Sadie knew she wasn't going to the after-party. And there was no way she was going to use Cruz's jet. When he was gone, she pulled out her cell phone and stared down at it for a moment, wishing Max would choose this moment to finally return her countless calls and texts. But her phone stayed silent, the screen as lonely and empty as her heart.

She texted Amalia. **I need to get the address for Max's cabin. I need to take matters into my own hands.**

As she sent the text, there was a tap on her door and Tasha walked in, magnificent in a glittering sea-green mermaid gown and sky-high heels she somehow made walking in look effortless.

"Tasha. You look incredible," she said.

"I could say the same for you." Tasha came to stand beside her and they surveyed themselves in the mirror. "You ready to do this thing, Sadie?" Tasha came to Sadie's dressing room every single night to ask her this question. It always made Sadie feel like she was Tasha's equal, like they were a real team and she wasn't just her opening act.

Now she wanted to tell Tasha everything—and ask her for help. But she couldn't do that. She needed to handle this on her own. So instead, she repeated what she said to Tasha every night. "I was born ready."

Tasha was holding a little package and she handed it to Sadie. "This is for you—but open it later. We don't have time for tears and makeup redos."

"No, no, not so fast." Sadie went to her dressing table and retrieved Tasha's gift: it was a locket she had found at a Christmas market on a tour stop in Germany. Inside it, she had put photos of the two cats, Johnny and June, that Tasha left behind when she went touring. "Same to you. Open this later, and then we can do our crying over how much we're going to miss each other once the lights go out."

"Hmm," Tasha said, her expression now thoughtful. "That might just be my next hit song." She hummed a tune and sang, *"I'm gonna do my cryin' over you, once the lights go out, babe."*

Sadie laughed. "Do I get a writing credit?"

"You get a lot of credit, Sadie Hunter. I don't want this to be the last I see of you. We need to talk about your next album, and those tracks of yours Cruz has. I want to hear them, the second you're ready to share. But for now, see you out there." Tasha waved as she left the room.

When Sadie was alone, she pulled up a flight-booking app on her phone. There was a satisfying *ping* as the app confirmed her flight booking for later that night. Destination: Calgary, Alberta. She'd miss the wrap party, and saying a proper goodbye to all the friends she'd made.

But the bottom line was: she had to solve her Max Brody problem.

13

Max

Banff, Canada
December 14

There were only two sounds in the cozy cabin. Max's quiet strumming on his guitar as he worked through a riff, and Patsy's shockingly loud snoring.

Max glanced out the window, noting that the snow that had been coming down steadily all night was slowing. He couldn't believe he'd been away from Nashville long enough that the snow was back for another year. Max had only intended to stay for two weeks, but somehow almost eleven months had passed. Some days he wondered if he'd ever go back.

He strummed for a moment longer, humming the tune as he did, then with a restless sigh set the guitar back down. Things were not going as well as he'd hoped, musically speaking. Actually, things weren't going as well as he'd hoped, *period*. The hint of cabin fever mixed with a touch of guilt, which seemed to ramp up with every month that passed, wasn't helping.

Max needed a distraction. He turned on the ancient television and flipped through the few channels he could get in this isolated wilderness. *News. More news. Weather.* Some sort of kitchen appliance infomercial. And a movie that he hadn't seen but could tell based on fashion alone was at least thirty years old.

"This will have to do," he muttered, grabbing a beer from the fridge and then sinking down on the couch beside Patsy. She nudged his hand holding the beer.

"Hey, no judgment, okay? I know it's only . . ." Max picked up his phone and the screen lit up. "It's only nine a.m. Shit, how is it only nine?" He tried not to think about Holden, and how beer for breakfast was on-brand for his father when Max was growing up. *I'm nothing like him,* Max thought. He set the unopened beer on the coffee table.

Glancing again at his phone, he saw the string of missed calls and messages—some having arrived days ago, others weeks ago. A wave of guilt rose up. Then the movie went to commercial break, and Patsy's head poked up from under her blanket. She let out a short, sharp bark.

Max looked from Patsy to the television, where a mattress commercial was playing.

"What the . . . ?" He sat forward and listened intently. The commercial ran often and the jingle was very familiar. Then he slapped a hand to his forehead and leaned back against the couch. Patsy crawled into his lap and lay her head up against his chest, watching him. Waiting for him to sort out what she already had.

"That's what I've been playing, and humming, isn't it?" Max covered his eyes, then squeezed the bridge of his nose.

"I can't believe I lifted a Canadian mattress company jingle for my song. Of all the . . ." He let out a frustrated groan. "Patsy, your dad is officially washed up at twenty-eight."

His phone pinged again, and this time Max read the text. It was from his manager, Bobbi, and she was not pleased.

You need to come home.

He watched the ghost dots wiggle, and then,

A little reminder via video (also, you signed a contract, remember?)

Another series of ghost dots. Finally,

"All I Want for Christmas," Max Brody, is you back in the studio. You don't even have to put a bow on your head for it to count as my present!

Max chuckled at that, then clicked play on the attached video.

It was a clip of Max and Sadie, singing their holiday cover of "All I Want for Christmas." He struggled to watch it, his hurt feelings still close to the surface.

He and Sadie may have been faking a lot of things, but the magic they created together, both on- and offstage—you couldn't fake that. But he had misjudged both her and the situation. He still felt sick when he remembered Sadie's tears and cutting words the night they'd won.

He had since ignored her calls and texts. Most of his time in Banff had been about trying to pretend that Sadie Hunter didn't exist, even if the rest of the world still believed that they were an item. It was immature and, quite frankly, self-destructive, but he also didn't see a way out of it now.

L̲ater, after another failed attempt at songwriting (and watching the video a half dozen more times), Max decided to head into "town." The snow had picked up again, and so he wore his ski goggles for the walk—it might have been an odd look to some, but here it was a perfectly normal sight during snowstorms.

About twenty minutes later Max arrived at the base of the hill, to what the locals referred to as "Fox's Corners." It was named as such because of the Fox family (headed up by Marty Fox), who owned the only three buildings in town—a repair shop with one gas pump, a small but surprisingly well-stocked general store, and a bar, with its popular comfort-foods menu.

The best part about Fox's Corners, aside from the bar's French onion soup, was that here he didn't have to be anyone other than "just Max." He was one of the "regulars," meaning he wasn't a permanent resident, but he also wasn't a tourist. Yes, the townspeople knew precisely *who* he was, but in Fox's Corners you were more revered for your hunting and fishing skills than any sort of musical celebrity, which suited "just Max" just fine.

A bell chimed above the repair shop's front door as he opened it, and smells of gasoline and metal, with a hint of something sharp and acrid, like rubber burning, filled Max's nose. There was a small, fake Christmas tree in the front window, which—with its dusty boughs and only about half the lights working—had seen better days. A young woman popped her head out of the tiny office at the back.

Mary Fox was Marty's daughter, and she helped her dad out when she was home for university breaks.

"You're still here, eh? Thought you'd be long gone by now," Mary said, giving him a hug.

"You and everyone else." Max gave Mary a lopsided smile.

"So, what brings you by?"

"Just wanted to drop this off. An early Christmas gift."

He pulled a large package, wrapped in candy-cane paper that he'd found in the cabin, out of his backpack.

"Oh, you didn't have to do this!" Mary took the wrapped package in her hands, then shook it a couple of times.

"They're scarves," Max said. "For your whole family."

"Well, personally I prefer to be surprised by a gift . . ."

Max laughed, mumbled an apology for ruining the surprise.

The Foxes had often invited Max, his mom, and his sister to join them for dinner at the bar when they were at the cabin while Holden toured. In some ways he felt more at home in Fox's Corners than he did back in Nashville.

"Anyway, I should probably head out," Max said. "Merry almost Christmas, Mary."

"Same to you," Mary replied.

Max said a final goodbye and shut the door behind him. He considered heading to the bar for some lunch, but then his phone vibrated in his coat pocket. He expected to see Bobbi's name flash on the screen, but it was his sister, Becca.

He frowned, contemplated calling her back when he got to the bar, but he had a rule that he never ignored a call from Becca. Ever since that night at the Sparrow when she had been trying to reach him—with the hardest news he had ever received—and he'd blown off her calls.

"Hey," he said.

"Get your ass back to Nashville, Max. Pronto." There was some shuffling in the background. He pressed the phone tighter to his ear.

Max stopped walking. "Becca? Is everyone okay?"

"Everyone is fine," Becca replied. "But can we say the same for you?"

Max ignored her comment. "You can't stress me out like this. Are you sure everything is fine? Where are you?"

"I'm home. In Nashville."

"Since when?" Max asked. Becca lived in England, and didn't get back to the States all that often.

"Oh, since about four hours ago," Becca replied. "Look, Max, I don't know what's going on with you, but you need to come home. It's almost Christmas. Don't you want to see your favorite sister?"

"*Only* sister," Max replied. "And of course I want to see you, but Christmas isn't for another couple of weeks."

"It's eleven days away, Maximillian," Becca said. "Speaking of Christmas, how's Sadie?"

"Not your best segue, Becks." Max sighed. "Why are you asking about Sadie?"

"Because she's your girlfriend?"

"Okay, did Bobbi call you? Don't bother, I know she did. And she never should have—"

Becca cut him off. "You've gone AWOL, Max. You won't even answer texts anymore apparently? So you can hardly blame me, and Bobbi, for worrying. Seriously, baby brother, what are you doing? It's been eleven months."

"I'm coming home soon," Max replied. "Leave it be, please."

There was a pause, then Becca said, "Fine. But stop ignoring the people who care about you."

They hung up and Max shoved his phone back into his pocket, raising his eyes skyward and taking a deep breath, a few errant snowflakes tickling his nose as he did.

A truck pulled up—"Fox's Autobody" printed on its side—towing a beige sedan with a dinged-in front fender. Marty Fox stepped out of the driver's side, a shock of white hair poking out from below his well-worn woolen toque, which Max had knit for him many Christmases ago.

"Hey, Marty!" Max called out. He started to make his way toward the truck when he was stopped in his tracks. There was someone else sitting in the passenger seat. She was trying to gather her belongings, so he couldn't see her face, but he would recognize Sadie Hunter anywhere.

Seeing her, Max felt like time was moving through a vat of molasses. He could not comprehend what was happening, or why (how?) Sadie was here, in Fox's Corners.

"Max, what serendipitous timing!" Marty held open the passenger-side door. "I have your girl, Sadie, here. She told me she was on her way to visit for a few days, and a snowbank got in her way."

"What? Is she okay?" Max tripped over an ice chunk in his

haste to get to the truck, still feeling disoriented by Sadie's sudden appearance. He caught himself before he landed flat on his face.

Sadie stepped out of the truck and thanked Marty. She still hadn't acknowledged Max, or even looked his way yet.

"No worries at all, young lady, I'm just glad I was there at the right time." He shut the door, rubbed his bare, well-calloused hands together. "Those damn rental car companies at the airport should know better than to send someone up the mountain in a car like that."

He clapped a hand against Max's upper arm. "Nice to see you, Max. I was wondering if you'd headed back home."

"Not yet," Max replied, staring at Sadie. His breath hitched. Goddamn, he was powerless against her. A strong wave of something moved through him—and he realized it was longing, with a tinge of regret. He had *missed* her. There was no denying it.

Now Sadie stared right back at him, her expression difficult to read. When they didn't speak, or immediately embrace, Marty glanced curiously between them.

Then Marty said, "Well, I'll leave you to it, kids. Sadie, don't worry about your rental car, that's what insurance is for, and I'll take a look besides."

Now Max glanced at the beige sedan, with the bent fender, then quickly back at Sadie. "Are you sure you're okay?" He looked her over, wanting to see for himself that she wasn't hurt. She seemed unscathed. She looked as beautiful as ever. It had been so long since he'd seen her, he was struggling to think clearly.

Sadie looked away first. "It was a slow slide into some snow.

I'm fine. The rental car, maybe not so much. But luckily Marty came along after it happened."

Max noticed how she was dressed: too lightly for the weather, in ankle boots that were no match for the deep snow, and a toque with the embroidered words "Kiss Me in Calgary" on her head.

As though reading his mind, Sadie smiled sheepishly, tugging the toque lower. "I got this from the airport."

Max merely nodded.

Sadie walked over to him, close enough that he could smell the familiar scent of vanilla. His chest constricted.

"I knew you were here," she said. "But I didn't expect to find you *right here*."

"Why are *you* here?" Max asked, raising his goggles on top of his head. His eyes were not playing tricks on him. Sadie Hunter was in Fox's Corners.

"What happened to your face?" she asked, instead of answering his question.

He ran his fingers over his short, coarse beard, which had come in in a light reddish tone versus the dark brown hair on his head. "You don't like it?"

"Not particularly. It doesn't suit you."

Max laughed and shook his head. He had the sudden urge to shout at her to go back to Nashville and leave him be. Or to take her in his arms and kiss her. *What the hell, Max?*

Max kept his tone light, trying not to let her get under his skin (too late). "So, how can I help you this afternoon, Sadie? You obviously didn't come two thousand miles, without any snow gear, to comment about my beard."

"You haven't answered your phone or replied to the, oh, two hundred text messages I've left you."

They stood there a moment longer—and then Max said, gruffly, "What do you want, Sadie?" He no longer had the energy for pithy commentary.

"I want you to come back to Nashville with me." For a moment, Sadie looked like she might cry. Max noticed a few other things: the light purple circles under her eyes; the slight red rash she always got on her cheeks after having to wear heavy makeup for shows; the two braids poking out from the toque—which was how she wore her hair after a show, to give it a rest from all the teasing.

"Did you have a show last night?" Even if he hadn't talked with Sadie, he had been following what she'd been up to.

Sadie nodded. "It was the last stop on tour with Tasha. I ditched the wrap party to come here."

"How did you even know where to find me?" He hadn't remembered ever talking to Sadie about the cabin in the Rockies, but even if he had, it wasn't exactly easy to find on a map. The directions were more like, *Drive toward the mountains, then when you hit the fork in the road turn left, and after the row of seven evergreens, take a right at the Fox's Corners sign . . .*

"Bobbi gave me the address."

"Did she now?" Max tried to garner irritation toward Bobbi, but he felt as tired as Sadie looked. "Look, I'm sorry you came all the way here. And the whole 'car into the snowbank' thing. But I'm not going back with you. End of story."

Sadie suddenly looked furious. "*End of story*? Oh no, Max Brody, you do not get to 'end of story' me. We had a deal."

"Trust me, Bobbi reminds me frequently about my 'contractual obligations,'" he grumbled. Max had to hand it to Sadie—Bobbi had been calling and leaving voicemails relentlessly, but she had not gotten on a plane and showed up in a snowstorm to get him. "But I'm not skipping out on anything, okay?"

Max waited for her to berate him further, but she had gone quiet and looked pale. He set his hands gently on her upper arms. "Are you going to fall over on me?"

"I'm okay," she said, but her voice betrayed her.

"Oh, I know you are," Max said. "But we should get out of the cold—I can barely feel my fingers and toes. And when was the last time you had something to eat?"

"I don't remember," she replied. "But I can't be bribed with a good meal, Max. You're coming back with me."

She moved closer still, and the scent of vanilla was oddly soothing, even if the expression on her face wasn't.

Sadie

Banff, Canada
December 14

Max led Sadie down the snowy road, her bag slung casually over his shoulder, as if it weighed nothing. The tavern they were headed toward was strung with unruly Christmas lights, half of them burnt out.

"I'm guessing this place isn't exactly known for its food," Sadie said. The wooden sign, hanging askew, said "The Local" in uneven, fading lettering. Her stomach growled and she wished she could give it some sort of warning that it shouldn't get its hopes up too high. She wished she could send that same message to her heart. The moment she had seen Max it had started racing as fast as it did before she went onstage. And she hadn't been telling him the truth about the beard not suiting him. He looked rugged and handsome—and more relaxed than he did in Nashville. Almost like he was an entirely different guy.

But he wasn't. He was still the same guy who had ghosted her for almost an entire year. She had come all the way to Banff to get him—and he still refused to come back.

"Trust me, they have a killer French onion soup served in a bread bowl, and great poutine," he was saying. "I come here all the time. It's not a bad spot, really."

Inside, the bar was dingy yet charming, a post-and-beam-style cabin with sawdust on the floors and kitschy art everywhere. There was one entire wall covered in Canadian two-dollar bills. Some of them were brown, some red, some featured Queen Elizabeth staring out benignly while some had little brown robins instead.

"Hey, Maxy. Haven't seen you for a few days." The woman behind the bar was pretty, in a fresh outdoorsy way. Sadie couldn't help it, she felt a pang of jealousy.

"Kara, you know wild horses can't keep me away," Max said, grinning back.

Sadie was standing awkwardly beside Max, not sure what to do or say. Was he really flirting with another woman in front of her? True, Sadie was just his fake girlfriend, but this Kara, with her strawberry hair in soft waves almost to her waist, and her big green eyes, didn't know that! Sadie cleared her throat and Max glanced her way as if he had just realized she was still there. "Oh. Kara, this is—"

"Sadie Hunter. I've seen you on TV together, but I was beginning to think Max had made up the fact he was dating you." Kara grinned, then beckoned them to have a seat. "Come on, sit. Fireballs, on the house! It's a town tradition if you drive into a snowbank. News travels fast in this town."

Fireballs? Sadie gave Max a quizzical look, but he just

laughed. She hoped they were some sort of delicious food—but doubted it. She perched herself on a barstool beside Max, peanut shells and sawdust crunching under the stool legs as she moved them.

"A Fireball is exactly what it sounds like," Max eventually said, which was not reassuring at all.

There were a few other patrons, all focused on a hockey game playing on a television in the corner. "Canucks game," Max said, by way of explanation. Most of the people watching the game had on toques or jerseys bearing a logo with a huge, angry-looking whale swimming its way out of a giant "C." A man walked over to the jukebox in the corner and moments later, the blare of AC/DC's "Mistress for Christmas" filled the room. Sadie grimaced.

"Not your favorite Christmas song?" Max shouted over the din.

"Calling this a song is a stretch," Sadie shot back. "It's sexist—definitely not my favorite."

Max accepted two shots of light brown liquid from Kara. "Thanks, sweetheart," he said to her, and Sadie felt another jealous pang. She hated when Max called *her* "sweetheart"—but apparently didn't want him calling anyone *else* sweetheart, either. She grabbed a shot glass and slammed it back without thinking, then started coughing and sputtering while Max looked on, amused.

"Hey, you might want to go easy," he said. "You look exhausted."

"Hasn't anybody ever told you never to tell a woman she looks tired?"

"Hmm, I do think my sister mentioned that once," Max

said, with a crooked smile that looked even cuter underneath his new beard.

"Anyway, I'm fine," Sadie insisted, even though her entire throat felt like it had been coated in hot cinnamon.

"Okay, then, tough girl. Want another?" Max drawled.

To prove him wrong, Sadie nodded. "I sure do," she said in a strangled voice. "Two more, please."

"And two bottles of Export," Max said, glancing at Sadie. "Mind if I order some food for us?"

"Be my guest."

"Also, two French onions. And a large poutine to share."

Kara gave them their drinks and left the bottle on the bar. "Honor system, okay?" She winked at Max and Max winked back. Sadie grabbed another shot and drank it back. This time she didn't cough.

"Whoa there, cowgirl, you haven't even eaten yet," Max said. "I don't really want to be carrying you back home later. Maybe you need to slow down?"

"Back home? Who says I'm going home with you?"

"This town has exactly zero hotel options, and you have no car. I'm stuck with you."

Sadie rolled her eyes, then pointed at the two shots sitting in front of him. "Why don't you drink one of those to numb the pain of having to deal with me, then?"

"Nah. I'm a one Fireball a night kind of guy, really."

"Fine, then. I'll have yours." She reached for one of his shots and glanced at him. "So . . . you and the bartender, huh?"

"What are you talking about?"

As if on cue, Brian Johnson shout-growled *"Mistress!"* on the speakers.

"She likes you."

"Well, I would hope so. We've been friends since we were kids, and she's engaged to one of my buddies out here."

"Oh. Well. Great, then."

Max looked down at his watch, then back up at her.

"What?"

"Yep, this is about right," Max said. "You haven't eaten in a while, right? This is the point when you start to get extremely irritable."

"What are you talking about?"

"You're like a gremlin. Back in Nashville, I needed to keep you fed every few hours or you'd turn into a beast."

"Keep me fed? I wasn't your pet, Max."

His smile faded somewhat. "No. I guess you weren't," he said, turning his attention to the game, even though Sadie had never heard Max say he followed hockey.

Despite her annoyance with Max, the whiskey's heat was now dulling into a pleasant warmth that spread through her chest and all the way down to her toes. Kara appeared from the kitchen, two steaming, cheese-covered bread bowls in her hands.

"Poutine'll be up in a moment," Kara said.

Sadie dug into the soup immediately.

"That better?" Max asked after she'd had a few bites.

"You're right, this is really good," she said, her mouth full. She noticed the bar was starting to fill up; most of the tables were now taken. "Why is it so busy in here in the middle of the day?"

"It's karaoke day."

"Karaoke *day*?"

"Yeah. Once winter sets in and it starts to get dark early around here, nobody tends to go out much at night. Way too dangerous on the roads—or the roads are closed on account of snow. So the wise owners of this here tavern decided to have their karaoke night during the day. It just makes sense."

"I'm sure it does."

"Most people just snowshoe or cross-country-ski home later—and there are a few volunteers out patrolling the paths, making sure no one who's had too much to drink falls in a snowbank and freezes to death."

"Sounds perfectly reasonable."

"Yeah, but it's pretty awful. I personally am of the mindset that day-drinking and karaoke do not mix."

"It actually sounds like fun," Sadie said.

He cocked his head and raised an eyebrow. "That, ma'am, is because *you've* been day-drinking."

"We should do a song."

"Out of the question," Max said, turning his attention to his soup. "No way."

Sadie stopped eating and picked up a shot glass, shaking it gently at him. "Well, I guess *this* is the only fun I'm going to have today," she said, knocking it back.

"Seriously, Sadie, you're going to be on your *ass*—"

"Well, that's fine, because I need to drown my sorrows." She hadn't meant to say that, and tried to smile to make the words go away.

But Max tilted his head. "Sorrows?"

Suddenly, she felt a bit queasy. He was right—she shouldn't

have been so liberal with the whiskey drinking on an empty stomach. Kara arrived with the poutine and Sadie dug into that as a way to avoid Max's question.

"Sadie. What's going on?"

"Oh, I don't know," Sadie said, finally gaining control of her emotions. "I've been back in the States, working my ass off, and you've been . . ." She looked around. "Here, avoiding everything? I've been trying to reach you all year to try to talk to you about that night, and you just disappeared on me. Have you thought about me, or anyone who's been trying to help you, at all?"

"Let's talk about that night, then, Sadie," Max said, his expression now cold.

She opened her mouth, then closed it again—realizing she couldn't. But not for the reason he thought. After too many whiskeys, if she told him about her gran, she knew she would completely fall apart. The tears were still stinging at her eyes but she blinked them away. You didn't unbottle something you'd kept inside for so long in a tavern filled with strangers, in the middle of the afternoon. "You let me down," she said, knowing that wasn't quite fair, but also that it was at least part of the truth.

"Come on. It was a *fake* proposal."

"That's not what I mean! It wasn't about the proposal." She lowered her voice. "We can't go back in time. I know that." She also knew that if she *could* go back in time, she would have told him everything, the night they won *Starmaker*, about why she was so upset, why she had to take off so fast. But it was too late for that. "And things aren't great between us, but we still have to see things through. I wish you would come back with me and finish what we started. You know that's why I'm here, Max. To bring you back."

Max just nodded and looked away again—even though *he* had asked her to tell him what was on her mind.

Sadie put down her fork.

"That's it? No comment?"

"Nope," he said.

She released a blustering sigh. "You're impossible, Max, did you know that?"

"You keep telling me so. And, well, you're not exactly . . . possible," Max muttered. Sadie glanced at him sideways and suddenly felt a tipsy giggle build up inside her.

"I'm not exactly . . . *possible*?"

He just shook his head and frowned. Sadie took another bite of her soup and looked around at the full tavern. There was a warm buzz in the air as conversations rose around them and someone put Willie Nelson's version of "Pretty Paper" on the juke. It was one of her favorite Christmas songs and helped pull her back from the edge of her dark mood. She hummed along for a bar and thought of her gran—but this time, it didn't feel like a knife was stabbing into her heart. She could almost hear her gran's voice, telling her to get over what was bothering her. "You can be right, or you can be happy, Sadie Jane," Gran always used to tell her. Max wasn't going to budge, at least right now. But she was in a tiny, snowy town that was actually quite quaint. She was eating good food and listening to good music. Max could be his miserable, broody self—but maybe she could try to be happy, for just a little while? She turned to him. "Aside from you being here," she quipped, "this place is not half bad, you know."

"It's not even a little bit bad," Max said. "There's a reason I want to stay. It's good here. For *me*." His gaze moved up, to a space above the mirror behind the bar, where a series of photos were affixed.

"I guess that's all that matters. What works for *you*," she countered, immediately forgetting about her decision to try to have a good time.

"And why exactly do you think it would be right for *you* to keep up this charade?"

"We don't all have a standing invitation to sing at the Grand Ole Opry, Max."

"I don't have a *standing invitation* to—"

"But you will. And you know it. You won't even have to do anything to get it, either. It's in your bloodline. You're Holden Brody's son. You can disappear for a year and come back and everyone will welcome you with open arms."

"That's bullshit," he said in a low voice. "I work hard."

"So that spot on *Starmaker*, the fact that they were contractually obligated to not kick you off until the final episode—you earned that?"

"Hey. You seem to be forgetting you might have been kicked off if it weren't for me."

"Exactly! Because my way wasn't paved for me. And *you* seem to be forgetting you didn't stand a chance against Johnny King if it hadn't been for me. For *us*."

"Is this why you came here? To rehash the past?"

"No. I came here to bring you back. And then—"

"And then what, Sadie? And then we do our song and never talk to each other again?"

He was staring at her so intently, and she didn't know why

the stab of sadness was back. Did the idea of never speaking to Max Brody again make her that miserable? Sadie watched Max as his eyes returned to the space above the bar. She followed his gaze and it landed on a black-and-white photo of a man and a woman standing on the tavern stage, singing into the same microphone, eyes closed, rapt.

Sadie was about to ask him about the passionate couple, when Kara returned, a bit breathless now. "You two want a couple more whiskeys?"

"Fine. Why not?" Max said. "Sadie here is clearly trying to show herself a good time."

"Make it two," Sadie said. Despite him saying he was a one Fireball kind of guy, Max slugged back one of his shots as soon as Kara was gone. Meanwhile, Sadie kept staring up at the photos on the wall.

"That's your dad, right?" she said. "For a second, I thought it was you. But you'd never dress like that. In a Stetson. And that's your mom?"

"That photo is probably thirty years old." Max said. "Dad bought the cabin after they were married, as a wedding gift for my mom. She always said there was nothing like a fresh snowfall to help you remember how beautiful the world could be." Max smiled at the memory, his eyes on the photo, and Sadie nodded because she understood. It felt good to be in a snowy setting. It was almost like going home.

"They were here that night, celebrating Mom's last album release," Max continued. "Actually, her only album release— and they performed one of her songs together." He glanced back at the small platform with the stools and the karaoke machine on it. "Right up there, as the story goes."

Holden Brody and his wife, Maren, were staring into each other's eyes like fate had decreed they would never fall out of love. Sadie wished she could take that photo down and get a closer look, so she could discover any secrets it held that might help her understand Max and convince him to come back to Nashville. But maybe she also wanted to look at it so she could understand true love. And maybe she couldn't stop staring at the photo because the way Holden and Maren Brody were looking at each other reminded her of herself and Max when they sang together.

Sadie glanced back at the karaoke stage. If they could sing together, she and Max, would that help? Would it start to feel like old times—when they were getting along and making great music? She glanced over at Max to see if he felt it, too, but it was impossible to read his expression.

"Do you think your mom regretted not pursuing her career?" Sadie asked. After Maren Brody became a mother, she just dropped out of the music business, and never sang publicly again.

"Of course not," Max replied, with a hint of defensiveness. "She wanted what we had as a family. Can we drop this?"

Sadie realized that maybe Max was just as invested in guarding his pain as she was. She felt a wave of empathy for him. The walls he had built around himself were so well-constructed.

In the background, someone was testing out the karaoke mic. Moments later, a group of young women took the stage and launched into a version of "These Boots Are Made for Walkin'." There were five of them, all crowded around one mic. The one in the middle had her head thrown back, and Sadie felt a tug. She understood that joyful abandon. She knew that when she was down, or anxious, there was only one thing that could make her feel better: singing. Impulsively, she walked up to the stage and wrote a fake name down on the sign-up sheet—but the young man running the machine recognized her.

"Sadie Hunter! I don't think anyone will mind if you jump the line. What song do you want to do?"

"Tasha Munroe's 'Don't Come Callin',' " Sadie said, thinking fast.

"You and Max planning to treat us to a duet? Should I wait for him to start the music?"

"No, I'll go ahead. He's not in the mood," Sadie said with a laugh.

"Alright! Sadie Hunter is in the house," he crooned into the microphone. The bar erupted in hoots and hollers. The only one not cheering was Max. He looked like he wished the sawdust and peanut-shell-covered floor would open up and swallow him.

Sadie took the two steps up to the stage and nearly stumbled, but stayed upright. She grabbed the microphone and felt that familiar burst of energy. Even though she was in a tiny northern town singing karaoke in the middle of the afternoon, it felt just the way it did when she was on tour with Tasha. She loved this.

Sadie sang the opening verse, about a woman who was on a mission, at a bar to drown her sorrows and forget about her man. She found herself beckoning to Max and mouthing, *Come on*. He didn't move, but she no longer cared. Suddenly, it felt like she was singing out all the hurt she had felt as months had passed and she hadn't heard from someone she had grown to care about. Someone who wasn't giving her the chance to say she was sorry for being so harsh during a very bad night. *"Baby, I know you've got my number . . ."* She closed her eyes and shimmied her hips.

When she opened her eyes, she thought the whiskey had caused her to hallucinate. Was that Max Brody, stepping onto the stage beside her, his smile tentative? Then he grabbed the mic and sang a verse, shooting her a wink halfway through. Even after a year, they could still pick up where they left off—onstage, at least. *"You act like you're all high and mighty, but you know what? You're just too flighty."* He was grinning down at her as she sang, and she smiled up at him—and wondered for a moment if the two of them looked just the same as Holden and Maren, all those years before. She grabbed back the mic and sang her musical rebuttal, feeling the warmth from the whiskey turn into full-on heat. *This always happens when I sing with Max,* she reminded herself. *It doesn't really mean anything. It's probably just that I haven't seen him in such a long time.*

That was why the heat felt so strong today.

Everyone in the bar had moved to the dancefloor now. Sadie and Max bumped hips—and Sadie was almost sure she saw sparks of electricity between them as their bodies touched, even briefly. If she didn't know better, she'd think Max was actually having fun, too. The song ended with the two of them crooning into the mic together, *"Whatever you do, babe . . . don't come callin' me! Cause I'm not home . . ."* And the crowd in the bar went as wild as they would have if Sadie had been standing in a stadium with Tasha herself. *"See ya,"* Sadie growled into the microphone as the song ended, doing her best Tasha impersonation. Max put his arm around her waist and leaned in. He took the mic out of her hand.

"You're plastered," he said softly. "Let's go outside for some air."

She made her way unsteadily down the steps of the stage and toward the door, smiling at patrons who waved their phones in her face and took photos.

Outside, she spun around. "Why'd you always have to be telling me what to do?" she slurred.

"Last I checked, you came all the way here to try to tell *me* what to do."

He was standing close, looking intently at her. His breath was even more cinnamon-scented than usual, because of the whiskey.

"Why'd you come up onstage with me if you said you didn't wanna sing?"

"I came up there because . . ." He stared into her eyes for a long moment. "Because I had to. Because I couldn't *not*."

Their lips were close and Sadie felt electricity flow through her body. She wanted him to kiss her, she realized. The very idea of that was making her dizzy. She tried to take a step back and get her bearings, but nearly stumbled and lost her balance. Max grabbed her and held her steady. They swayed for a moment, there in the gently falling snow. Like they were dancing.

"I'm sorry," Max said softly.

"What exactly are you sorry for, Max?" She pulled him closer to her, avoiding his gaze. She thought she could feel his heartbeat underneath her cheek.

"I'm sorry I didn't call," he said. And he did sound genuinely sorry. Before she could think too much about what she was doing, she reached up to touch the new beard she liked so much.

"Sadie . . ." He put his hand to hers. "Why are things always so difficult between us?" He looked agonized, and suddenly Sadie wanted him to be happy. She didn't want things to be difficult between them. She wanted everything between them to be as easy as it was when they sang together. As it had that last night together onstage when they won *Starmaker*. And in the minutes before, in her dressing room, when she had actually thought that this was someone she wanted in her life forever.

But for now, she gave in to the kiss. The spicy, familiar taste of his lips, the new scratchy feeling of his beard on her skin, the way his hands felt on her back as their bodies were pressed close, making her feel shivery all over, but hot at the same time. It wasn't clear who had kissed whom first. When they finally came up for air, she kept her body where it was, warm against his.

"Sadie," Max said.

She looked up at him as the snow fell softly around them. "Let's go back to your place," she said, realizing as she did that there was no place in the world she'd rather be.

15

Max

Banff, Canada
December 15

Max hadn't slept a wink. But at least this third pot of coffee was helping to clear some of the fogginess away. The sleepless night also meant he'd finished another dog sweater, this one joining a dozen others going to the rescue where he'd adopted Patsy. Max may have been struggling with his music at the cabin, but he'd been prolific with his knitting—every closet was full of projects, in various stages of completion.

He glanced at the closed guest bedroom door, behind which Sadie slept. She was plumb tuckered out, between the tour and the flight to Banff, and he wanted to let her sleep as long as possible. She would likely have a rough morning regardless, after all that whiskey.

That got him thinking about the bar, their karaoke singing . . . *that kiss*. Max could still feel the softness and warmth of her lips, which had been a welcomed contrast to the chilly temperatures last night. He could still smell the heady vanilla scent swirling around them, the taste of spicy cinnamon on her lips, the feel of his heart racing like a herd of wild horses.

A pained groan escaped from the guest room. Max rapped his knuckles softly against the door. "Sadie? You up?"

There was no answer, and he pressed an ear to the door. Hearing nothing still, he knocked again, a touch louder. Another low groan in response.

"There's coffee," he said.

"Okay, thanks," Sadie mumbled. He heard the sound of items shifting on the nightstand, then a loud *thud* followed by some cursing.

"All good?"

"Yeah, all good," she strangled out. Max knew from personal experience that Fireball hangovers were *the* worst.

A few minutes later Sadie emerged from the guest room, and Max handed her a glass of water and two ibuprofens, for which she seemed grateful. Then he filled a mug—the saying "Country Music: Cheaper Than Therapy" on its side—with coffee. "You take it black, right?"

"Thanks. I really needed this." She took a sip, but then cringed as she put her hand on her forehead. She looked green around her mouth, the dark circles under her eyes even more prominent today. "My memory is spotty, and what I *can* remember, well, I hope it isn't true?"

Max's stomach flipped. Was she regretting the kiss? *Well, of course she is, you ding-dong,* he thought. Sadie Hunter needed Max, but not in that way. She had drunk too much—he couldn't read into anything about last night.

But then she said, "Did I get sick? Outside the cabin?" She looked mortified. "Oh God, I did. Didn't I?"

He was relieved. So, it wasn't about the kiss after all. "Don't you worry about that."

Sadie put her coffee down and covered her face with her hands. "This is so embarrassing." Then she looked at Max, her blue eyes holding his dark ones. "Did anything else happen?"

Max paused, remembering the feel of their bodies pressed together, full of desire, white-hot even through their layers of winter clothing. Things could have gone differently when they'd returned to Max's cabin, but he would never take advantage of a situation like that.

"Joe gave us a lift back on his snowmobile, and then you wisely got rid of a few of those Fireballs into the snowbank. Don't worry, I held your hair back," Max said, chuckling slightly at the look of horror on her face. "Then I gave you a big glass of water and got you to bed."

"I appreciate you getting me back here in one piece." Sadie rubbed her temples and looked around the cabin's living room. He tried to see it through her eyes. It was rustic but plenty comfortable, with warm touches, like woven tapestries on the walls and a large stone fireplace. The fire Max had started crackled and cast a bright orange glow into the space.

"It's so cozy. The perfect spot to recover from too many Fireballs." She gave him a weak smile. "Thanks again for taking care of me, Max."

"You're welcome," Max replied. "My pleasure."

She snorted. "I highly doubt that."

He smiled, then handed her a fluffy white bath towel. "A hot shower will make everything better."

After he heard the water go on, Max stoked the fire and tried to avoid thinking of Sadie in the shower. Instead, he thought about how he'd carried her into the cabin and tucked her into bed. He liked taking care of her. Max wasn't sure about a lot right now, but that much he was certain about.

An hour later they sat on the couch in the living room, the fire raging and keeping the cabin toasty. The snow came down steadily as they listened to John Denver's *Rocky Mountain Christmas* album and drank hot cocoa. Sadie was dressed head to toe in red-plaid fleece loungewear, which had been his sister's and fit her well, if not a touch long in the arms and legs. Her cheeks were still rosy from when they'd taken Patsy out on a short walk about twenty minutes earlier.

"Hope the cocoa's not too hot," Max said, joining her on the couch with his own mug, marshmallows bobbing on its surface. He patted the cushion between them for Patsy. "Come on, girl. Up."

But Patsy stayed where she was—sitting on the floor beside Sadie.

Sadie reached into her mug and pulled a mini marshmallow out with her fingers. She held out the tiny sweet treat to Patsy, who gleefully ate it in a split second, then licked at Sadie's fingers.

"Sadie! She doesn't eat marshmallows!"

"I think she does, in fact, eat marshmallows. Three, so far," Sadie retorted, scratching under the dog's chin.

"Well, before today she's never had a marshmallow. Who knows what that's going to do to her digestive system." Max pointed at Sadie. "You are cleaning up the mess if anything goes sideways."

"Deal," Sadie replied. "You know, I don't blame you for running away here."

"I didn't 'run away,'" he said. "I needed to think, to work without distraction, and this is where I feel my best, okay?"

Sadie took another sip from her mug. "Why this place?"

"My mom was from Canada. Did you know that?" Max swallowed hard. Some days he couldn't believe she was gone, even if it had been years now.

"I didn't." Sadie blew across the surface of the cocoa, keeping her eyes on Max.

"Grew up on Vancouver Island, then came to Nashville to do what singers do—try to hit it big."

"Well, she certainly followed through on that plan," Sadie said. Max felt pride at that, and gratitude toward Sadie for recognizing his mom's talent even though her career had been short. By the time Max was born, Maren Brody—poised to be nearly as famous as her husband, Holden—had happily left the stage for the title of "Mom." She had been the most constant, loving force Max had ever known, and part of him had disappeared after she died.

"You must miss her. I understand why you ran—sorry, came back here. This is where you feel closest to her."

"It is," Max said softly, then he cleared his throat. "So, how about a refresher?"

Sadie held out her mug, a bit of sticky white marshmallow fluff above her upper lip.

"You've got a little . . ." Max put his finger on his lip.

Sadie looked at him in confusion. "What?"

"Here. Let me." Max took a napkin and shifting closer to her, gently pressed it against Sadie's lip.

Their eyes locked—and Max held his breath. Her eyes still on his, Sadie leaned forward slowly and gently brushed his lips with hers.

Oh. My. God. He cupped her face with his hands, kissing her deeply. Forget what everyone said about the magic that happened when they sang. *This* put their onstage chemistry to shame.

All he could think about was how good her lips felt against his, the tantalizing taste of her: sweet cocoa and marshmallow. Until he heard her whisper, "Wait . . . Max."

Immediately, he pulled back. "Are you okay?"

"I'm not sure."

"Are you going to throw up on me again?"

"Oh my God . . . Did I throw up *on* you?"

"Stop your fretting," Max said, laughing gently. They were inches apart, the heat of their bodies adding to the warmth of the space. Max wanted nothing more than to keep kissing Sadie, but only if she wanted the same thing. "You don't have to, you know, do this."

"I will say the same to you." Sadie raised an eyebrow, and when he raised an eyebrow back she laughed, before kissing him again.

Once they broke apart, Max touched his forehead to hers and closed his eyes. "I . . . I need to tell you something."

Sadie looked at him in concern. "What is it?"

Max could barely concentrate. His heart raced, knowing he was about to let his guard down and not knowing how his next words would be received.

"I know our history is . . . complicated. But I don't want to be fake with you, Sadie."

She was silent. Max held his breath until he couldn't bear it any longer. "If you don't feel—"

"I don't want to be fake with you, either," she said at the same time.

Max felt a weight lift off him. And then confusion set in again. "Wait, you know what I mean, right? Like, I can't pretend to have feelings for you, because I *have* feelings for you."

She leaned in and whispered, "I have feelings for you, too, Max Brody, in case that wasn't clear."

This suit is ah-mazing." Sadie held out her arms and turned around in a circle, the neon colors bright against the snow. She was wearing Maren Brody's still-pristine, one-piece ski suit, which was white except for a neon-colored rainbow that cut across the top and wrapped around the back. It fit Sadie nearly perfectly, the white belt with the delicate gold buckle cinched around her small waist.

"Glad you like it," Max said, laughing as he watched her spin around. *She looks fine in everything she puts on.* He wanted to toss her over his shoulder and carry her back inside (maybe they could save the sledding for tomorrow), to continue kissing her in front of the fire. She stuck out her tongue and caught a falling snowflake, her face lighting up with a smile when she looked at him. His heart felt like it stopped right then, being under her gaze like that. Knowing his feelings were reciprocated, and that they didn't have to pretend anymore.

They were on the hill behind Max's cabin, having hiked to the top, Max dragging the old wooden toboggan behind him. If you had asked him yesterday morning how he'd spend today, it *would not be* sledding with Sadie Hunter. And it would definitely not include what had happened *before* they went sledding. Every time he thought about the feel of her lips . . . well, he could barely concentrate on anything else.

Trying to stay focused on the task at hand, Max shifted the toboggan so it was perched at the crest of the hill, its front end wobbling slightly as it rested above the steep incline. He crouched, setting one gloved hand firmly on the wooden slats, the rope tight in his other hand. "Ladies first."

Max had one heavy snow boot on the toboggan's slats behind Sadie, the other still planted in the snow. "Once I jump on, it's 'go' time."

"I grew up in the Midwest," Sadie replied. "I'm not exactly a sledding virgin. So stop talking and get on."

"Yes, ma'am." In one swift movement Max jumped on behind Sadie. One second the wooden slats creaked as the sled adjusted to the weight and movement, the next they were flying down the hill, carving a deeply grooved swath through the snow.

It was exhilarating, and not just because of the speed. Max had wrapped his arms around Sadie, and she leaned into him as though it was the most natural thing to do, a whiff of vanilla hitting his nose.

But then the sled hit an unseen bump in the terrain and they were suddenly airborne. Max didn't travel far, sliding off the back and rolling once before the snow stopped him. But Sadie—much lighter than Max—wasn't as lucky: she flew off the toboggan like a rag doll. The rainbow on her suit was a dizzying kaleidoscope as she tumbled over and over, finally resting facedown in the snow about twenty feet from where Max was. The sled kept going another few feet before it caught an edge and flipped on its side.

"Sadie!" Max scrambled to his feet and raced down the hill toward her. He knelt beside her. She *was* crying, but not out of pain. "Are you . . . Wait, what's happening?"

Sadie was laughing so hard she could barely catch her breath. "That . . . was . . . awesome!"

Max laughed, too, then sat beside her in the snow, relieved she wasn't hurt.

"This is the most fun I've had in a while," Sadie said.

Max reached out and reset her toque so it covered her ears.

He was just about to kiss her nose, which had reddened with the chill, when she said, "I know you don't want to come back, Max. And being here, well, I can't say I blame you. But you need to, okay?"

Max sighed. "Can we not do this right now?"

"When else?" Sadie asked, with a lilt of frustration. "I know it's easy to ignore our 'Nashville problem' here, but—"

"I don't have a Nashville problem," Max retorted. He grabbed a handful of snow, formed it into a ball, and then tossed it down the hill. A second later it disappeared into the white abyss.

"You do," Sadie said. "*We* do. It's almost Christmas. We have to record our song. We're on contract. You know what Cruz is like. A lot rests on what we do next. Careers depend on us, Max, and not just our own."

If only he had the guts to tell her precisely *what* the issue was: that he was terrified of going back, because he finally felt like himself again. Sure, he wasn't making music the way he'd hoped, but cabin life and Fox's Corners suited him. Here no one gave a shit about his celebrity, and he got calls not for a silly autograph but to help dig out a stuck-in-the-ditch truck. The thought of being back in Nashville took all those good feelings, scrunched them into a tight ball, and set them on fire. If only he and Sadie could stay here indefinitely.

"I'll think about it," he finally replied, saying none of what he really should.

She gaped at him. "Do you have any idea . . . ?"

"Don't blow a gasket, Sadie." Max stood then, brushing snow from his pants. He immediately regretted his tone. Why did he have to go and ruin what had been one of the most amazing days of his life? It took two to tango, he reminded himself. But now he had a new problem. Max's romantic feelings toward Sadie were in direct competition with his irritated ones, and he had to pick a side within himself. He opted to call a truce, putting out his hand as an offering to help her up from the snow. But Sadie angrily stood and stomped past him, ignoring his outstretched hand. He watched her slip and slide up the hill, muttering to herself as she did.

"Sadie, stop. Please."

She turned back, hands on her hips, her eyebrows raised questioningly. Looking exquisite, like a rainbow Snow Queen, but pissed as hell.

Max grabbed the toboggan's frayed rope, then walked to where she stood. "Can we put this on the back burner for now? We're stuck here for a few days at least, until these storms pass, and I can think of better things to do than fight."

The weather report was calling for yet another blizzard, right on the heels of the last. Fox's Corners had barely begun to dig out from the first dump of snow, and flights were all back-logged. Max knew from experience they weren't going any-where anytime soon. He said a silent prayer of thanks to Mother Nature, because being snowed in with Sadie Hunter was exactly what he hoped for.

He reached his gloved hand out again, and after a moment of hesitation, Sadie took it.

"I know I'm a pain in the ass, Sadie," Max said, holding her hand tightly. "Can we enjoy this winter wonderland and take a break from our goddamn 'Nashville problem,' just for a few days?"

Sadie set her hands on his shoulders, which wasn't easy due to the snow boots and uneven ground. She huffed in frustra-tion, but then kissed him.

"Fine, Max. You win this round," she said, her breath warm against his lips.

Max grinned, then let go of the toboggan and wrapped his arms around Sadie's waist. "You know, I was going to suggest another ride down the hill, but you seem like you've caught a bit of a chill . . ."

"Maybe we need to head back inside?" Sadie said, even though she was plenty warm in his arms.

"I think that would be best." Max nodded solemnly, then turned around. "Hop on."

Sadie laughed. "You're going to piggyback me up this hill?"

"I sure am, darlin'." Max gestured for her to jump on his back.

Sadie jumped, but the bulkiness of the ski outfits made it tough for either of them to get a solid grip, and they toppled sideways.

She landed on top of Max, and it winded him slightly. "That went differently in my mind," he finally said, laughing.

"I actually think this turned out okay." Sadie shifted so they lay facing one another, the deep snow creating a nest around them.

"Me, too," Max said, thinking about nothing but the feel of her warm lips on his, the snow falling steadily around them.

16

Sadie

Banff, Canada
December 18

Sadie sat on the deep, comfy couch in Max's cabin, half watching her favorite holiday movie, *Miracle on 34th Street*, and half watching Max, who had fallen asleep with Patsy on his chest. In between Max's soft snores, Sadie could hear the tiny puffs of air whistling out of Patsy's adorable snub nose.

She looked out the window. It was snowing outside—it seemed to have been snowing steadily since she arrived here, four days earlier, but the flakes were lighter today, dancing down from the sky and floating in front of the window like white fireflies.

She eased herself off the couch, careful not to disturb Max. They had been up late the night before. She had found the game

Rummoli in a dusty box in one of the cupboards. It had been a favorite in the Hunter household when Sadie was growing up. "My gran loves this game," Sadie had said to Max when she discovered it—and then hadn't known how to correct herself. So, she hadn't. She had decided not to bring her sadness into the happy moments they were having. She and Max had curled up on the floor at either end of his live-edge wood coffee table, wrapped in blankets. They drank fragrant, hot tea and laughed together, learning a new game as the fire crackled behind them. And it had been, like so much of these recent days with Max, perfect.

The truth was, Sadie was happier than she had been in a long time, secluded here in the snowy mountains with Max. She was seeing another side of him—and liking what she saw. The rest of the world seemed like it existed on another planet. So she had decided she wanted to keep it that way, for just a little while longer.

She wandered into the guest bedroom and sat down on the thick quilt. Sadie had been sleeping alone at night, while Max slept in his own room. They were constantly touching one another—kissing, holding hands, snuggling up to watch movies—but things hadn't gone further than that. Not yet. Sadie got the sense that they were both being very careful, given that the chemical cocktail created when they were together had far too easily exploded in the past. But here, in the quiet and calm of Banff, their chemistry might actually have staying power instead of ending up a failed experiment.

She closed her eyes and recalled their good-night kiss the night before. With Max's lips on hers, Sadie had felt heat rising within her—and she wanted to pull him gently into the bedroom with her. But then Patsy had started whining to go out and the moment had passed. After that, Sadie had cuddled under the thick blankets alone, listening to Max out in the main room, shutting things down for the night. She had wondered if taking things further would be a good idea. She was still wondering. She knew it would be good between them—probably astronomically so. But their relationship was already so complicated.

Sadie's stomach growled, interrupting her thoughts. Back out in the kitchen, she opened Max's freezer and looked inside. They'd eaten its contents over the past few days—frozen pizzas, mostly—and all that was left was freezer-burned ice and something unidentifiable and brown in a Ziploc bag. The fridge wasn't much better: mustard, a few beers, coffee cream. Typical bachelor stuff.

She closed the fridge and made a decision. Then she walked to the door and picked up a pair of snowshoes.

The clock was ticking, and Sadie knew it. She had turned off her phone, but when she finally turned it on again it would be overloaded with messages. Everyone in Nashville wanted Sadie and Max to come back to town.

But tonight, she would change things up, make it special—and see where it all went.

Outside, the air was fresh and cold. Sadie breathed it in deeply. The snowflakes were gone, and the clouds above were thinning. Rays of sunlight cast ladders into the distant mountain range. Although the several feet of powdery snow was more than they ever had in Wisconsin, she still felt at home in the winter wonderland. Max's cabin wasn't too far from the town, only about a half hour down a gentle mountain slope.

Soon, Fox's Corners came into view: the autobody shop, the tavern, and the tiny general store.

The snow may have stopped, but the main road hadn't been cleared yet. There was traffic—but it consisted only of people on cross-country skis or, like Sadie, on snowshoes. Sadie was charmed; it looked as cozy and heartwarming as a holiday movie set.

As she passed the autobody shop, she saw Mary standing outside, closing the hood of a pickup truck with chains on its tires. She smiled and waved when she saw Sadie plodding along the snowy street.

Sadie stepped into the tiny general store, where the owner was restringing an ancient looking pair of snowshoes. She found a bag of decent-looking frozen shrimp and a bake-from-frozen baguette. She added a dusty box of penne to her basket, as well as cream, parmesan, lemon, garlic, and a clamshell container of cherry tomatoes. She even found California strawberries in the small produce section. "Lucky girl," the man said when she got to the checkout. "Those go fast." She added a package of taper candles to her basket, and she was done.

After she paid for the groceries, she packed them all into the small backpack she had brought along and headed back up the mountain to Max's cabin. She felt her anticipation grow with every step. She had only been away from him for just over an hour, but she missed him. And it was a good feeling.

Max was just waking up when she opened the door. He rubbed his bleary eyes, confused. "Where'd you go?"

"Just into town," Sadie said, closing the door behind her.

"You should have woken me, I would have come with you."

"You looked so peaceful, and you were obviously worn out from my kicking your butt all night at Rummoli."

He rolled his eyes. "Yeah, yeah. I held my own."

Max stood and greeted her with a kiss, but then frowned when he noticed her phone sitting on a side table. "You really should have brought your phone with you, Sadie. It's not safe to be trekking up and down the mountain without one."

"It's not snowing, there was plenty of light, and it's a direct and easy path from your place to town," Sadie said lightly—but she was touched by his worry for her. She picked up her phone but couldn't turn it on, not yet. She didn't want to think about the real world. She would focus on their safe little haven inside the cabin instead, and making it a perfect night.

"What do you have there?" Max asked, coming up behind her and sliding his arms around her waist, then nuzzling her ear. She leaned into him.

"I'm making you dinner," she said.

"Now, wait a minute. You can sing, you're smart, you're not so bad to look at, and you can cook? Hot damn, I am one lucky man!"

"You really are," she said with a smile.

"What can I do to help?" he murmured, his face close to hers.

"We-ell, as enjoyable as *this* is, it's probably not helping much," she said. She pulled away from him reluctantly and gave him the cherry tomatoes to wash. "Maybe put on some music when you're done?"

He went to put on a record from his mom's extensive stash

of vinyl. She smiled as the familiar music from *Merry Christmas with Patsy Cline* began.

"My gran loved—" she said, then stopped and swallowed hard.

"I bet she *loves* this album."

"Oh yeah." Sadie recovered as fast as she could. "It's her favorite. Mine, too. Good choice, Max."

Outside, the sun was starting to set and the light in the cabin was dim. Max found old wine bottles to put the candles in, as well as a dusty bottle of Amarone in a high cupboard. "No idea if it'll be any good," he said as he popped the cork. He brought her a glass and kissed her nose. "Thanks for doing this, Sadie. You're making me feel real special."

Sadie kissed him back, banishing the sadness she had been feeling earlier about her gran. But, she decided as she took a sip of wine, she was going to tell him about Gran during their meal. She knew she had to let him in. It would hurt, but then it would be over.

The meal came together quickly, a dish her mom had taught her to make. She explained the steps to Max as she sauteed the shrimp in butter and garlic, added the tomatoes and cooked them until they burst, splashed in some of the cream, and plated it with parmesan and lemon wedges.

"Sadie, this is *so* good," Max said, taking his first bite of the pasta when they were seated at the table.

"It's really nothing," Sadie said. "But I wanted to show you how much I appreciate . . ." She looked around her at the cabin, which looked especially enchanting in the flickering candlelight. "All this. This week was just what I needed."

He looked at her for a long time, the candle flames dancing in his eyes. "Me, too, Sadie," he said gently.

"There's something else I need to talk about," Sadie said. Her heart was pounding, but she knew what she had to do.

"Anything, Sadie," he said. She took a deep breath—and then noticed a red spot on his neck.

"Max! Are you having an allergic reaction?"

"Oh. I'm okay," Max said, looking a little embarrassed. "You were about to tell me something?"

"Max . . . are you . . ." She looked down at the shrimp tails on her plate, then back up at him. "Are you allergic to shellfish?"

"We-ell. *Allergic* would be a strong word. It's not fatal or anything. I just . . . get a temporary rash when I eat shellfish. But I had sort of hoped I had grown out of it. I really didn't want to tell you I couldn't eat the meal you were making me. It's no big deal, really."

Sadie jumped up from the table. "Max! You should have told me. You could end up with anaphylaxis. You risked your life to eat this dinner!"

Max laughed and stood, catching her by the arm and pulling her gently toward him. "Sadie, I am not going to die."

"Do you have any Benadryl?"

"I don't think so. I really think I'll be okay. I feel fine."

"Okay. Well, *stop* scratching your arms. Take off your shirt," she commanded.

"What? What does that have to do with—"

"Just to make sure it isn't getting worse," Sadie said.

Max did what he was told, revealing his firm, muscled chest—no rash.

Had he stopped breathing, or had she? She looked up at him and saw that his expression wasn't pained—he was watching her, his eyes now full of the same desire she was feeling.

"I really think you should take off your pants, too. Just in case," she suggested, her hand hovering above the waistband of his jeans.

Max merely nodded, undoing his zippered fly and then taking off his jeans. A moment later he stood in front of her, wearing only a pair of boxers. There was no question what was going through his mind.

"Well, this took a turn, didn't it?" Sadie murmured, very aware of how little clothing Max was now wearing.

"It did. And now that you know I'm okay, I think it might only be fair if you take your clothes off, too," he whispered, helping her stand back up. "I mean, only if you want to . . ."

"I do," she said quickly.

"Happy to help," Max said, his fingers gently tugging on the hem of her shirt.

She gave a nod and lifted her arms, allowing him to pull her shirt over her head, leaving just her lacy black bra on. "I'll get that in a sec," he murmured, his breath hitching, making her knees quiver.

"You're so perfect," he whispered, touching her shoulders, moving his hands down and around her back to undo her bra. His movements were slow, yet purposeful. "Okay?" Max asked, his fingers on her bra clasp. She nodded, and a second later the bra released. He slid the straps from her shoulders, allowing one hand to graze her breast, setting his other hand on her waist. In one swift move he pulled her to him, kissing her hard. She gasped, locked her arms around his neck, and kissed him back.

These kisses were different from the ones they had shared over the past few days. They were deep and hungry. They both knew what they wanted.

She kissed his face, his chest, making her way down his body until she reached his boxers, which she tugged down without a moment's thought. He groaned, then said, "Time to even things up again," and tucked his fingers into the waistband of her underwear, pulling them down with the same determination she had. They stood there for a moment like that, both of them breathing heavily, both realizing what this meant: there would be no pretending now.

Sadie reached out and let her fingers intertwine with his, then she led him to the couch and pushed him against the cushions, letting him take a good look—she had never felt so wanted. He made a sound in the back of his throat and reached for her. She let him pull her on top of him, the two of them breathless and wanting. They stayed like that for a time, Sadie moving against Max until she was almost dizzy with desire.

"Hang on," Max whispered, shifting her slightly to the side so he could reach for his jeans. He pulled a small packet from his back pocket, and Sadie laughed.

"Did you have that in there this whole time?"

Max grinned, then shrugged, carefully ripping open the packet. "I was hopeful."

A moment later Max pulled Sadie back onto his lap, and she lowered herself onto him. Max let out a groan and she clung to him, pausing only a moment longer before she started moving her hips. "Oh my God, Sadie," Max whispered against her neck, the heat of his breath agonizing against her skin.

"Don't take this the wrong way," she murmured, pressing

closer to him. He clasped her hands in his, then set them against her lower back, pulling her in deeper. "But I'm not sorry about your shellfish allergy."

Max chuckled, leaving a trail of soft kisses across her collarbone, moving slowly inside her. Sadie shivered in his arms, even though she felt she was burning up. "I've never been so happy about anything," he replied.

S adie opened her eyes as the morning light shone through the bedroom window. She stared up at the wood-beamed ceiling above her, then ran her hands across the soft flannel sheets. Her hand hit something—or, more accurately, some*one*.

Max Brody.

She closed her eyes and let it all wash over her: the night before, and the passion they had shared—on the couch and in this bed, well into the early hours of the morning. She had asked herself over and over if this was the right thing to do—but in the end, it had felt perfectly natural. And this morning, she felt happy, with no regrets.

She watched Max for a moment as he slept, then eased out of bed, sliding on a pair of his slippers and a robe.

As she headed to the kitchen to make coffee, she saw her phone, still turned off. She picked it up and looked down at it. Her finger hovered over the power button.

She could handle this, right? Turning her phone on and seeing the messages there? Now that she and Max were so close—in every way—*they* could handle this together, couldn't they? She turned the phone on. It took a moment, but soon the screen came to life—and, as Sadie had expected, began to fill with unanswered texts. Some of them were from Amalia, but most of them were from Cruz.

> Hey, girl, we're just doing some holiday cleaning at the studio and your master tapes are here. Should they go in the garbage, or are you ever coming back?

> Just kidding! I'd never throw them away, of course. ;-) But I'm getting a little worried. You okay? Get eaten by a Grizzly? Send an update on Operation Bring Brody Home ASAP, plz.

Sadie sighed and put her phone down. The coffee had finished brewing. She filled two mugs and went into the bedroom. Max's face was so peaceful. She almost hated to wake him—but they needed to talk. About the future that waited in Nashville—and their obligations. It was strange, though. It all felt like the last thing she wanted to deal with now.

Maybe she could delay reality, just a little while longer? She put the coffees on the end table and dropped the robe, climbing back into bed beside Max and tucking her body against his. Max didn't even open his eyes, just sighed and moved against her, too, kissing her softly at first and then with more urgency until they were twisted and tangled in the sheets.

"You sure do know the right way to wake a man up, Sadie," Max said to her later, with a smile.

"There's coffee," Sadie said, leaning up on one elbow. "But I think it's gone cold . . ."

Just then, Patsy leapt on the bed and wriggled her way between them. She stood staring at them, her little tail wagging as if to say, *Okay, I've left you two lovebirds alone long enough, now where is my breakfast?* Sadie laughed and scratched Patsy's adorable ears, marveling at how at home she felt here. How, in this moment, she, Max, and Patsy felt like a little family.

"Yeah, yeah, I'm on it," Max said, climbing out of bed and pulling on some boxers. They were emblazoned with little red candy canes.

Sadie leaned against the pillow and closed her eyes, listening to the sounds of Max in the kitchen filling Patsy's dish with her special freeze-dried kibble.

"Your phone is lighting up like a Christmas tree," Max said, startling Sadie as he walked back into the bedroom and tossed her phone on the bed.

Sadie picked it up and looked down. Her heart sank and she felt a flash of guilt. There were even more messages from Cruz now, coming in fast and furious:

I've been thinking about it and you were right that Max's only true talent is the one he comes by genetically. He's Holden Brody's son and that means you still need him, but I swear once you're done with him you'll be a star in your own right. I'll make it happen for you. You have my word, and it's obviously worth a lot more than the prince of Nashville.

Sadie winced. She remembered that conversation with Cruz on a particularly bad day, when her frustration over Max refusing to respond to her calls or texts had reached its peak. She had spoken out of anger; she hadn't really meant those things, and had tried to explain that to Cruz afterward. But Cruz was the kind of person with a selective memory. The texts were incriminating. It was possible he wanted them to be.

Bing.

Send me an update!!

Sadie looked up from the screen and met Max's eyes, but he looked away from her—and she knew.

"Max, I . . ."

"No, no, don't bother apologizing. Those are your personal texts; I shouldn't have looked."

"You know what Cruz is like," she began. "But still, it's no excuse. I—"

"This isn't necessary," he interrupted. And there was no mistaking it—his tone was now icy as a glacier. She shivered and pulled the sheet up, covering herself.

"We should talk about this," she said, but he just shrugged and turned away.

"What's there to talk about? Besides, it's obvious you and Cruz have been doing enough talking."

"Please, Max. Just hear me out. I came out here to drag your ass back to Nashville, yes. I was upset with you—and I know you were upset with me, too. We left things on a bad note. But I found something very different here than I expected to. This week, you and I have—"

"I said it isn't necessary." Max's tone was so abrupt she felt as if she'd woken from a dream. "You don't need to make a big production out of this, Sadie."

"Oh, come on, Max, really?" She stood, keeping the sheet tight against her body and picking up the robe she had discarded on the floor earlier. "None of this means—"

"Sadie, *don't*," Max said, and now he looked a bit anguished, but he quickly covered it up—and her heart sank. He looked distant and cold. It was an expression she hadn't seen since they were in Nashville together. It was a Max she didn't understand. A side of him he didn't *want* her to understand. The walls were going back up—and she knew it was partly her fault.

"I always knew I had to go back. And I was planning to. You didn't need to bother coming all the way out here. Should have saved yourself a trip, sweetheart. Now, I'm going out to the shed to start locking things up."

"Fine," was all Sadie could say.

But Max was already gone, the door of the cabin slamming hard behind him.

Max

Nashville, Tennessee
December 19

The next day, Max arrived at Cruz McNeil's recording studio a few minutes early. He decided he'd wait for Sadie before heading in, and stood in front of the enormous Christmas wreaths—gaudy, if you asked him, because of both the size and the spray-painted gold greenery—that hung on the building's front doors.

It took everything in him not to turn around and get back in his truck. Spending the entire day traveling had been exhausting enough, but he couldn't stop thinking about Cruz's text to Sadie (. . . *you were right that Max's only true talent is the one he comes by genetically. He's Holden Brody's son . . .*) and how badly he had misjudged her intentions. How much of her coming to get him in Fox's Corners had been Cruz's idea? It made him ill, thinking of Sadie and Cruz in cahoots, and it took him back to the night of the finale, when he'd seen them huddled together.

However, there wasn't time to wallow. In true Max fashion, he planned to ignore the problem (and that damn text), in the hopes it would just go away. He would put on that *genetically gifted* Brody smile and pretend like what Sadie had said to Cruz hadn't cut him up inside. Like he was *fine*. Which he most certainly was not.

"Mornin'," Max said to Sadie, who had just gotten out of a black town car.

Sadie barely nodded at him, though she gave Patsy a nice scratch under her chin. Max couldn't see Sadie's expression behind her oversized sunglasses, and wondered if her thoughts were as scattered as his were. She'd been upset, too—but he couldn't figure out if it was because he'd seen the text, or because of what it implied.

She was wearing two sweaters and cozy sheepskin boots—it was balmy compared to the weather in Fox's Corners, but Nashville in December was cool enough to require layers. He asked if she was cold—*obviously, Einstein,* Max thought to himself, but damn, he was just trying to make conversation, because they had to work together—and she shrugged, saying nothing. It was hard to fathom that only a day ago they had been in Max's bed, together, wearing no layers at all.

Guess this is how we're going to play it. Max fought the urge to make some snappy comment about her frosty reception, like, "Well, aren't you a grey sprinkle on a rainbow cupcake today."

"After you," Max said instead, opening the door and letting Sadie walk through first. The bells chimed their arrival—someone had set the tone to "Jingle Bells"—but the reminder that it was almost Christmas only made Max's anxiety increase. He had pushed things too far, staying so long in Banff. They were quite nearly out of time to write their song.

Sadie stepped into the warm lobby ahead of him, which smelled of cinnamon sticks and clove-studded apples. "Thanks," she said, her voice coming out in a strangled croak.

"Whoa, what's the matter with you?"

"Nothing," Sadie said, but clearly that was a lie. She sounded like she'd swallowed sandpaper. "Look, I don't need this today, Max."

"Need what?" he asked, confused. *What the hell had he done now?* She was the one bad-mouthing him to Cruz.

"*This,*" she replied, waving her arms between them. Then she grimaced as she swallowed, and Max's irritation evaporated. Clearly, she was not well.

"Don't take this the wrong way—but you sound like a frog with laryngitis."

She set her sunglasses atop her head. "You always know *just* what to say, Max." Sadie pushed past him as she headed toward the elevators, which were outlined in rows of red and green twinkle lights. Whoever had been in charge of the holiday décor at the studio was clearly a fan of Christmas.

"Hey, *hey*," Max said, reaching for her arm before she got too far. "Seriously, are you sick?"

She gave him a worried look. "Maybe? It started at the airport yesterday. I must have caught some sort of bug?"

"Do you have a fever?" He set his coffee on the floor and lay a hand on her forehead, the way his mom used to when he was sick. She did feel a touch warm . . . and it reminded him of how her body had felt when she was on top of him. *Pull it together, man,* he thought.

Sadie shifted away from his touch. "This is bad, Max. I can't sing like this. *They are going to freak out,*" she whispered, meaning their managers—and, of course, Cruz McNeil. It was just over a week until showtime, and today they were supposed to lay down opening tracks with Cruz for the *Starmaker* Christmas song.

Max ran his hand through his dark hair, trying to think. Then he set his fingers under Sadie's chin, lifting her eyes to his. He was on an emotional roller coaster, but now was not the time to get off the ride. Max pushed down his hurt feelings, focusing instead on this more pressing issue. "Do you trust me?"

"Do I have a choice?" she croaked out, but granted him a genuine smile.

"Good enough." Max pulled out his phone. While he waited for the person he was calling to pick up, he said, "Saxie forever, right?" Her subsequent laugh, even strangled by her sore throat, was music to his ears.

After a couple of phone calls, the two drove to Amalia's office in Max's truck, where they sat huddled with Bobbi and Amalia at a conference table.

"Okay, here's what we're going to do. We can buy you one day, but that's probably it," Bobbi said. Then she turned to

Sadie. "Do you need to see a doctor, or do you think it will pass with some rest and lozenges?"

Sadie whispered, "No doctor. Rest should help."

A ribbon of guilt moved through Max. If Sadie hadn't come to Banff to drag him back, she could have properly rested after the tour.

"Sadie's a pro," Amalia said. "She's dealt with this before. She'll be good to go by tomorrow."

"Go have a rest day, then, and take care of that throat. But make sure to also be 'seen,' okay?" Bobbi raised an eyebrow at the couple, and Max understood what she meant: make sure the paparazzi got photos.

"What will you tell Cruz? He just texted me, wondering where we are," Sadie asked, the croak in her voice making everyone wince. Max not only felt pained by the sound of her voice, but also by the mention of Cruz sending Sadie a text. He pushed the memory of Cruz's other text aside—he couldn't focus on that right now.

Bobbi shrugged. "We'll tell him the lovebirds needed a day off after traveling. Christmas shopping, a nice meal out, yada-yada-yada." Max swallowed hard at the thought of playing up #Saxie for the cameras, after the tranquility of Fox's Corners. But he'd faked it before, and he could do it again.

E verything in here is beautiful . . . and *expensive*," Sadie said under her breath to Max. They were in Louis Vuitton at The Mall at Green Hills—the ideal place to play up the couple they were pretending to be, and to "be seen," as Bobbi had requested. "This is beyond my budget."

"Louis Vuitton isn't about budget, Sadie," Max murmured. They'd dropped Patsy off at the Brody estate (Becca promised to look after her, after giving Max a ten-minute lecture followed by a long hug) and then swung past Sadie's apartment so she could change into something more photo-friendly. The faded jeans she'd chosen fit her like a glove, showcasing her long legs. She had paired them with a black cashmere sweater and boots, and a white-and-black-plaid wool coat. With her hair pulled back in a messy bun, and a mauve lipstick, Sadie Hunter looked the part. Country music ingenue, on the arm of her Nashville prince boyfriend.

They held hands as they moved through the store. Sadie's fingers felt warm in his, and he almost forgot that things had changed between them. What he wouldn't give to go back to Banff.

But right now, Max could feel the stares from fans and curious onlookers. He knew they had been recognized, both at the coffee stand where he bought Sadie a hot candy-cane-flavored tea for her throat and once they'd waltzed into Louis Vuitton.

"Let's do a lap," he said, bending his head to hers and murmuring softly. "Go try on some stuff. Don't worry, you don't need to buy anything."

While Sadie looked around, Max inconspicuously scanned the store and its surroundings. He saw a few cell phones pointed in his direction, and in Sadie's, and knew Bobbi and Amalia would be happy. Acting unaware of the cameras, he went to the front cash register and leaned across the counter to talk to an employee who was wearing a monogrammed tie and matching pocket square.

A few minutes later Max headed over to where Sadie stood in front of a mirror, turning this way and that, a cross-body bag swinging against her coat as she did.

"Sweetheart, that was made for you," Max said, coming up behind her and wrapping his arms around her. She startled slightly, but then leaned into him and turned her face, giving him a smile.

"Thanks, babe," she said, and Max kissed her cheek. In the mirror he could see another cell phone pointed their way, so he stayed like that for a moment, making sure whoever it was got the shot. Then Max turned to the saleswoman. "Would you mind giving us a moment, darlin'?"

Max felt Sadie stiffen somewhat in his embrace, but at least she didn't pull away.

"I have something for you," Max said, his lips close to Sadie's ear. "Close your eyes."

Sadie had a curious look on her face.

"Please," Max added, watching her in the mirror. She closed her eyes.

He took the scarf he'd just purchased and carefully wrapped it around her neck, making sure it was cozy but not tight. Her hands rose to the material, cashmere, her fingers running the length of it. She raised her eyebrows but kept her eyes closed.

"Okay, open up," he said.

He could tell she loved it. Her eyes widened as she took in her reflection, and her look of surprise was delightful. "Max, it's gorgeous. And my favorite color!" She admired the deep magenta pattern of the scarf. "How did you know I love this color?" She turned to face him, and her smile this time was genuine.

"You're welcome, Sadie," Max said, his resolve to remain unaffected by her rapidly dissipating.

I could sleep for a week straight," Sadie said in her gravelly voice.

"If you do, I can't promise you'll wake up to a song you actually want to sing." Max glanced over at her, glad to see her smile at the joke, even if it was short lived. "Maybe we should skip dinner, huh?"

"No way. I may be exhausted, but I can always eat."

They were seated on a bench inside the vast Opryland Hotel atrium, Sadie nursing a hot peppermint tea and Max a hot chocolate. The memories had hit Max when they'd first walked through the front doors of the hotel a couple hours ago. The Opryland Hotel at Christmas was something else—a must-see for visitors to Nashville during the holidays—and it had been an annual tradition for the Brody family. He had especially enjoyed seeing it from Sadie's perspective, as someone who had never experienced the hotel's over-the-top holiday extravaganza.

It was like Christmas had exploded inside the massive atrium: there were floor-to-ceiling twinkle lights, including hanging panels that gave the impression of a Christmas lights rainstorm; festive greenery and brilliant red poinsettias had been placed throughout the space, in between palm trees and emerald green palm fans that made it feel like you were in the tropics during the holidays; oversized Christmas ornaments made of tiny white lights hung from the ceilings, and garlands of evergreen with red bows were woven around light posts and railings. It was beautiful, if not slightly overwhelming for the senses, as the place was also overflowing with Nashville residents and tourists alike. If there was somewhere to "be seen," this was it.

They had already strolled the space, enjoying the lights and the decorations, stopping at the impressive Christmas tree for a few photos and to sign autographs for fans. Then Sadie convinced Max to take the riverboat "cruise," which traveled the indoor river that snaked through the hotel's atrium. It was packed, and they sat shoulder to shoulder. The boat was filled with a group of seniors on a tour, so miraculously no one recognized them. At one point Sadie yawned discreetly, then rested her head on Max's shoulder. It was the best fifteen minutes of the day, as far as Max was concerned.

But he could see Sadie was fading. Her voice was a touch better, thanks to the copious amounts of warm tea and the throat-rescue lozenges she'd been popping all day, but he could tell she needed to rest.

"How about dinner in bed?" Max asked, once they got off the boat. Sadie raised her eyebrows.

He laughed. "That came out wrong. Let me try that again—why don't we get a room instead of going out for dinner?"

"I'm not sure that's better, Max," Sadie replied, giving him an amused look.

"Third time's a charm. I'm going to get us a room here for the night. We can order room service, and you can sleep, and I can keep an eye on you. In case you spike a fever, or need a peppermint tea at three a.m."

"I guess that *is* the ultimate 'be seen' move, right? Staying here overnight? Bobbi and Amalia would probably approve." Sadie paused. "Okay, let's get a room."

Max held out his hand, which she took. But as they walked toward the front desk, she turned to face him. "Don't you think they're sold out?" she said, looking around the packed atrium. "This close to Christmas?"

Max chuckled. "Have you met me? I have the last name Brody and this is Nashville. There isn't a thing I can't make happen in this town."

"Too bad you're so insecure," Sadie said sarcastically. "Maybe you should work on that?"

Max, happy with the easy peace between them at the moment, tugged on her hand again to follow him to the front desk. "I'll try," he replied. "But only because you asked so nicely."

Ten minutes later, Max and Sadie walked into the hotel room. It was an enormous suite, with a dining room table and six chairs, a living room area with a couch and two stuffed armchairs, a full bar, and a separate bedroom.

"Wow," Sadie said, looking around. "This is bigger than my apartment."

Max had grabbed some cold medication from the hotel's sundries shop (they didn't have nondrowsy, but Sadie said she was fine with something to help her sleep tonight), and after Sadie took a dose they ordered room service—a fried chicken sandwich for him, hot chicken noodle soup for her, and pints of ice cream for dessert. Soon after, Sadie started yawning.

"Let's call it a night." Max tugged back the duvet, and fluffed up the pillows on the king-size bed.

"I don't have a toothbrush," Sadie said. "Or anything to wear." Max wanted to quip that not long ago that wasn't a problem—in fact, not having clothes on had been a *bonus*—but he simply opened the closet.

"Here, you can wear this." He handed her a monogrammed robe. "And I bet there's a toiletries kit in the bathroom."

"Thanks," Sadie said, her fingers brushing his as she took the robe from him. A shot of electricity moved through Max, and he cleared his throat and took a step back.

"Why don't you get ready first?" Max said. Things felt different between them here—far more complicated than they'd been in his little cabin in the mountains.

Sadie agreed, shutting the bathroom door behind her. Max tried not to think about the fact that she was changing out of her clothes and into the robe . . .

He pulled out his phone to distract him. *You need to focus on the music. On the song. That's it.*

He texted Bobbi to update her, and she let him know the day had been a success. There was tons of chatter in the media about Max and Sadie's Nashville staycation. He checked Instagram—finding screen after screen of tags—and scrolled the photos (he and Sadie snuggling on the boat cruise, him laughing at something she'd said; the two of them in front of the Christmas tree, his arm around her shoulders and grins on both their faces). They certainly looked like a couple who couldn't stand to be apart. A couple in love.

The bathroom door opened and Sadie stepped out in a robe far too big for her. She laughed as she held out her arms, the fabric hanging far beyond the tips of her fingers.

Max helped her roll up the arms of the robe. Then he folded

the bedding down and patted the mattress. Sadie obliged, sliding under the Egyptian cotton sheets and letting Max tuck the duvet up around her shoulders.

"You can be such a gentleman." Her voice was weak and she looked exhausted, but she gave him a smile that reached her eyes. It made him feel damn good.

"I can't remember the last time I felt this tired." Sadie shifted closer to Max. He lifted one arm so she could get into the crook, and she lay her head against his chest. Could she feel his heart racing?

"You've earned a good night's rest, sweetheart," Max said, pulling her a touch closer. "Just settle in."

But she shifted onto her elbow, so they were face-to-face. "Max . . . I'm really sorry. About those texts." She paused for a moment, and he heard her breath hitch. Then she cleared her throat, which still sounded sore as heck. "I wasn't at my best. I was angry and spoke out of turn to Cruz. You didn't deserve that. And for what it's worth, I don't believe it. You are incredibly talented, all on your own."

His mind whirled in a dozen different directions, and he tried to focus on slowing his hammering heart. He smiled at her, then nodded. "No harm done, Sadie."

She returned the smile, a look of relief coming across her face. "You're one of the good ones, Max Brody," she murmured, snuggling back into the crook of his arm. She yawned again.

"Ah, that's a high compliment coming from you," Max replied, certain now there was no way she wouldn't feel his heart beating practically through his chest.

Sadie was still for a moment, and he wondered if she'd

fallen asleep. But then she spoke, and her voice was sleep-heavy and soft.

"Max, at the cabin, there was something I wanted to tell you . . ."

He waited, but when her breathing evened out Max knew she was asleep. Whatever she'd been about to say would have to wait until morning. He turned on the TV and flipped through the channels, finding the show he was looking for, watching the silent images of the two of them flash across the television screen as he held her.

18

Sadie

Nashville, Tennessee
December 20

Sadie could hear the shower running in the next room, and the rumble of Max's voice as he sang in the shower. She turned and saw a little tray on the bedside table. There was a French press filled with coffee, orange juice in a champagne glass, a basket of muffins, and a note: *Didn't want you to get hangry while I was in the shower. :) Hope you slept well.—Max.*

Sadie smiled back at the note, then reached for the orange juice. She winced as she swallowed, in anticipation of the pain her sore throat would likely still cause—but there was no pain at all. The chicken soup and night of rest had done the trick. Sadie listened to the water continue to run in the other room, and Max's singing voice growing louder. She felt happy—but nervous, too. Things had chilled so quickly between them in Banff. She had apologized for the texts Max had seen from only good when they were alone. But the rest of the world was waiting outside the window. She pressed her body against his and felt him wake. He started kissing her neck, which was all it took to ignite her desire for him again.

Her phone rang on the bedside table but she ignored it, wrapping one leg around him to keep him close as their kissing intensified. But whoever it was hung up and called back, once, then twice, until finally, a laughing Max disentangled himself from Sadie and handed her the phone.

"Hello? *Mom?* Is everything okay?"

Max raised his eyebrows and covered her up with a sheet. *Busted*, he mouthed as Sadie clutched the phone to her ear.

"I have a surprise for you," her mom said, sounding nervous. "I'm *here*!"

Sadie pulled the sheet tighter over her chest. "You're where?"

"In Nashville. I decided it should be a surprise. Otherwise, you would have told me not to come."

Sadie knew her mom was right. She had done a good job of shutting out her feelings this past year—and shutting out her mom, too.

"Well, anyway," Lynn continued, "I just couldn't face Christmas on my own this year. So, Grandpa is with your uncle Blair. And I'm here."

It made perfect sense, and Sadie should have invited her. Of course a grieving single mother would want to come spend the holidays with her only child. Except there was the problem of nothing about their mother-daughter relationship being natural right now. And there was the problem of Sadie being in bed with Max Brody at the moment. In the mirror on the dresser across the room, Sadie could see that her cheeks were turning pink.

"Where are you staying, Mom?"

"I'm just pulling up to my hotel in a taxi now. It's pretty fancy—I decided to cheer myself up by splurging. And I got a big enough room that if you wanted a break from your apartment for a few days, you could definitely come stay with me."

"Which hotel?" Sadie asked again, but she had a terrible feeling she knew exactly which one.

"The Opryland Hotel! Oh my, it's *gorgeous*. Do you want to come meet me? And can you bring Max with you, too? I'd really like to meet him. Your gran had such nice things to say about your boyfriend—and I just feel like I need to get properly caught up on your life, Sadie."

Max was idly tracing a pattern on Sadie's bare arm. His hand then started to wander beneath the sheets, but she pulled away. "Actually, I'm staying at the same hotel as you are, Mom. I was doing a photo shoot yesterday and they gave me a room," she lied as she turned her body slightly away from Max's. "I'll meet you in the lobby in twenty minutes, okay?" She hung up before her mom could ask which room she was staying in.

"Well . . ." she began. "My mom is here."

"I gathered that."

He took the phone out of her hand and kissed her gently. "I'd love to meet your mom. Do you think twenty minutes gives us enough time to . . ." He was moving his hand underneath the sheets again but she put her hand on his chest.

"I have to go downstairs and meet her. By myself."

Max's smile faded. "But I'm sure she'd also be happy to

meet your *boyfriend*. Right? Why'd you tell her you were here by yourself?"

"I just figured it wouldn't be your thing. I'm giving you a free pass!" She smiled as big as she could, trying to convince him everything was fine.

Max was silent, and Sadie wondered if she'd gone too far by shutting him out. But then he picked up his phone and started tapping, looking nonchalant. "At least let me get you two a brunch reservation at my favorite restaurant," he said. He stopped tapping and looked up. "Hey, wait. I'm surprised your gran didn't join your mom this time?"

Sadie's cheeks were really burning now. She knew she should have told Max when they were getting close at the cabin—and that now she had left it too long. "Yeah, weird," was all she could manage to say. *What in the hell are you doing, Sadie Hunter?*

She hopped out of bed and made a dash for the shower before Max could see the sudden tears in her eyes.

Lynn was standing in the lobby of the hotel, right in front of a fully decked-out Christmas tree that sparkled with lights and almost touched the high ceiling. With her dark bobbed hair and bright blue eyes, Lynn was often mistaken for Sadie's sister. When she saw Sadie, she waved and rushed toward her.

Camera phones clicked as they hugged. "What in the world," Lynn murmured into Sadie's ear.

"It's not like home. Here in Nashville, people kind of follow my every move."

Lynn pulled back and smiled down at her daughter. "You're famous now. It's partly why I wanted to come here. I needed to see it all for myself." Her expression grew serious. "And we need to talk about—"

"Right, so anything heavy we should talk about privately, okay?"

It took all Sadie's strength not to fall apart. Sadie had kept herself so busy all year that she and her mother had never properly discussed what had happened last Christmas. And while Sadie had come to understand her gran's need to keep her declining health a secret—Gran thought knowing the truth would have put Sadie's career at risk—being kept in the dark about Gran's health still stung. Sadie had never been able to say a proper goodbye—and Lynn could have changed that, if she had wanted to. But now it was too late.

As if reading her thoughts, Lynn spoke in a low voice. "Sadie, I just need you to know, she wasn't going to let me do anything to jeopardize your chances of winning. Please, understand that. I came here to—"

"Not now," Sadie said, her expression full of forced cheer. She heard another camera click. "We can't talk about that here." She spoke through her smile. "You must be hungry. Max made us a brunch reservation."

Lynn's expression brightened. "Will he be joining us?"

"He's busy. He sends his regrets."

"Well, I do hope I get to meet him at least once before I go home. Your life is such a mystery to me now."

My life is a mystery to me, *too,* Sadie thought as they settled themselves into the back of a cab.

"I was hoping to stay over Christmas," Lynn was saying. "I

know you'll be busy but seeing you sing at the Grand Ole Opry was a dream of your gran's, and since she's been gone, I've found it's become a dream of mine, too."

A lump had formed in Sadie's throat. All she could do was nod and stare out the window. They cruised toward the restaurant, each wrapped in her own thoughts.

"Well," Sadie finally said as the restaurant came into view. "Nice to have family around for Christmas. Almost as good as being . . ." She had been about to say *home* but the word dried up in her throat.

Gran had been home.

And seeing Lynn only reminded her of this—which was why, fair or not, Sadie had been avoiding spending time with her mother for almost a year.

Soon, they were pulling up to the front of Margot. It had been Max's favorite place to have holiday brunch with his mother. "Make sure you get the beignets," he said before she left the hotel room. "No, wait, make it the croissant French toast. No, *wait*, the savory crepes."

Inside the restaurant, Christmas carols were playing on the speakers and the vibe was warm and festive. The host gave Sadie and Lynn a four-top in a quiet corner, with a view of the sunny street. As Sadie had predicted, a few photographers had gotten wind of her arrival.

"How do you get used to that?" Lynn asked.

"You just do," Sadie said, even though that wasn't exactly true. After the quiet week in Banff, she was finding all the attention hard to become accustomed to again. She tapped her fingers on the table along to the beat of the Ronettes singing "Sleigh Ride" to distract herself.

"I'm proud of you," Lynn continued. "But worried, too."

"Why would you be worried?" Sadie picked up the menu so she could avoid her mother's eyes.

"I can sit here with you and smile and pretend it's all fine but I *know* you, and I love you, and while you're smiling on the outside, your eyes tell a different story. We have to talk, and I mean *really* talk." Lynn paused, and angled herself away from a photographer who had come right up to the window. "We've been at odds for far too long, and of course when you came home last year after the finale, with what had happened with your gran, we both needed time to grieve. And then, when you stopped in during your tour, it was just such a whirlwind. I know you're upset with me for not telling you how sick Gran was. The thing *is*—" There were so many flashbulbs going off outside the window now that Lynn had to stop talking. Sadie and her mother watched out the window as a dark-haired man moved through the crowd toward the front door of the restaurant. Then Lynn's mouth dropped open. "Oh, *my goodness*. Is that Max Brody? But you said he wasn't coming!"

Max parted what had become a sea of photographers and glided into the restaurant. He smiled hesitantly when he caught Sadie's eye, and held up two bouquets of flowers. Any normal person would have been overjoyed to see him. She forced a big smile—*flash, flash*—as she wiped her sweaty palms on her jeans. Max placed a bouquet beside her mother's plate, then Sadie's, before taking Lynn's hand. "It is so nice to meet you, ma'am."

"Please, call me Lynn," Sadie's mom said as she blushed with pleasure.

"Coffee, Mr. Brody?" the server asked immediately.

"I've already had coffee today. But they have the best mimosas here this side of the Gulch and I'm kind of in the mood." He raised an eyebrow at Sadie, and now she was the one who blushed despite her bleak mood. "Maybe a round of those. Since we're celebrating and all."

"What are we celebrating, Max?" Sadie asked.

"Me finally getting to meet your mom. After meeting Elsie already—who, by the way, I miss and wish could be here—it seems to be about time to meet your mom, too, doesn't it?"

"I miss her, too," Lynn said, while Sadie stared down at the tablecloth. "And that's nice of you to say, Max. Yes, let's order a round of mimosas. In Elsie's honor."

The mimosas arrived in short order, and Sadie did not get her Christmas wish that the ground would open up and swallow her before they did. It wasn't that she wasn't happy to be near Max, or even that she didn't want to introduce him to Lynn. It was just that she still hadn't told Max the truth about Gran, still hadn't fully absorbed the painful truth herself. And now it all felt like it was closing in on her.

Max raised his champagne flute, and Sadie and Lynn followed suit. "A toast," he began. "To Elsie."

"Yes," Lynn said, her voice full of emotion. "May she rest in peace."

The next few moments were a blur.

Max was so shocked he spat out his sip of mimosa, and it seemed like every server in the restaurant rushed over with a napkin to help him clean up the mess. When the chaos finally cleared, Max was looking at Sadie imploringly. And all Sadie could do was stare down at the stained white tablecloth and shake her head.

She had to hand it to Max. He was a good actor. After the initial outburst, which he pretended was just a bad swallow, he acted like he wasn't shocked to hear this news. Because, of course, if he really were her boyfriend—which everyone, even her own mother, believed—this wouldn't be news to him. He would already know that on the night they won *Starmaker* and Sadie got the biggest career break of her life, she also suffered the biggest heartbreak of her life.

After the meal, Lynn excused herself to go to the restroom and Max turned to Sadie. "I'm so sorry," he said. "I had no idea. Why didn't you tell me?"

"I just . . . couldn't."

"But we spent so much time together last week. You couldn't open up to me?"

"I wanted to. I really did." It didn't sound convincing as she said it—because it wasn't exactly the truth. In Banff, she had been happy for the first time in a long while. She had wanted it to stay that way—and that decision had been a mistake. "It was just too painful," Sadie began, while Max's expression remained anguished.

Lynn was already returning, and he shook his head to compose himself, then signaled to the server for the bill.

"Smile for the camera, Sadie!" one of the paparazzi called out as they left the restaurant hand in hand. Sadie did—but she knew there was no hiding it. Her grief had cracked open. It was written all over her face, and there was no going back.

19

Max

Nashville, Tennessee
December 21

By morning Max was still trying to sort through the whip-lash of the past couple of days. First, there was the night (and morning) he and Sadie spent at the Opryland Hotel. *Heaven*. It had been a much-needed boost for Max, after how his and Sadie's time in Banff had ended. He'd accepted and appreciated her apology, and as far as he was concerned, that was the end of that. Max wouldn't let Cruz ruin things again. But then things were upended once more, when he learned of Elsie's death. Max had been both devastated for Sadie and upset she hadn't trusted him enough to share her heartbreak.

But could he really blame her? Max hadn't exactly been around. He'd taken off to Banff, not returned a single one of her calls, and acted like a selfish jackass. Max decided he didn't care anymore about what (or who) may have led Sadie to come to Banff—ancient history now. All that mattered was she had shown up, they had had an incredible week, and he was crazy about her.

All he could do now was prove to her that he was there for her—that she could count on him, no matter what.

"I have some makin' up to do, Pats," Max said to his dog, the two of them alone in the studio. Unable to sleep, he'd decided to head in early, and had been inspired to start a new knitting project for Sadie.

Max started to unwind the yarn, then put the ball down and picked up his phone.

Morning–can't wait to get our songwriting vibe going.

His finger hovered as he tried to decide which emoji to close with. A heart? (Too much?) A winky face? (Too cocky?) A music note? (He was trying too hard.) He chose the smiley face, then pressed send.

A moment later his phone pinged and he saw her reply.

See you soon.

Max frowned. Sure, it was hard to convey warmth via text, but that was a blunt reply. Something felt off.

What's going on, Sadie?

By eight-thirty Sadie still hadn't arrived, and Max was concerned. He checked his phone again, but she hadn't texted since her last message.

Max was sure Sadie knew what time rehearsal started (eight a.m.)—they'd discussed it yesterday after brunch, before she'd left with her mom.

He called, but it went straight to voicemail.

"Hope she's alright," Max murmured.

He paced the room, trying her phone again but it went to voicemail again. With a sigh of frustration Max set his phone down and picked up his guitar.

"Morning, doll. Where's Sadie?" Bobbi poked her head in the studio. She had a meeting with Amalia, Cruz, and the rest of the *Starmaker* brass today. Something about the run of the show for the Christmas special, she had explained.

"On her way," Max replied, and continued strumming softly, the feel and rhythm of his fingers on the guitar strings almost meditative.

"Okay. Well, I just saw Cruz heading upstairs looking *all* business," Bobbi said, tapping her fingers against the doorjamb.

"We're all set," Max said, wishing they could do this without Cruz.

Bobbi nodded and went to leave, then turned back. "Well done again on the whole 'lovers in Opryland' thing," she said. "You two really sold it."

Moments after Bobbi left, Max's phone pinged again. The text was from an unfamiliar number, and simply said:

FYI, your "girlfriend" isn't who she pretends to be . . .

"What the . . . ?" The message also contained a link, within which Max could see both Sadie's and Cruz's names. He was hesitant to click it. This was his personal phone, and only so many people had the number. But it was strange that whoever sent the text, and link, hadn't identified themselves.

Who is this? Max typed back. He felt compelled to click the link, but had the sense he wasn't going to like what he saw once he did.

No answer arrived, no ghost dots showing there would be one. Max paused a moment longer, then opened the link. His eyes scanned the article, widening when he got to the photo buried in its middle. A photo—a bit grainy, a bit dark—of Sadie and Cruz looking awfully snuggly on a couch. Their heads were so close together Max had to zoom in to make sure they weren't actually kissing. He felt a hit of relief to see they weren't, though with barely an inch between their bodies, it was possible that they had just been or were about to. Either way, it was clearly an intimate moment.

He reread the article, his anger cresting.

HotStarGossip.com

BREAKING #SAXIE NEWS: Is There Trouble in Paradise? Sadie Hunter, We Know What *You* Did Last Summer . . .

Moments ago, an anonymous source leaked this verified photo of Nashville royalty Max Brody's girlfriend, Sadie Hunter, and top Nashville producer Cruz McNeil getting hot and heavy at Stagecoach last summer. The two were leading separate lives at the time, with Brody holed up at his songwriting retreat in Canada and Hunter on tour as

Tasha Munroe's opening act. But we still believed they were the happy couple we'd seen win *Starmaker* months earlier. Or were they?? Not long after, *a rumor* began to swirl that maybe the whole thing was faked . . . Could it be true? #Saxie, a sham?

Combined with photos taken this morning of Max and an upset-looking Sadie with an unidentified woman some sources say is Sadie's mother, Lynn Hunter, it seems that something most definitely is amiss. Are those tears in Sadie's eyes? Does she really look like a woman who is brunching with the love of her life?

Now take a look at McNeil and Hunter cozying up on that couch and try to tell us we're not seeing what we think we are. When HotStarGossip reached out to Cruz McNeil for a comment, here's what the lawsuit-embroiled restaurant owner and mega producer had to say: "Sadie had confided in me about a death in the family—she was heartbroken, obviously—and I was comforting her."

We'll keep doing our best to reach our #Saxie stars, or their reps, for a statement! Hang on to your hearts, there's surely more to come . . .

His jaw tensed as he stared at the photo, wanting to disbelieve what he was seeing. But pictures didn't lie, right? Then the texts on Sadie's phone from Cruz popped into his mind, and he couldn't ignore it any longer: the two *had* been collaborating all along—*against Max*. He'd been manipulated, and he'd let it happen. He thought about Sadie's apology at the hotel . . . Had it been merely a tactic? Well, if it was, he had fallen for it: hook, line, and sinker. He felt sick to his stomach, thinking about what a fool he'd been.

As the anger, hurt, and embarrassment bloomed in his gut, Max knew he had to get out of there. Right now.

He had just packed up his guitar when he heard: "Max? What are you doing?"

Sadie stood in the doorway, bundled in layers, a confused look on her face.

"You're late," Max said.

"Yeah, sorry." Sadie looked at the clock on the wall—it was 8:41 a.m. "I had breakfast with my mom and traffic was . . . It doesn't matter. I'm here now. And Cruz is stuck in a meeting apparently. But you look like you're going somewhere?"

"Well, I am not staying here." He barked out a short, mirthless laugh. She looked even more confused now. Max pulled out his phone, open to the article with the photo of Sadie and Cruz. He held it out, watched as the color drained from her face as she quickly read through the caption on the photo.

Sadie shook her head. "Where did you get this?"

"Does it matter?"

But Sadie seemed not to hear him. "Amalia texted, telling me to call her right away. I was with my mom and didn't think . . ."

"Looks to me like you and Cruz got pretty darn cozy at Stagecoach," Max said. "You know, even with the creepy age difference you two don't look half bad together. No, really," he added, "I think this is a good look for you, Sadie. At least for your career. I mean, *Cruz McNeil*." Max whistled softly. "So glad he could be there for you in your time of need."

They stared at one another.

"You don't know what you're talking about," Sadie replied. "Nothing happened."

Max laughed then. "Ha! Oh, you keep telling yourself that, princess. But this picture tells a different story. According to some updates to this article, sources are now saying you two are an 'item.'"

"You are the last person who should believe some tabloid story!" Sadie crossed her arms, her eyes shining with anger. "*Nothing happened*. Cruz was drunk, and I got stuck in a room with him, and he got a bit . . ."

She sighed in frustration. "Why won't you believe me? After everything? Besides, even if something had happened—and it never would—you and I, well, we were *nothing* at that point."

"Exactly, we were nothing. We *are* nothing. If Cruz is your type, your *confidant*, as much as that makes me feel like throwing up," Max said, "who am I to stop true love in its tracks?"

Sadie was close to tears now, and he couldn't stand to see her upset. But he steeled himself—she had brought this upon herself, and all he wanted now was to get as far away from her as he could.

"Please, Max, you're not listening. Cruz had—"

"Save it. I'm leaving." He slung his guitar over his shoulder, and picking up Patsy's carrier, he strode toward the studio's door.

"We have to rehearse! Max, stop, please. Would you just stop? What do you expect me to tell Cruz?"

"Is that all you care about?" His mouth in a taut line, he

pushed past her and heard her breath catch. "Make something up. You're good at that."

"Fine, Max," Sadie called out after him. "Do what you always do, run away and let everyone else pick up the pieces!"

Max kept walking, held up an arm and gave a wave without turning around.

20

Sadie

Nashville, Tennessee
December 21

After Max was gone, Sadie sat down at the piano, her elbows landing on it with a discordant clamor. She put her face in her hands for a moment and let herself absorb everything.

It was over between her and Max.

This was twice now—three times, if you counted the proposal that never was—that they had gotten close and then it had blown up in their faces. She wasn't going to keep getting burned, time after time.

She could see why he was hurt that Cruz knew about her gran's death and he didn't. Why seeing all those texts from Cruz on her phone confused and hurt him. And yes, she knew, she hadn't exactly been the most forthcoming with him when she'd had the chance. But did she really deserve to pay for this so dearly? He had walked out. Yet again.

She ran her hands over her face and got out her phone, to take another look at the photo herself. It was blurry, but unmistakable that she and Cruz McNeil were embracing on a couch. The article that accompanied the photo was filled with salacious speculation, and the comments were just cruel.

> Sadie Hunter was a nothing and a nobody until Max
> Brody came along. And she'll be nothing and
> nobody after this, too.

> What a tramp!

> The only reason to be interested in Sadie Hunter is
> because she's dating Max Brody. And now she's
> gone and messed up her fifteen minutes of fame . . .
> time to cancel her! #saxieover #sadiethetramp

> Well, I guess now we know the real reason Sadie
> Hunter got as far as she did on *Starmaker*

What had been going on in that photo had not been the first time Cruz had crossed a line with her. It had started when she began recording songs with him: he'd brush a stray hair from her shoulder, allow his hand to linger on her arm too long when he greeted her, brush against her in a hallway when there was plenty of space for him to walk by. Sadie should have said something then—but she hadn't, because it had felt like she needed Cruz's support and approval to record a hit album. If she had called him out on his behavior, would anyone have believed her? There was not a single thing she would have been able to prove.

Her phone rang in her hand. "Care to give me a backgrounder on that photo?" It was Amalia and she wasn't happy.

"That photo is not what it looks like. Amalia, I would never—"

"Sadie, things are never what they appear with men like Cruz—and I know you well enough to know this isn't the avenue you'd go down. But if we're going to deal with the public relations debacle this is becoming, I need some intel."

"I was at Stagecoach with Tasha, and it started out as the best day. But you know what I was going through then. I was still in so much pain about my gran. But that day, I let myself relax a bit. I let myself enjoy singing in the festival. I was in the greenroom, when Cruz and the guys from Saddle 'em Up came in . . ."

"Oh, dear. Jäger bombs?"

Sadie winced. "Yes. I was going to head back to the tour buses and see what Tasha was up to, but then I had two shots with them, and we were just laughing and chatting but then it all just hit me. I went to sit on a couch to try to pull myself together and suddenly I was crying. Cruz came over to comfort me. It was a weak moment—and I told him about my gran dying. He gave me this long hug, and it got uncomfortable, but I just sat there and let it happen. I should have pushed him away, but I didn't."

"*You* did nothing wrong. Cruz is known to be handsy. I wish I could have been there for you. Why don't you come to my office and we can talk and try to strategize on some damage control? I'll send a car."

"Can we do that later? I think at this point the damage has been done. Max is angry at me. I'm angry at myself. And I really just need to be alone."

Amalia sighed. "Alright. But, Sadie? If Cruz McNeil is the only person you can confide in . . . honey, you have a problem. You can't stay a lone wolf forever. You do have friends, you know. People who care about you. And one last thing? I know it hurts. I've lost people I cared about, too. But let me tell you what *doesn't* work when you're dealing with grief: pretending it doesn't exist. You're going to need to deal with it. Allow yourself some closure, or you won't be able to move forward."

After she hung up, Sadie stood still, thinking about what her manager had just said. *Closure.* Maybe Amalia was right. Closure was exactly what she needed—and was possibly the only thing in her life she could control right now. Suddenly, she heard her gran's voice, saying: *One bite at a time, dear.* This was something Gran would always say to her when Sadie got herself into a pickle with too much overdue schoolwork, or too many gigs booked, or any other mess she'd ever managed to get herself into in life. Now, Sadie decided, she *was* going to solve one of her problems—and then see what she could do about the rest of them.

Out in the lobby, the studio assistant, a young woman named Yasmin, looked up from her phone with a guilty look, like she had just been looking at the photo of Sadie with Cruz.

"Anything I can help you with, Miss Hunter?"

"Could I get a car service, please?"

"But Mr. McNeil is upstairs waiting. He's here to work with you and Max. He won't like it if you—"

"Mr. Brody had to leave," Sadie said firmly. "If he doesn't have to be here, neither do I. Now, if you could please get me a car service?"

It worked. Yasmin busied herself on the phone, and Sadie went outside to wait.

A black town car pulled up, and Sadie hopped in the back, collapsing against the cold leather seat in relief as she gave the driver the address of her apartment. As the car moved through Nashville, it seemed every place she passed sparked a memory of Max: the Opryland Hotel, the building that housed the *Starmaker* soundstage, the restaurant they had taken Gran to, Margot, and the costume shop. This pain wouldn't last forever, Sadie hoped—but it certainly felt very raw right now.

The car had arrived at her apartment. She asked the driver to wait for her while she went inside to get something she needed.

Upstairs, her gran's jaunty knit blanket was draped across the couch, and Sadie felt a pang as she looked at it. She headed into her bedroom to find the cookie tin she kept the letters in. The ones she had been writing to Gran all year when she missed her too much, telling her the things she would normally have told her on their frequent FaceTime calls. She lifted the lid of the tin; it was so filled with letters she had written, mostly while on tour, that they spilled over the edge and out onto her bed.

Dear Gran, I can't believe it, I'm in Prague. I love it so much! You would, too. It feels like it's haunted, but not in a bad way. I had one day to myself and probably should have rested but instead I went to the State Opera alone and watched a performance of Tosca. *Malin Byström sang the lead. She was incredible.*

> *. . . We're in Santa Barbara. We just performed at The Bowl and then after, everyone was planning to go to some after-party, but I said I thought I'd just go back to my hotel. I ran into Tasha and she said she was heading to a friend's, and that I should join her—and this friend turned out to be OLIVIA NEWTON-JOHN. All I could think about was how much you would have loved to be there. Remember we used to listen to her records together? Olivia made us lemon chicken, and about a dozen different salads, and instead of wine there was beet-kale juice, which was more than fine with me.*

> *Hi, Gran, I could really use your advice. Max won't respond to any of my messages. I'm starting to think he might never reply, and soon, all this is going to be over. What would you say to me? That I don't need Max Brody to have a successful career? But what if I'm just a flash in the pan without him? I need to finish my album. I need some perspective, and you were always so good at giving it to me.*

Sadie stuffed the letters back in the tin, adding a heavy paperweight from her desk and forcing the lid shut. She put on a baseball cap, tucked her hair inside it, found a pair of large, dark sunglasses, and left the apartment with the tin tucked under her arm.

"John Seigenthaler Pedestrian Bridge," she instructed the driver when she was back inside the vehicle. She held the tin against her body, realizing as she clung to it that she might have a hard time letting it go. *But you have to do this,* she told herself. *You have to let this go so you can move on from your grief. You need closure.*

The bridge was strung with holiday lights, shining bright green and red even in the afternoon. The bridge was fairly quiet. She walked to the middle and looked down at the navy-green water of the Cumberland River, then out at the buildings of Nashville on the left and the trees and paths of Cumberland Park on the right. Someday soon, she would find the time to process all the things that had happened to her this past year: *Starmaker*, Max, Gran's death, touring with Tasha Munroe, Max again . . .

But now was not that time. Now she just needed to release it. She looked around to make sure no one was watching and felt a pang of guilt about littering (she'd make a donation to the Clean Streams Initiative, she decided), then dropped the tin straight down into the fast-flowing water and watched it get carried away downstream. It sank, and was gone.

Okay. Now all she needed to do was stand here and have a good, long cry. Let it all out. Gran was dead. There was no changing it. When Gran had come to visit Sadie as a surprise last Christmas, she had already been diagnosed with an incurable arrhythmic heart condition. She had told Sadie she had the flu, and Sadie had pretended nothing was wrong. In some ways, Sadie could understand why Gran tried to protect her from the truth. She knew she would have done anything, even forgo her chance to win *Starmaker*, to be with Gran in her last moments. But how could anyone, Gran or Lynn or anyone else, have believed that taking away that choice wasn't going to cause her a great deal of pain? *This sucks, Sadie. It's terrible. Go ahead, let it all out.*

Nothing happened. So Sadie kept thinking about the dark moments she had been avoiding. She remembered fleeing the *Starmaker* set when her mother finally realized it was getting to be too late. She had stayed in Wisconsin for the funeral and had felt completely numb the entire time. She could barely even look at Lynn, so she shut her out even though she knew she was grieving, too. And then Sadie had returned to Nashville after a few days—but at that point, Max was already gone and wouldn't take her calls. The only person she told about her gran's death was Amalia. She knew she couldn't deal with her feelings about her gran's death and certainly didn't want to have to do it through the lens of the media. And then her professional life had started to pick up steam. The Tasha Munroe tour, starting to record with Cruz. She had hoped she could keep herself busy enough to leave behind her pain. That hadn't worked.

She was finally allowing herself to feel—but she couldn't cry. Instead, she stood on the bridge, looking down at the water and the path the letters had taken away from her now washed away by endless, flowing water. She felt frozen. Unable to release what she had come here to release.

Sadie looked up at the clouds that had gathered above her, heavy and thick. They were full of *snow*. As she craned her neck up, a few fat, lazy flakes floated down, landing in her hair and on her shoulders. Impulsively she stuck her tongue out and caught a few plump snowflakes. They lingered for seconds, icy, cool, evocative of home, then melted away into nothing.

She *had* felt something for a moment, hadn't she? Some

childhood memory, a shadow of the carefree, innocent person she had once been. Someone much more in touch with herself and her emotions than she was now. But the moment was gone.

And suddenly, she had the creeping sensation that she was being watched.

She spun around, but no one was there.

Up ahead, the few pedestrians on the bridge were looking up in wonder, too; it was rare for there to be any snow at all in Nashville in December. But by the time she got back to the car, it had stopped. It was as if the little flurry of festive snow-flakes had never happened. The sky was grey, and she felt grey, too.

All she wanted was to talk to her gran, to tell her every-thing about her difficult day. She opened up her phone's con-tacts folder and scrolled through them, hovering over "Gran" but never deleting it. She kept scrolling, thinking about what Amalia had said to her about the fact that she did have friends in Nashville—that there were people here who cared about her. She thought about calling her mom, but she knew how upset Lynn would get when she learned the vile extent of the music industry gossip being directed her daughter's way. So she clicked on "Tasha Munroe." She texted: **Can we talk?**

Tasha replied right away. **Absolutely. I'm at home. Come on over.**

S weetie, take a blanket instead of standing there shivering and have a seat." Tasha was sitting outside by her heated pool, looking gorgeous and serene, surrounded by flawless landscaping.

Sadie did as she was told, relieved that Tasha had clearly heard the nasty rumors and she didn't have to relive any of it by explaining.

"Sadie, I *know* this is hard. I have been where you are, many a time. Some people insist pictures never lie, but pictures *do* lie. They almost always lack context, or are given context by the people who stand to earn money from them."

"It really wasn't what it looked like," Sadie said. "All I wanted from Cruz was for him to be a professional mentor."

"Cruz is many things, but professional is not one of them. Genuine, by the way, is not one of them, either. Max Brody, on the other hand—"

"I really don't want to talk about Max," Sadie said, looking away.

"Really? I thought Max would be the one bright spot in all this. Surely, he knows that photo is absolute hogwash?"

"No, Tasha." Sadie paused. "It's over. Believe me."

"I don't, actually." Tasha's expression was gently stern. "Max is not one for—well, you know him. He's pretty guarded. But when you're around, it's written all over his face: he has fallen head over his cowboy-booted heels for you. That's the plain truth, whether you want to believe it or not."

Sadie tried to protest but Tasha halted her with another pointed look. "It's been obvious since the moment he laid eyes on you—which, by the way, I witnessed. He tried to shrug it off, but I'm inclined to say it was love at first sight, songbird."

Sadie shook her head. "We just don't work together, okay? Max refuses to ever stick around long enough to deal with any of his emotions, and I'm not exactly dealing with mine, either. My gran died, and I didn't even tell him!"

Tasha put her hand to her heart. "What? Sadie, when did this happen? I'm so sorry, I know how much your gran means to you. Please say it didn't happen while we were on tour, and you were afraid to ask for time off, because——"

Tasha's eyes widened with empathy as Sadie explained that it had happened the night of the *Starmaker* finale and she hadn't told anyone except Amalia. "But then, at Stagecoach, I made a mistake: I told Cruz. I was having a hard moment, and he witnessed it, and I trusted him. And it totally torpedoed things between Max and me. I hadn't even told him."

"Oh, Sadie," Tasha said, taking Sadie's hand. "I feel for you. We work together, yes, but I'm also your friend. You know that, right?" Tasha continued. "That means I'm here for you. And I'm not going to let this industry make a meal out of you."

Sadie knew that this was a person she could trust. She had a friend, and a mentor—two roles she should never have looked to Cruz McNeil to fill.

"I'm such a fool," Sadie said. But Tasha shook her head.

"Okay, let's lay some ground rules of our friendship. There is no negative self-talk—you and I both know the critics and the naysayers can take care of that for us. The second rule is we talk about hard things. Okay?"

Sadie nodded.

"Third rule: we speak the truth. And the truth is, I cannot let you throw away your relationship with Max over something like this. Because that boy has it *bad*. And you do, too. Just look at you. You're not just grieving your gran, I know that much."

Sadie sighed. "Tasha. In accordance with rule number three, I have to tell you that my relationship with Max has been nothing but a publicity stunt. Yes, we did start to develop real feelings, but Max has a bizarre way of showing it these days."

"Sadie, if this were only a ruse, he wouldn't have had any reaction at all. He'd be sticking around because there wouldn't be any big-ass emotions for him to avoid. Don't you see?"

"Maybe. But it's just too late," Sadie said.

"Fine, maybe this relationship of yours started out as a publicity stunt—which a lot of people on *Starmaker* did suspect, by the way. But it is not a stunt anymore. What's between you is *real*. You're going to let Cruz McNeil get in the way of that?"

Sadie pulled the blanket tighter around her. It was getting late in the day now, and the sun was sinking behind Tasha's tall hedges. The massive yard was decorated for Christmas, with feather wreaths tied with big red bows on every surface that would hold one, evergreen garlands entwined through the many pergolas, and the lights inside the pool slowly and mesmerizingly fading from red to green to white.

"Yes, we have had some special moments," Sadie reflected. "But it's over now."

"You're going to give up just like that? This isn't the determined, ambitious woman I spent four months of this year touring with." Tasha's expression was serious, her words affectionate but stern. A lot like the way Gran used to talk to Sadie. Sadie now felt her eyes filling with the tears she had been hoping to shed earlier that day.

"It's okay, let it all out." Tasha leaned forward and rubbed her back.

"You don't know the half of it," Sadie said.

"So *tell* me the whole of it," Tasha countered. "Everyone in this town can't be trusted, but you *can* trust me. And letting it all hang out is what friends are for."

Sadie smiled through her tears as she finally accepted them, then started to talk to her friend.

21

Max

Nashville, Tennessee
December 21

After Max walked out on Sadie, he'd sat in his truck in the studio's parking lot, trying to figure out what to do next.

He wrestled with what he knew he *should* do—be the professional he claimed he was, and get to work—versus what his heart was telling him to do. Sadie had cut him deeply. He kept picturing her nuzzled up to Cruz, knowing she had chosen him as her confidant, possibly more.

How did I misread her so badly? Max was typically astute when it came to character—he had good practice, thanks to Holden. But Sadie had somehow fleeced him, and he was both sad about it and royally pissed off that he'd so epically let his guard down.

He closed his eyes and leaned against the truck's headrest. "What would you tell me to do, Mom?"

Just then Patsy let out a bark, and Max opened his eyes. She was staring at him, her paws up on the console, panting excitedly with her tongue hanging out. He nodded and said, "Okay, girl, that's what we'll do. But first we have to swing by the house. Let's get you buckled in." A moment later Max pulled out of the studio's parking lot and headed south.

The Underdog Rescue pet shelter came into view, and Max couldn't help but smile when he saw the sign at the entrance:

"It's all fun and games until someone ends up in a cone. Donate, Rescue, Volunteer Today!"

Maren Brody had been an active volunteer with Underdog—an animal lover, Max's mom had spent hours every week walking dogs, fundraising, and then working on the rescue's board of directors. She had enlisted Max to volunteer, too, as soon as he turned fourteen. And this was the very place he had rescued Patsy from four years ago.

Patsy loved visiting the Underdog Rescue. She squirmed in Max's arms until he set her down. "Hang on there, girl," Max said, breaking into a run to keep up with Patsy.

"Well, I'll be darned. Max Brody! We have missed you, young man." An older woman with long silver hair sat at the reception desk.

"Sorry, Eve. I know it's been a long while since I've visited," Max said.

The woman came out from behind the desk and hugged Max. Then she crouched and gave Patsy a belly rub. "Okay if she has a romp in the playground?"

Max nodded and looked over at the large room to the right of where they stood, and noted with both a heavy heart and a sense of pride the plaque above the gate's archway:

Maren's Mutt Haven

"Oh, before I forget. I brought a few things for the pups who will be here over Christmas." Inside the bag he had picked up at home were two dozen hand-knit stockings, in a variety of festive colors, along with the sweaters. "I'm also leaving a check so the stockings can be filled." Max took an envelope out of his back pocket and placed it on the counter.

Eve placed a hand on his arm. "Your mom would be proud of you."

Max smiled, though it was forced. He thought back to how he'd behaved that morning, not to mention over the past year, and wasn't sure that was the truth. "Thanks for saying that, Eve, and Merry Christmas." Then he watched as Patsy ran in circles in the playground for a solid minute.

He had thought coming here would make him feel better, and to some degree it had. But he still carried something heavy in his chest.

Max knew where he needed to go next.

Max left Patsy to play at the shelter for a few hours, and then made a quick stop at the nearby corner store before going to the cemetery. Someone had visited recently, because there were fresh flowers in a vase beside the headstone—yellow and orange and pink ranunculus, Maren's favorite, their blooms stunning against the grey December sky. Even during Christmas, when it was difficult to get summertime blooms, his mom had filled the house with vases of brightly hued flowers that evoked memories of sunshine and summer cicadas.

After placing his hand on top of Maren's gravestone, he sat on the grass and pulled the bottle out from the paper bag.

"Hey, Mom——" He didn't know if he could continue, but he knew he had to.

"I know it has been a long time," he said. This was difficult. He opened the bottle and took a long swig. "Mom, the truth is . . . I've missed you."

The whiskey burned from his throat down to his stomach. He took another sip. Max rarely drank hard liquor—scared that he'd become a drunk like Holden—but he had needed a touch of liquid courage to come here today. He had some explaining to do to his mom.

So, between sips of whiskey he filled her in. Told her about *Starmaker*, and Sadie. By the time he finished downloading what had been going on in his life for the past year, he'd finished most of the bottle. Drained from everything that had happened—and drunk as a skunk—he asked: "What should I do, Mom? What do you think I should do about Sadie?"

He had wanted it to be simple. When he'd walked out of the studio that morning, he had every intention of not going back and never seeing Sadie again. But the longer he sat there, the less simple it all became. In a flash he realized the problem: he loved Sadie Hunter. He *loved* her.

He. Loved. Her.

And he had to tell her.

Taking his phone out of his jeans pocket, he scrolled

drunkenly through his contacts. "Bingo," Max said, seeing her name. It went to voicemail.

"Sadie, hi. It's me, Max. Max Brody." He hiccupped, and then cleared his throat. "Things this mornin', well, I'm sorry for storming out like that. I'm a piece of work, I know it." Max swayed, his elbow slipping off one knee, causing him to almost drop the phone. "I'm not sure what's going on . . . with Cruz . . . but I need you to know something. I don't know how in the hell it happened, but I love you. Simple as that. *I love you, Sadie Hunter.*"

He took a deep breath, let it out slowly, then said, "Okay! Now you know. And that's all that matters. Okay, then. Bye-bye."

Max hung up, lying back on the grass and watching the clouds up above, glad he had *finally* told her how he felt. He was also feeling quite dizzy from the alcohol, and it occurred to him he was stranded at the cemetery, because there was no way he was going to be able to drive. At that moment his phone rang, and he fumbled and twisted on the ground, trying to get it out of his pocket. For a moment he hoped it was Sadie returning his call, but squinting at the screen, the name fuzzy, he realized it was Bobbi.

"Howdy," he said.

"Where the hell are you? I just got out of the meeting and Sadie told me you took off. Of all the stunts, on all the days . . . You need to get your ass back here, Max, like *now*." Bobbi barely took a breath. "Cruz is madder than a mule chewin' on bumblebees! I made up some story about how you had a photo shoot for a deodorant brand."

Max chuckled. "Deodorant, huh?"

"I panicked! You know how he just sidles up and then is, like, right there in your face. Besides, I don't think he bought it. Seriously, what's going on with you?"

"I needed some air," Max slurred. "Look, I know you're pissed at me but it's okay. I'll pay the money back to *Starmaker*. It's fine." He sat up, but rested his head on his bent knees as the world spun around him.

"It's the opposite of fine." Bobbi sighed heavily. "I can't keep bailing you out, Max. Sadie can't keep bailing you out. Paying your portion of the money back might—and I'd like to emphasize *might*, because they could sue you—get you off the hook, but it won't help Sadie."

He didn't know what to say to that.

"Where are you?" Bobbi asked.

"I'm visiting my mom."

"Oh, Max." Bobbi had worked with the Brody family for long enough to have known Maren well, to have seen Holden spiral to the point where his drinking almost ended his career, and to have watched Max deal with it all. "Hon, have you been drinking?"

Max squinted at the bottle by his feet, and saw about an inch or so left at the bottom. He pressed his thumb and index finger close together, even though Bobbi couldn't see the gesture. "Maybe a teensy bit?"

"For the love of God, Max, do not put your keys in the ignition. You hear me?"

"Yes, ma'am," he replied.

"I'm sending someone to come and get you. Hang tight."

There was a knock on the driver's-side window. Max cracked an eye—with some effort, because everything felt heavy—and saw Landon peering in at him. Landon had long since moved on from being Max's *Starmaker* assistant and had been working for the studio all year, so this was clearly a favor Bobbi had called in. He made an "open up" gesture, and Max unlocked the doors.

Landon gave a low whistle. "Wow, this truck smells like the inside of a whiskey barrel."

"Well, helloooo to you, too, Captain Obvious." Max grunted as he twisted around to a seated position, hanging on to the dashboard as the horizon tilted. "Oh, boy."

"Are you going to vomit?" Landon sounded alarmed.

"No, but *bless your heart* for being so concerned." Max's tone was sarcastic, but Landon was too focused on trying to get the driver's seat forward to notice.

Max raised an eyebrow. "You've driven a truck before, right?"

"Of course I've driven a truck," Landon mumbled. "I grew up in the South, too, you know."

Landon started the truck, and Max leaned his head back again. He felt like he was underwater, his body moving in rhythmic waves.

"I find taking some deep breaths helps." Landon looked in the rearview, then pulled out onto the road.

Max didn't reply, but gave it a go. Breathing in and out. And again. He did feel a touch more clearheaded, actually.

"So, what brings you out here, Mr. Brody?" Landon asked. Then, remembering where he had picked Max up, stuttered, "Oh, I'm sorry. That is none of my business. Are you okay, though?"

It was at that moment that Max—still three sheets to the wind and obviously not thinking clearly—had a sudden urge to confess everything.

"Having some girl problems, if you must know," Max said, the image of Sadie staring at him just before he walked out on her this morning burned into his memory.

Max let out a deep sigh, pressed a hand to his chest. Landon glanced over, but didn't say anything. "I have a secret about Sadie. Do you want to know what it is? Okay, here goes . . . She's not really my girlfriend."

"Did you two have a fight?"

"We are *always* fighting, Landon. That woman is . . . Well, she has her nose so high in the air she could drown in a rainstorm." Max closed his eyes, picturing Sadie with her arms crossed over her chest, a look of irritation on her beautiful face, her blue eyes flashing.

"But damn, if she isn't whip smart. And gorgeous. And that voice. She sure can sing. Thing is," Max continued. "*Thing is*, Landon, Sadie and I are not together."

Max let his own words sink in. He shifted in his seat so he could see his former assistant's reaction. "For a hot second it seemed it was gonna *become* real, but not anymore." Max thought about Cruz, and the photo of him and Sadie, and he almost had to ask Landon to pull over.

"What was never real, Mr. Brody?" Landon asked.

"Me and Sadie. Why are you so formal all the time? Just call me Max, okay? And Ms. Hunter is Sadie."

"Of course. Won't happen again." Landon changed lanes, checking his blind spot twice. "But here's where you're wrong, Mr. Brody . . . Max." Landon's sudden change in tone was surprising. "I worked with both of you. I've seen things. And what you have with Sadie? Well, if that ain't real, I don't know what is."

"We fooled you, Landon. We fooled everyone. The judges. The fans. The paparazzi. Even our families," Max said quietly. "We fooled everyone."

"Max, I'm sorry, but I'm just not following you."

"There is no such thing as Saxie, man! It was all fake. The relationship. The stories about us being in love. We faked it all because that's what the show wanted, what the fans wanted. And we wanted to win, so we did what we had to do."

Landon was silent, likely trying to sort out the truth from his drunken babbling.

"But you two seem so together. In love."

Max let out a strangled sigh. "She's a good actress, man. A damn fine actress."

"What about you?"

"What about me?" Max asked.

"Are you a good actor, too?" Landon kept his eyes on the road.

"Nope, never have been," Max replied after a moment. "You wanna know the truth, Landon? I love her. Like, *really* love her. And I once told her I don't wanna fake it anymore, and that's still true."

Max stumbled out of the truck, catching himself before falling to the ground. Landon had come around and was trying to steady him.

"Thanks, man. But I got this," he said. "Just grab my bag from the back, would ya?"

Max went to open the Brodys' front door, but it was locked. He sighed, patted down his jeans looking for the key. He'd sold his condo after leaving for Banff, so he was stuck staying with Holden until he found a new place—whether that was in Nashville or somewhere else, Max wasn't yet sure.

"Is this it?" Landon asked, holding up the truck fob's key ring.

"Sure is." Max grabbed for the ring, missed it, and pitched forward just as the front door opened. Holden caught Max and righted him.

"Alright there, son?" he said, glancing at Max's face.

Max just scowled, straightened his shoulders. "Why wouldn't I be?"

Landon handed Holden the keys and bag. "Nice to see you, Mr. Brody. Your house looks really festive." Wide boughs of greenery wrapped around the marble posts that flanked the home's porch, with white lights poking in and out of the boughs, casting a warm glow. Two large nutcracker soldiers stood guard at the front door, surrounded by swaths of cotton batten meant to look like fresh snow.

"Thank you kindly, Landon," Holden replied. Max was surprised that his father remembered Landon's name. That wasn't really his style, to pay attention to details that didn't immediately concern him. "I really appreciate you bringing my boy home. Do you need a ride home yourself?"

"I'll call an Uber," Landon said as he retreated down the front porch's stairs.

"Nonsense," Holden said. "We'll get you a ride. Just let me get Max inside, alright?"

Once Holden shut the door behind them and arranged a ride for Landon, he turned to Max. "This isn't how we handle things, son."

Max knew then that Bobbi had already called his dad, which he should have expected. Bobbi had managed Holden's career, and had taken over Max's at Holden's request.

"Speak for yourself, old man," Max said, giving a scoff and hiccup simultaneously.

Holden paused, watching his son, then took off his Stetson and hung it on the coatrack by the front door. "Max, I don't want you making the same mistakes I did, alright?"

"Oh, don't you worry about that. I'm *nothing* like you, Dad."

Holden sighed and grabbed Max. "Let's get you to bed, so you can sleep this off. Trust me, things will look a hell of a lot brighter by morning."

Max ripped his arm out of Holden's hands. "I can take care of myself."

"I know you can, Max." Holden's voice was soft. "You always have."

Max pointed a finger at Holden. "No thanks to you, I might add."

"No thanks to me." Holden nodded. "Come on now. Let's get you a prairie oyster."

A "prairie oyster" was a drink made of tomato juice, one

raw egg, a dash of Worcestershire sauce, salt, pepper, and a shake of Tabasco, meant to cure a hangover or stop one from happening. It was as disgusting as it sounded, and Max was a pro at making them—having done so many times as a kid when Holden came down for breakfast, still drunk from the night before.

"I don't need anything from you, Dad. Can't everyone just leave me the hell alone?"

With that Max made his way up the staircase—clumsily, slowly, as his fingers got caught in the pine garland and twinkle lights that were wrapped around the railing. He checked his phone to see if Sadie had called back, hazily remembering the message he had left her, before collapsing on his bed, letting sleep take over him.

22

Sadie

Nashville, Tennessee
December 22

Sadie stepped inside the studio building and looked around, hoping to see Max already there, waiting, ready to work. The night before, after their heart-to-heart, Tasha had insisted she was going to call Max. Sadie hadn't heard anything from her yet and had a sinking feeling the call hadn't gone well. But she was here, even if Max wasn't going to be. She wasn't giving up yet.

Her phone pinged. It was a text message from her mom. They had gone shopping two days before, but Sadie hadn't seen her since. She juggled her phone with the two coffees she was carrying, one for her and one for Max—because it was his birthday, and even though things weren't good with them, she wasn't going to let the day go by without acknowledging it. She glanced down at the message. **Hi, honey, I'm sorry we missed each other for dinner last night. Just wanted to say I hope you have a good day!**

No mention of any of the tabloid furor, which Lynn must have seen. Sadie quickly texted back, **It's a busy day for me but I'll call you later**, and felt the customary guilt. Her mother was now in the same city she was, and Sadie was still avoiding her. But there was only so much she could deal with at once. *One bite at a time*, she reminded herself. Lynn had insisted on remaining at her hotel, and seemed to be enjoying herself as a tourist in Nashville. She seemed to understand how busy Sadie was and had told Sadie she was looking forward to attending the holiday extravaganza at the Grand Ole Opry the next day. Lynn didn't have to know the show might not be happening, Sadie told herself. These were all problems she had to take care of on her own.

The studio's lobby was empty except for Yasmin, who was sitting behind her reception desk wearing a Santa hat.

"Cruz is upstairs, waiting for you," Yasmin said.

"Any sign of Max?" Sadie tried to make her voice sound natural when she said his name, but heard the waver in it—and the hope. Maybe he was already there. Maybe Tasha was right, he cared about her as much as she cared about him—no matter how much baggage the two of them were carrying around.

"He's not here yet," Yasmin said, adjusting her Santa hat, which had fallen down over one of her eyes. "But as I said, Cruz is eager to get to work. He's in the live room, and he wants to do some intimate-sounding recording today. So it's just him up there waiting. I'll buzz you up."

Sadie felt like she was walking a plank as she headed for the upstairs studio's live room. *Come on, Max,* she mentally willed. *I need you here.*

She took a deep breath and entered the room. Cruz spun around in his chair, two large coffees in his hands. "Mornin', sunshine! Figured we might need these. But I see you're way ahead of me there. Thanks." He took one of the coffees from her, the one intended for Max, and handed her one of his. "Sit. Please. His Highness's team just called to tell me our boy Max isn't feeling so hot today and is going to be late, if he shows at all." Sadie's heart sank. "But that's okay. We need some alone time. Shall we deal with the elephant in the room? Let's just dive right into that."

"We really should." She took a deep breath. "Cruz, what I told you about my gran was a secret. It's not okay that you said anything about it to the press."

Cruz's expression seemed appropriately chastened as he dumped sugar packets into one of his coffees. "Sadie Hunter, I am so damn sorry. First off, I know I behaved like an idiot at Stagecoach from what I remember. Those Saddle 'em Up guys sure do like their Jäger bombs." He rubbed his forehead as if still nursing a months-long hangover. "I was having so much fun with you that day, just hangin' out." He put his coffee down and put his hand on her arm. "And *you* know it was all good fun, right? We were *all* drinkin', yourself included, *all* just havin' a good time. Whoever took that photo—" He shook his head. "Now, *that* person did not have the best of intentions. It happens, in this industry. The bigger you get, the more people want to take you down. Trust me, I know. You don't get much bigger than Cruz McNeil."

"It's just I really needed that information about my personal life to stay—"

"There ain't much we can do about it now but move on. You and me are a great team. So today, let's just put our two heads down and do some good work."

"Three heads. Max is going to get here eventually."

"I kinda doubt that. Seems the boy went out and got plastered yesterday."

This surprised Sadie. She knew Max, and he wasn't a big drinker. "Are you sure?" she asked.

"Sure as shootin'. Took a page out of his old man's book a little too soon, if you ask me. You have to actually *be* a megastar before you can start exhibiting rock star behavior. But perhaps we both know the truth about Max Brody: that he's no match for his old man."

Sadie bristled at this. "I don't agree with you, Cruz. Max is just as talented as Holden, but in a different way—"

Cruz laughed off her words and shook his head. "You don't have to pretend with me, Sadie. Remember? I know the truth. That you two have been fakin'. Here, with me, you can be real. And I think you know that, since you do seem to make a habit of confiding in me. Maybe Max is going to show up, maybe he ain't. But if you stay here today I'll agree to work on a song with *you*. And it could up your chances of actually getting to perform at the extravaganza. If you've got a song, you've got a shot. Who knows, maybe they'll just decide to throw Johnny King up there with you."

He shrugged nonchalantly, but Sadie sensed there was more afoot here than met the eye. Her throat felt dry and she tried sipping her coffee, but it didn't help. Meanwhile, Cruz tapped his cup against hers, as if everything was settled. "You've made the right decision. I admire you, Sadie. You have what everyone in the industry is starting to realize is a once-in-a-lifetime voice. So, let's get to it."

Everyone in the industry. Once-in-a-lifetime. Was he speaking the truth? Surely she'd be a fool to walk out now. She had to take her own shot here. She had to be strong. And time was running short. The Grand Ole Opry performance was supposed to be the next day, and the song was supposed to be pre-recorded so fans could stream it immediately. They had to get something down.

"Hey, Cruz, once we're done here, do you think we could talk about those master tapes of mine you have?"

"Sure thing, doll, sure thing."

Sadie didn't entirely trust him, but he was right about one thing. They simply had to get to work.

Cruz stood, patting her arm in a patronizing manner as he picked up a guitar leaning against the wall. "I've got a few ideas for a song that will work for you and Max. Why don't I play it, you see what you think, maybe we lay down a few vocal tracks and hear how it sounds? When and if Max surfaces we can edit him in, okay? We're not cutting him out entirely. Fans are expecting Saxie to perform and we may just be able to make that happen for them. However, Max won't get a writing credit, and that's just how it's gonna go."

Sadie wanted to argue, but the reality was Max wasn't there. She was writing the song with Cruz, not Max. She was also growing concerned about something else. If Cruz was claiming a writing credit on this, what else of hers was he going to try to hone in on? "What about my songs?" she ventured. "Do you get a writing credit on those, too?"

"We said we were going to stick with one thing at a time, right? *Your* songs we can talk about once we get this one done. Now, come on, let's get to work, princess."

Excuse me a moment, Sadie? I need to make a phone call. But why don't you play back what we've got down here."

After Cruz left, Sadie listened to the song once, then twice. The third time was not a charm. The song was lackluster. It was called "Christmas Love Train" and it followed the story of two lovers on a romantic holiday getaway together. There was nothing wrong with it, per se. Cruz insisted it had everything it needed to become a huge holiday hit. And it did, as Cruz insisted, have some shades of Kenny and Dolly to it. But Sadie knew she could do better. She knew she and Max, if they finally gave themselves a chance, could do better.

She checked her phone for the tenth time to see if Max had reached out, but there were no messages from him—just one from Tasha, asking her to call ASAP. But Tasha wasn't picking up.

Sadie hit play on the song again. The weird thing was that try as she might, Sadie was unable to see where Max was going to fit into the song—or to picture him singing at all.

She stopped the playback and picked up her phone.

Hey. Happy Birthday, Max. Any chance you're feeling better and can get here soon? I really need you here.

She hit send, before she could think better of extending an olive branch, just as Cruz reentered the room. "Texting your boyfriend?" he said, and she could hear the air quotes around the word *boyfriend*.

She didn't answer him.

Cruz gazed at her intensely for a moment, but then smiled. "Well, we can't get any further on an empty stomach, now can we?" He lowered his arms and leaned in. "How about lunch? Sound good?" He hit the intercom button.

"Hey, doll, can you order some vittles for us?"

"Sure, boss, the usual?" Yasmin asked.

"Thanks, make it two, please. And add in a bottle of Sancerre."

He turned off the intercom and hit play on the music Sadie had been listening to before. "Christmas Love Train" filled the room—and Sadie tried not to cringe.

Cruz seemed delighted with it, nodding his head along to the music. "A song like that gets me right into the Christmas spirit," he said. "And a song like that is also the kind of song that allows a stellar voice like yours to shine." He turned down the volume and stood to pace the room as he spoke. "I can make you a star. You know I can. It's the whole reason I got involved with *Starmaker*: to find the next big thing. And the next big thing is *you*, doll. Not Max Brody. Not even Johnny King. Sadie Hunter, all on her own. My next label headliner. Isn't that what you want?"

Sadie tried to keep her voice casual and calm, even though the panicked sensations she'd been having were growing stronger by the minute. "To be the next big thing is what everyone in Nashville wants," she said as noncommittally as possible. *I'm just not sure you're the right producer for my songs, and I have to get my tapes back.*

There was a tap on the door. Lunch had arrived. Yasmin, still in her jaunty Santa hat, set it up on a small folding table and the room filled with the scent of fried food: battered catfish and French fries. "Come on, dig in, lady first," Cruz said, dishing her up a big paper plate when she didn't make a move toward the oily food, and pouring her a glass of wine, too. "It's not as good as Cruz's Catfish, which I very much hope will be up and running again soon, but it's a close second."

Sadie put the wineglass on the table and fished her water bottle out of her bag instead, as Cruz dug in to his heaping helping of fried catfish. Eventually, she put her nearly untouched plate down on the table and checked her phone, but there was still no response from Max.

Cruz refilled his wine and looked pointedly at her untouched cup. "You sure you don't want any?"

She shook her head. "If I have wine now, I'll need a nap soon enough."

"Well," Cruz said, taking a slug of wine. "This place is *full* of couches. I might just snuggle up beside you."

Sadie knew she could no longer ignore how uncomfortable Cruz was making her feel. But when she opened her mouth to say something to him the words dried up in her throat. What exactly was she going to call him on? He would say he had only been joking, and that she was being too sensitive.

"Anyway," Sadie said. "We should get back to it."

"Right. That's my girl. You're goddamn relentless." He

tipped his glass toward her. "You're the real deal, Sadie Hunter. Now, come here, sit close, I want to show you this new technique with the mic I think will give your voice more depth. Make it sound sorta like you just got out of bed, you know?"

Reluctantly, even though every technique Cruz suggested seemed to make her voice sound hollow, she pulled her chair over a few feet closer, but he grabbed the arm of it and pulled it right up against his. "Don't be shy," he said, and she smelled the wine he had been drinking on his breath. "A lot of people out there think we're an item now, and you're used to playing, aren't you? It's okay to sit close." He winked and she looked away. But he grabbed her hand and put it on the mic. "Okay, so you hold the mic like this, and tilt your head like that"—he now had his hand on her jaw; his fingers felt greasy. "And then, I press this button like so, and you start singing."

She sang a few bars of the Christmas train song, but the position of her head was too awkward. She had to stop eventually and rub at a crick in her neck. Cruz jumped up and stood behind her. "Here, let me take care of that for you," he said, his hands on her shoulders.

She moved her chair forward, away from his touch, but Cruz followed with his hands. "Really, Cruz. I'm fine. I just don't think that technique worked for me, that's all." She tried to pull away again, but his grip was firm.

"I'm just trying to find ways to get the most out of you. Wait, I have an idea." He stopped rubbing her shoulders and came around in front of her. He leaned down, and the catfish and wine on his breath was almost too much to bear. How had she ever admired this man, thought he could ever be a part of her path to success? "What if we tried to channel some of that same passion you and Max have? Surely it isn't just him. You can turn it on with anyone, can't you?"

"Excuse me?"

The next thing she knew, Cruz's fishy, oily lips were on hers. She struggled to move herself back, but he was a lot bigger than her, and he was holding her tight.

"Cruz!" Her voice was muffled because his lips were pressed so hard against hers.

He pulled away then, but only by millimeters, holding her to him with his other arm. "Come on," he said. "You can't deny we've been vibing all day. This is just a natural progression of our professional relationship and is going to bring out the best in your voice."

"Get your hands off of me, Cruz!" Sadie pushed him away so hard he nearly fell over. As she did, she thought she saw movement out in the hallway, but no one entered the room.

"Hey!" he said, collecting himself. "What is your problem, doll? We're making beautiful music. That is all we're doing. This is just how it's done. If you were anything other than an amateur, you'd know that."

"No," Sadie said, standing up. "I am not an amateur, I'm a professional. You are not. And we are not making beautiful music, by the way. We're making lackluster music, and *you* are making me uncomfortable. You've crossed a line, and I'm not going to take it anymore. I don't *have* to take it anymore. I have a contract to record a song with Max, for *Starmaker*, and that's what I'm going to do. I don't need you, Cruz."

He laughed as if she'd just delivered a punch line to a hilarious joke. But then his expression morphed into an ugly sneer. "In this town, *everyone* needs me," he said. "And congratulations, you're finished. You've just made the second biggest mistake of your life—the first one was ever getting involved in a fake relationship with Max Brody in the first place."

"Screw you, Cruz."

"Screw you, Sadie Hunter. You and your master tapes, which belong to me."

As she gathered her things and got the hell out of there, all she could think was that if this was what getting ahead in the music industry looked like, it was time to find a new dream.

23

Max

Nashville, Tennessee
December 22

Max woke up hazy, with absolutely no clue what had happened. It had been a long time since he'd had a hangover, and he lay still for some time with his hands over his eyes.

"Happy Birthday, baby brother," Becca said, from the doorway. Max squinted at her in the semidarkness as she set a wrapped present on the bedside table.

"It's a book. Two hundred knitting patterns. Figured based on everything that's been going on, you're probably up to your eyeballs in yarn."

"Becca, it's the middle of the night." Max put his hands back over his eyes. His voice was hoarse, like he'd been singing for hours.

"Actually, Maximillian—it's almost nine."

Max let out a groan. He was normally at the studio by seven.

"Dad wanted me to make you that disgusting tomato juice and raw egg concoction, but I brought you some OJ instead."

"Thanks, Becks." He sat up gingerly and took a sip, the cold sweetness soothing on his throat. "And thanks for the book."

Becca went over to the windows and opened the blinds, letting in the morning light.

"Whoa!" Max shielded his eyes with his arm. "Give a guy a chance to come to before you do that."

"No time for that. Bobbi called. She said, 'Get his ass to the studio in whatever manner you see fit.'" Becca put her hands on her hips, and it was then Max noticed something new about his sister.

"Um, don't take this the wrong way, sis, but you look . . . different."

She threw a pillow at him and he ducked, spilling juice on his bare chest. "You know better than to ever comment, in any way, on a woman's figure."

But then she smoothed her sweater over her stomach, smiling. "I honestly can't believe it took you this long."

Max's eyes widened. "Is that . . . Are you . . . ?"

"Pregnant? Sure am." Becca rubbed her belly, grinning. "You're going to be an uncle, Maximillian. Which means it's time to grow the hell up. I expect you to be a good role model for this peanut."

"Becks, how did this happen?"

Becca raised an eyebrow. "Do we need to talk about the birds and the bees?"

"Hush up." Max scowled at his sister's teasing. "*What I meant* is that you aren't married."

"So what? Since when are you so old-fashioned?"

"Does Dad know?"

"Of course. I told him straightaway. He's pretty excited to be a grandpa. Already planning a trip across the pond for when the baby's born."

"Well, I'm really happy for you, Becks. Though I still think your guy, Stanley, should get down on one knee, and soon by the looks of it."

Becca laughed. "Maybe worry about your own love life, huh?"

"Don't remind me," Max grumbled, and pushed the covers back, then swung his legs over the edge of the bed.

"Get dressed. I've walked Patsy and there's breakfast waiting. See you downstairs, birthday boy." Becca shut the door behind her.

After Becca left, he opened her gift—flipped through the pages, patterns and bright swatches of yarn adorning the pages. He thought about Becca's news, and that he was going to be an uncle. She was right. It *was* past time for him to grow the hell up.

Glancing at his phone, he saw a voicemail notification. It was from an unfamiliar number, and for a beat he hoped it might be Sadie. But he was disappointed to find out it was from Cruz, which was strange, because Cruz McNeil had never directly called him before. Regardless, it was a bit of good news. Cruz said he didn't need to come in until after lunch, something about a morning of meetings. It meant Max had time for a long hot shower, versus a short cold one. He pushed off the bed and, after pausing to let the light-headedness pass, headed to the shower.

————

Max drove to the studio, then parked and checked his phone. Sadie had texted while he was driving. He felt a moment of lift, seeing her name on his screen. Maybe they *could* sort this out. He sure as hell was going to try.

> **Hey. Happy Birthday, Max. Any chance you're feeling better and can get here soon? I really need you here.**

He was confused. Cruz had said to come in after lunch. With a sinking feeling he realized something was off and that he never should have trusted that message from Cruz. *Sadie needed him.* No matter what had happened, he had promised himself he would be there for her.

Slamming his truck door, he picked up the pace as he raced inside, guitar over one shoulder and a squirming Patsy under his arm. "Sorry, girl, no time for walkin'." But about twenty paces from the studio he abruptly stopped. Patsy grunted with the change in momentum.

"What am I gonna say?" he murmured. As he ran through apologies in his mind, he remained rooted in place.

Then in a flash, something his mom had said to him the night she gave him the guitar flooded his mind.

"Go chart your own course, my love," is what he always remembered her saying. But he had forgotten the second piece of her advice until now: "Never knock anyone down, or push them aside, to get where you're going."

It was both strange and comforting to remember this—like

the memory was a gift that he had received at precisely the right moment. Max had allowed his privilege and ego to cloud his judgment. He had been so single-minded about proving how different he was from his father that he had lost his way.

O nce he got to the studio, he grabbed the door's handle and took a deep breath. As he exhaled, he glanced through the small window, and then all the air left his body.

Sadie sat on a chair, with Cruz standing in front of her. But there wasn't nearly enough distance between them for two people who were no more than colleagues. Sadie seemed to be leaning toward Cruz. No, Cruz was leaning *into* Sadie.

Max was about to pull the door open, storm in there, and make Cruz back off. He no longer cared if Cruz worked on this song, or with him ever again.

But then Cruz leaned closer to Sadie, partially obscuring Sadie's face from Max's view. He pulled the door's handle and then . . .

Cruz was kissing Sadie, and Sadie was kissing him back!

Max let go of the handle like it was a hot potato, backing up a few steps so quickly he nearly tripped over his own feet. Sadie and Cruz *were* together.

So, maybe photos lie, but there's no denying what I just saw, he thought as he strode away from the studio.

Max was almost at the building's front door when he heard, "Hey, Max. Want me to take Patsy Canine so you can get to work?"

Landon stood a few feet away; the smile on his face dropped as soon as he saw Max's expression.

"Is everything okay, Max? You look ill."

When Max didn't respond, Landon added, "Should I let Sadie know you need a minute? Can I get you a glass of water? You're probably dehydrated after, well, you know, what happened yesterday."

"What happened yesterday?" Max asked.

Landon gave him a curious look. "Well, the cemetery? The whiskey? I drove you home, in your truck?"

Max stared at Landon, puzzled. "Right, sure. Hey, I don't mean to cut this short, but I need to go," he said. "But could you do me a favor and tell Sadie and Cruz I had to leave?"

"You bet," Landon replied. Then a moment later, "Hey, Max?"

Max stopped halfway out the door. "Yeah?"

Landon quickly closed the space between them. "I need to tell you something. After what you told me yesterday about how you and Sadie faked Saxie . . ."

Shit. He'd told Landon about Saxie? Goddamn whiskey. Max tried to look unconcerned. "I was pretty drunk, so you should ignore anything I said yesterday."

"But you also said you loved Sadie. Like, *really* loved her."

"Did I now?" Max didn't know what else to say.

"You did. So, I thought you should know that Cruz leaked that photo and story. He asked me to update his calendar last night, and, uh, I saw the messages between him and HotStarGossip. Sadie had nothing to do with it. It was all Cruz."

Max's jaw clenched. *Of course* it had been Cruz—that snake in the grass. He had the most to gain by putting a wedge between him and Sadie. But then Max thought back to the text fiasco in Banff, the way Sadie continuously held back bits of the truth from him. The puzzle pieces started to fit together in his mind. Maybe Sadie and Cruz *had* been working together all this time. Maybe even from the beginning. Maybe Max really was a fool, and her apology—however genuine it had felt at the time—was just another tactic.

As mad as he was at having the wool pulled over his eyes, he also couldn't ignore the burn of heartbreak. But, Sadie was with Cruz—that much was clear. Between Cruz's power and her star potential, it would be a golden relationship the media and fans would embrace. Sadie would be fine. While he wanted to storm back into the studio and punch Cruz in his smug face for all his backhandedness and manipulations, he knew the best thing he could do was to walk away. From Cruz, from *Starmaker*—even from Sadie.

Max was going to chart a different course.

"I appreciate you telling me, man." Max clapped a hand on Landon's arm. "But it doesn't matter anymore. I'm done with this town."

Max was nearly back at his truck when his phone rang.

"Hey, Becks. What's up?"

"Max, you need to come home. *Right now.*"

24

Sadie

Nashville, Tennessee
December 22

Sadie rushed down the hallway, nearly blinded by her anger—and walked smack into someone.

"Sadie!" Landon said. "Are you okay?"

"Not really," she said shakily. "Not at all, actually."

"Sadie, I have to tell you something. Max—"

"Is he coming?" Sadie's heart lifted. But then Landon shook his head.

"He had a family emergency. He was here, but he had to go."

Sadie's heart now sank to the bottom of her cowboy boots. *No. Please no.* "Wait. When? When was he here?"

"Just now."

"Did he seem upset when you saw him?"

Landon swallowed hard, then said, "Yes. He was. He was really shaken up. Ran out of there like a bat out of hell."

Tears flooded Sadie's eyes. "I need to get out of here. And, Landon? You might as well start spreading the word now. Saxie is *officially over*." She turned off her phone so she wouldn't have to see the oncoming barrage of tweets and texts, then turned on her heel and ran.

Sadie walked along downtown Nashville's main drag, not quite sure where she was going. She couldn't shake the feeling she was being watched, being followed. It was the same sensation she'd experienced on the bridge the day before, when she'd tossed her letters to her gran into the water—and she told herself that maybe this was just her reality at the moment, that she *was* being watched by paparazzi. But it wasn't always going to be that way. The official breakup of Saxie would be huge news for a few days—and then it would be over. Sadie forced herself to keep putting one foot in front of the other, and soon, she was in front of a familiar sign—and she realized maybe this was where she had been headed all along.

She stood in front of the modest-looking bar, its tattered awning and faded red curlicue name on the sign belying its status as one of the most legendary spots in Nashville. The Song Sparrow. Hallowed ground. She took a few steps closer and peered inside the window. It wasn't open yet but a server was inside wiping down the tables to prepare for the night ahead.

Sadie pressed her face to the glass—and all at once could almost see the ghost of herself in there, nearly paralyzed by stage fright years before. She pictured a younger Max, trying to get his footing in a town that was all too familiar to him, unaware that his life was about to change for the worse that very night.

The night I met you was the last time I was ever happy, he had told Sadie. And he had said he used to come to the Song Sparrow to reignite his passion for an industry that sometimes got him down. This was what had drawn Sadie here today, too. She needed a reminder, before she walked away for good, that there *had* been some good moments—it hadn't all been for nothing. She would say a last goodbye, and then call her mom and meet her at her hotel—and she would tell Lynn it was time for them to go home. Because Lynn had been right all this time. The music industry was only ever going to break her.

Sadie tapped on the door of the tavern, then opened it.

"Sadie Hunter! I am such a big fan!" The server inside the Song Sparrow had rushed to the door, realizing who she was. "You have the most beautiful voice I've ever heard. I came to Nashville after I saw you win *Starmaker* last year because I realized I had to at least try, you know?"

The server grasped Sadie's hand. "I'm Claire," she said. "I'm waiting tables for now, but I've met Maren Morris and LeAnn Rimes. Allen Shamblin was even in here one night—he wrote 'I Can't Make You Love Me,' which is the most heartbreaking song I've ever heard. And now I'm talking about music with Sadie freaking Hunter!"

"Thanks, Claire. I am such a huge fan of the Song Sparrow." Sadie paused. "I sang here years ago. And I was just standing here on the sidewalk remembering that night."

Claire glanced over her shoulder into the empty restaurant, then back at Sadie. "Did you want to come inside for a coffee? I'm the only one in there right now, doing the setup for tonight."

Sadie followed Claire inside. Dust motes floated in the

air—but inside the hallowed Song Sparrow, even dust managed to look magical.

The room was decked out in holiday garland and Christmas lights and there were big red poinsettia plants on either side of the bar. Claire saw her looking at them.

"I brought those in," she said. "This place may be legendary, but it needed some sprucing up. And they remind me of home. I'll be staying here this year because I can't afford to fly back to California." She reached up and touched one of the sumptuous red leaves, then passed Sadie a coffee. But Sadie left it on the bar top and continued to look around. She wandered close to the stage and found herself walking up the steps to lay her hands on top of the piano that stood sentry there. She looked down and thought of all the famous hands that had touched these keys, too.

Claire was watching her. "Go ahead. Have a seat."

Sadie pulled out the bench and sat, then stared down at the worn-smooth ivory keys. She played a few notes of the nostalgic opening bars of "I Can't Make You Love Me." She started to sing—then paused. "Hey, why don't you come on up here? And maybe sing with me?"

Claire's wide eyes grew even wider. She approached the stage and sat down beside Sadie.

"I'm no Max Brody, but I'll give it a shot," Claire said. Sadie felt a pang at the mention of that name. But she was going to let herself feel it, rather than sweep her emotions under a rug.

Sadie started to sing. She put all the pain she was feeling, all the heartbreak and regret, into her voice. And it felt damn good.

Meanwhile, Claire's voice was melodic and grew stronger

as Sadie played. Sadie kept right on allowing herself to feel everything the songwriter meant people to feel about love, and loss.

Sadie's hands stilled on the keys and the last notes sounded. She knew it was probably time to get going, but that song had opened up something inside her. Claire got up and smiled, telling her to stay as long as she wanted. Sadie sat still, staring down at the piano keys once more. Then her fingers began to move across the keys again and lyrics filled her mind. It was another love song, she realized. A song about Max Brody—and what it would be like if everything were different. If their love had somehow made it, against all odds.

Love. She was in love with Max Brody, she realized. And even if he didn't love her back, it meant something. She loved Max, it had to be acknowledged—and the best way she knew how to do that was with a song.

Sadie reached into her handbag and pulled out the notebook she always carried with her in case musical inspiration struck.

"Hey, Claire," she called out. "Are you sure I'm okay to stay a little while longer? Something just came to me. Something I've been waiting for." Her heart was racing. Maybe it was pointless, maybe it was all over—but she knew this song was good. She knew that even if the scenario she was writing about wasn't real, the emotion was.

"No one's due in for another half hour." Claire grinned and popped her earbuds back in her ears. "I'll make you a deal," she said. "I'll turn up my music so I can't hear the song you're writing, but I want front-row seats to your next sold-out show, where you perform it."

Sadie said yes but felt guilty knowing there probably wouldn't be any future sold-out Sadie Hunter shows. Cruz had said she was finished. But that didn't mean she couldn't keep writing music. She started to play again—and found herself singing the song to Max.

If nothing else, at least she'd have this song. A Christmas gift to herself. She would keep it with her forever.

Sadie tried to call Lynn on her way back to her apartment, but she didn't answer. She left her a voicemail, explaining that she was ready to go home for good.

Sadie entered her apartment's lobby to find the doorman, Reynold, standing on a ladder, putting a star atop a large Christmas tree. Sadie paused, taking in the glittery ornaments. As she watched, Rey's ladder wobbled. She rushed over to help.

"Thanks, Sadie," Rey said, climbing down gingerly. He was in his seventies and had once told Sadie he was retired but working part time as a doorman to raise extra money for Christmas presents for his many grandkids. "It is a fine tree, isn't it?" He turned to her. "Oh! I have mail for you, Sadie. Wait here."

He returned quickly with a large manila envelope—and Sadie's breath caught when she saw that her name and address were written on it in a heartbreakingly familiar script: her gran's.

"Who delivered this?" she managed.

"Sorry, I don't know," Rey said, returning to his post behind the high-countered desk. "I was taking my break, and when I got back it was sitting right here." He tapped the top of the counter. "Like a Christmas elf had come and dropped it off for you."

Sadie couldn't help herself. She ripped the envelope open.

Inside were several sheets of notepaper covered in more of her gran's familiar script.

Dear Sadie,

I'm so sorry. It's not our family's strong suit to talk about difficult things—and the most difficult thing you and I could ever have talked about was being apart. When I found out in the fall that I was on my way out, that I was too old for risky heart surgery, I swore your mother to secrecy. I knew it would ruin your chances of winning STAR-MAKER if you were preoccupied—and although I'm sure you'd disagree, I am the older and wiser one in the relationship. Until the day you surpass me in age, which I sincerely hope you will do many years from now, it's going to stay that way.

I did what I thought was right. You've had a year to deal with it. I hope it's getting easier.

I've had a long life. And although I'll never be ready to say goodbye to you or your mother, I can't complain. I got to see you grow. I got to help raise you. I got to see you come close to achieving a huge dream. I believe wholeheartedly that even if I do not manage to be here to witness it, you will prevail. You will, as always, make me proud. I have no way of knowing if you will win STARMAKER, but the world has heard your voice now. The sky is the limit for you.

I hope you have forgiven your mother by now for keeping you in the dark: she was just doing what I asked. And although you think she doesn't believe in your dreams, she wants you to be happy. She was cheering for you just as hard as I was.

Darling, I have something difficult to write to you. While I am very proud of myself for always encouraging you to chase your ambition and live without regret, there is something I regret. I think I may have given you a less than rosy view of romance and love. This might be an understatement. Your mother tried to protect you from any kind of heartache—and in doing that often pushed you away. My mistake is that I pushed you toward what I hoped would be a rewarding career because I started to believe I could protect you from the kind of romantic disappointment I experienced in life, and the kind of heartache your mother went through. And although I do see that you are independent and strong, well able to stand on your own, an impressive young modern woman—well, when I saw you with Max Brody I realized it might be possible for you to have the best of both worlds. Career success and a loving relationship. Strength and independence and someone to love you for everything you are.

I know your relationship with him is complicated, and has taken place in a fishbowl, but I also know you well enough to have been able to see the real feelings between the two of you the night I came to visit. I believe Max Brody is your match—in talent, in worth, and in stubborn willfulness. But I thought I'd wait a year to tell you and see what sort of job you did figuring it out on your own. I'm wondering what sort of obstacles you two created for your-selves over the year, and what sort of obstacles the world may have created for you. But I'm hoping you at some point decided to give things with Max a true shot. And if one year later, you and Max have not made a good, honest go of things, and if this is something you are regretting—I hope that it's not too late and my words may help lead you in the right direction. All I can do now is remind you that nothing and no one is perfect. That you are special. That Max saw that in you, and I witnessed him seeing that—and saw you seeing the same in him. The true love I sensed as a possibility between you is as rare as your beautiful voice. I'm no expert on love, but I do know it when I see it.

Speaking of true love, I love you with all my heart, and wish more than anything that things could be different than they are right now. But I'm always with you, I promise, watching you continue to chase all your dreams, believing in you always and forever. Merry Christmas, my darling.

Now, go on out there and make me proud.

Yours,

Gran

Sadie wiped away the tears that had rolled down her cheeks as she read the letter. "Oh, Gran," she whispered. "I miss you so much."

She felt a cold blast of wind as the lobby doors opened—and looked up to see a familiar figure walking toward her. "Mom . . ."

"Oh, honey. I'm so sorry!"

"But, why?"

"I hate feeling so much distance between us—and now I think I've waited too long. I've been following you around for the past few days trying to think of how to fix things between us, and . . . well, it's ridiculous. I'm no better than one of those paparazzi!"

"So these past few days, instead of touring Nashville, you've been following me around?" Sadie thought of the creeping sensation of being watched she'd had on the bridge the day before. Now it made sense. "Why didn't you just try talking to me?"

"I knew you were busy—and I knew you were struggling. I didn't know how to help you. I had the letter from your gran and wanted to find the right way, the right moment, to give it to you. I got it in my head that if I could find the perfect moment, maybe it would help. But today I realized there wasn't going to be a perfect moment. I knew I just needed to get over myself and stop holding you at arm's length—because you need me. And I need you."

"You're not the one who has been holding me at arm's length. I shut you out," Sadie said softly.

"Well, you learned from the best." Lynn pulled Sadie in for a hug. "I really am sorry, Sadie. I haven't been fair to you. I've been too afraid to treat you like an adult who can make her own choices, who knows her own heart well enough to know what she needs for her life."

"But you were right. I can't do this anymore. It's time for me to come home. I've been chasing the wrong dream."

"No, Sadie. I don't believe that. You've done nothing but prove to me this year that you were right to chase your dreams. You're an incredible talent, and now the world has seen it."

Sadie shook her head. "Really, it's fine. I've made my

decision. I want to come home." She clutched the letter to her chest. "And by the way, no matter how or when this letter got to me, it's still special, Mom. And you did manage to find the perfect moment. I've taken you for granted for far too long. That's one of the things"—she swallowed hard—"that knowing Max helped me realize. I saw how much he missed his own mom, even after all this time. And losing Gran, too—it's all made me realize that you need to hold your loved ones tight."

"Not follow them around at a distance?" Lynn asked.

Sadie laughed. "Right, maybe not that. You didn't need to hide, Mom. You didn't need to do any fancy footwork to make me believe in anything. All I needed was you. And now you're here. Which is perfect, because I need some help packing up my apartment, and I have so many things to talk to you about— and then, I want to go home. I don't want to spend another Christmas in Nashville. We can rent a U-Haul and haul ass out of here, okay?" *Sounds like a new Tasha Munroe song*, she couldn't help but think. But soon, she'd stop thinking that way, in Nashville terms.

Lynn frowned. "But what about your Grand Ole Opry performance?"

"Not happening. It's all over."

"Is this about Cruz McNeil and those photos?"

"It's about Cruz in some ways, and Max, too. But mostly, it's about me making my own decision. I don't want this anymore." It hurt to say it, and didn't feel quite right. But Sadie told herself that was because it was heartbreaking to let go of a dream she'd held so long. She'd get over it, though. She'd find something else to do with her life. She could still write music, but she could do that from Wisconsin for a while. "You've always been right, Mom."

"No, I wasn't right to ever try to hold you back." Lynn paused, then stepped closer to her daughter. "Sadie, do you remember those text messages your gran sent you, the night . . ." She swallowed hard, pain in her eyes. "The night she died?"

Sadie nodded, her heart aching. "I still have them."

"Those weren't from her. I typed those to you. I knew exactly what she would have wanted to say to you—but she was already too far gone to say them herself. And as I wrote them, I believed them. I finally understood this dream of yours, and why you *are* cut out to fight for it. I'm so sorry I didn't tell you. I'll try to do better at being more open and honest with you."

It took Sadie a couple of moments to absorb her mom's words, but she soon accepted that Lynn had only done what any loving mother would do. That Gran would likely have approved, too. That Sadie had needed to believe she was getting a final goodbye—and that nothing was ever going to change the fact that her gran was gone. "It's okay, Mom. Really. Come on, let's just go upstairs. We can talk more and soon you'll understand exactly why I can't stay here."

E ven after Sadie had told her mom everything, every painful detail, all the ways in which she had been broken by the music industry—she didn't have the reaction Sadie expected her to have.

"No damn way!" she said. "You are not letting that damn Cruz McNeil steal this dream from you. As your mother, I have to tell you—you are not making the right choice here. First off, Cruz deserves to be charged for what he did."

"No way. I am not going through that."

"So you'll just let him act however he wants? Do those things to anyone else he pleases?"

This did give Sadie pause, but she also knew that she alone was no match for someone as influential as Cruz. "I'll find ways to heal," she said. "Possibly with therapy. I promise, I won't just sweep it under the rug. But right now, I just hope I never have to see him again."

"I understand. I'll always support you however I can, Sadie. I just don't want to see you throw away your dreams because of someone like Cruz. Your gran would be livid with me if I did. And she wouldn't want you to forget how much you love music." Lynn paused. "Play that song for me. The one you said you wrote for Max at the Song Sparrow earlier."

Sadie got out the keyboard she kept at her apartment. She had to admit, despite everything, it felt pretty fantastic to play the song. She didn't realize until she was finished that Lynn was holding up Sadie's phone as she did. "Hey, were you recording me?"

Lynn shook her head and handed the phone to Sadie. "I may have gone ahead and made a phone call . . ."

It was Amalia. "Holy crap, Vanilla Twist! That song was *incredible!*" she shouted. "And you have got to stop disappearing on me, girl."

"Things have been tough, Amalia. I needed some time to think."

Amalia's voice was stern. "I heard from Cruz's team. Apparently you fired him? Why wouldn't you talk to me first?"

"Listen," Sadie said, her voice equally grim. "I don't want a career where I have to be near someone like Cruz ever again." She took a bolstering breath and explained to Amalia what had happened at the studio. After Sadie was finished speaking, Amalia was silent. Was she going to believe her?

"I'm sorry," Amalia said, and her voice was different now. In fact, her indomitable manager had never sounded so shaken up. "I've heard things like this about Cruz before. I even told you his handsiness was something that could be managed, but it's more than that, isn't it? I've chosen to turn a blind eye because he paints himself as so instrumental in building careers. But he's not—he's just a creep. I'm ashamed, Sadie. You did the right thing. But it would sicken me to see you walk away from what I know is going to be an incredible career because of something like this."

"Cruz said he would destroy me. I can't help but want to give up."

"You can, of course, make your own choices, and I'll support you. But I'm also your manager and advisor, which means it's still my job to tell you when I think you're wrong. That song is *gorgeous*. The world needs to hear it. You are talented—and it would be a crime to allow someone like Cruz to force you to give up on your dreams."

"But how? Cruz won't ever let me get ahead now that I've crossed him, and you know it."

"Maybe you're giving him too much power," Amalia said. "Cruz has created a persona, and everyone believes he is who he says he is—but you've seen differently, haven't you? He doesn't deserve to be in charge of anyone's fate, least of all yours. Don't you agree?"

"It's hard not to when you put it like that," Sadie allowed.

"*You* have a contract with *Starmaker* to sing at the Grand Ole Opry tomorrow night *with* Max Brody," Amalia continued. "I think the only logical next step is to make sure Max knows you are going to be there with a perfect song. It's got a simple melody he could pick up after just a run-through or two. I'll call Bobbi and explain that all he needs to do is show up for rehearsal tomorrow, and that I know you can get through the live performance together. You two have that off-the-charts chemistry to work with. I doubt that's gone anywhere, even with all the drama. Let me work on it, okay?"

Sadie hesitated, but her mom was nodding and giving a thumbs-up—with a twinkle in her eye Sadie recognized: she looked just like Gran. If Gran had been there, she would have told Sadie she had no choice but to give Max—and her dreams—one last chance.

And that, Sadie decided, was exactly what she was going to do. Life was too short for regret.

25

Max

Nashville, Tennessee
December 22

"Max, you need to come to the house. *Right now.*"

It had been only seconds since his sister had told him this over the phone, but it felt like an eternity, especially because he couldn't hear her anymore.

"Becks? Are you there?"

Max was frantically trying to buckle his seat belt and Patsy's, images of what might have happened at home swirling like a sickening kaleidoscope through his mind. Maybe Holden had suffered a heart attack, or fallen off one of his horses. Or maybe something had happened to Becca's baby? "Hello?! Rebecca!"

But the reception was terrible, and his sister's voice kept cutting out.

"What's happening? Are you okay?"

"I don't know . . . Dad . . . *hurry* . . ."

Max's heart leapt out of his chest.

"What happened to Dad? Becks!" Max put his phone on speaker as he backed the truck up. "Hello? I can't hear—"

But Becca had hung up.

Just then his phone rang again, and he answered without looking—assuming it was Becca calling him back.

"Becca, I'm on my way."

"Max? It's Tasha. Everything okay?"

Max sighed, pressing his foot harder on the gas. The truck sped up. "I have no idea how to answer that question right now."

"What's going on?"

He paused, pressed his lips together. *How to even explain?*

"Look, take some ibuprofen. I'm sure that headache of yours isn't helping things."

"How do you know I have a headache?" Max changed lanes carefully. The last thing he needed was to get in an accident.

"Well, you were drunk as a skunk yesterday," Tasha said.

"Huh? How did you know that?" he asked.

Tasha paused. "I know, because you called me."

Max tried to catch up. "Come again?"

"Well, it wasn't *me* you were trying to call, but I got the voicemail."

"Tasha, I have a headache that would make most people curl up on the ground, and something is going on with Becca, and everything in my life feels ass backward, so could you just come out with it?"

"You left a voicemail for Sadie, but you had actually called me instead." When Max said nothing, Tasha continued, her voice softening. "You declared your love for her, Max. You were slurring something awful, but that part I heard loud and clear."

"Oh . . . *no* . . ." A vague, distant memory of calling Sadie landed in his brain. He had told her he loved her, for the first time. *Over voicemail.* Or more accurately, he told Tasha he loved Sadie. Now his conversation with Landon made more sense. Apparently, he had been declaring his love for Sadie to everyone *but Sadie.*

"So, were you telling the truth?" Tasha asked.

Max was quiet for a moment, taking stock of the state of his heart. Then thinking about her kissing Cruz only minutes earlier, which made his stomach clench painfully. "It's the damn truth. Unfortunately."

"Look, it's none of my business, but Sadie paid me a visit," Tasha said.

"Sadie came to see you?"

"She did. And I'm not breaking any confidences here, so I can tell you this. She was pretty upset, Max. About a lot of things, including that photo, which, by the way, is total bullshit."

Max clenched his hands on the steering wheel. "You don't know what you're talking about, Tasha."

She sighed heavily. "You're a smart guy, Max, but sometimes you're as aggravating as a rock."

"And I appreciate you, darlin', but you are gettin' on my last nerve."

"*Nothing happened* with Sadie and Cruz, which I am sure you know deep down. So I don't get why you're choosing to be ugly about it. I mean, you of all people should know precisely who Cruz McNeil is . . . with your dad and everything."

His anger rose again as he thought about Sadie kissing Cruz in the studio. *Ugh*. He hated feeling this way.

"Sadie told me what happened at Stagecoach. Cruz was drunk, or high, who knows these days. She'd had a few drinks and started thinking about her gran. Tours are hard and take every last ounce of emotional energy you've got. She had a weak moment, and Cruz capitalized on that. He must have been keeping his eye on her, *the creep*—and followed her. He was not invited, I'll tell you that much," Tasha said.

"Wait, what?" Did Sadie want to be with Cruz . . . or not? He surely hadn't misinterpreted what had happened in the recording studio this afternoon, regardless of Stagecoach.

"She was trying to keep things friendly with Cruz, which we both know is an important business move, so she put up with him. She shared with him why she was upset, and about her gran, and he took advantage of that. She did nothing wrong, Max."

"Shit. Shit. Shit," Max said, slamming his hand against the steering wheel. All of a sudden, he knew the truth—which had been right in front of him all along, but he'd been too stubborn and self-absorbed to see it. Sadie wasn't kissing Cruz back . . . he had trapped her. She didn't have feelings for Cruz. Sadie had been treading water so as not to disrupt the ever-important relationship she—*they*—needed to have with Cruz.

Tasha paused. "Do you get it now, Max?"

"Yes," Max said, remorse heavy in his voice. "And as we both know, I'm a colossal jerk."

"As your lifelong friend, who knows you're not *this* guy— the one who flies off the handle about a stupid photo, accusing people of things you *know* can't be true, and then gets plastered to numb it all—let me give you a piece of advice: you need to get your head screwed on right. Or you're going to ruin both your careers. And even worse, you could lose her forever."

Max tried calling Sadie the second he'd hung up with Tasha, but it went straight to voicemail. He felt sick about what had happened in the recording studio, and hoped she was okay. But he had also just arrived at the Brody estate, and was panic-stricken about whatever emergency was going on there. Max grabbed Patsy and sprinted up the front steps, two at a time. He pushed open the door, afraid of what he was going to find. The memory of seeing his mom in the hospital, frail under the harsh ER lights, ran through his mind. His throat closed and he struggled to get enough air in.

"Becca! Dad! Martha! Where are you?" The house was quiet—too quiet. He ran into the great room, where the Christmas tree stood decorated, and found Holden on the couch, looking perfectly well. His dad had reading glasses perched on the end of his nose, a notebook on his lap. Holden looked over his glasses as Max burst into the room, surprise registering on his face.

"Maxy! What are you doing back here?"

"What's going on?" Breathless, Max bent over to put hands on his knees after he let Patsy down. The dog trotted to the couch and pawed at Holden's leg.

"Hey there, girl." Holden reached down to pick her up.

"Where's Becca? Her call cut out. Is it the baby?"

Holden set his 2B pencil into his notebook's spine. "Last time I checked she was perfectly fine. Baby, too. But shouldn't you be in the studio with Miss Sadie? Are *you* okay?"

"Clearly not." Max ran a hand through his hair. Waiting for his racing heart to slow.

Just then Becca came into the room. "Oh, hey, Max. Aren't you supposed to be at the studio?"

Max let out a strangled groan. "Yes, Becca. I *am* supposed to be at the studio. But I am here. Trying to reverse my heart attack, because you told me to hurry home!"

Becca gave him a blank look and then slapped a hand to her forehead. "Oh! I was out for a walk and it was pretty windy and the call dropped. Sorry."

"Becks, goddamn it! You told me to *hurry home*."

Becca shrugged. "I guess with the whole wind thing you didn't hear. Anyway, no, what I said was something like, 'I don't know if I can keep Dad from eating all the cinnamon buns, so you'd better hurry home after you finish up with Sadie.'"

She held up the plate in her hand. He stared at the gooey icing dripping down the side of the half-eaten pastry.

"You called me about cinnamon buns?" Max's mouth was agape.

"I have to say, they are almost worth moving back home for."

Max sat heavily in the chair closest to him, putting a hand to his chest. "Do you have any idea how much I have going on right now? Any idea how many times I almost crashed, trying to get home as fast as possible?"

"Again, sorry, little brother. Good news is there are still a few left, *if you hurry*." She took a huge bite of the bun.

Max was about to berate his sister again for scaring him half to death when he heard a voice in the hallway.

He twisted in his chair to see his manager walking into the great room, barefoot and with a large red purse over her shoulder.

"Bobbi, honey, you know you don't have to take your shoes off in this house." Holden gave her a kiss on the cheek. "But it's nice to see you, darlin'."

"You, too, Holden." Bobbi smiled warmly at Max's father. "And you know my father would have had my hide if I wore shoes in the house. Old habits." She shrugged, then hugged Becca. But when she turned to Max she did not have the same warm expression for him. She looked like she had a burr in her saddle, as Holden would say.

"This sure as heck does not look like a recording studio, where you assured me you would be today."

"Yeah, so about that . . ." Max stood, but Bobbi interrupted him.

"Look here, Max. I am busier than a moth in a mitten, so I don't have time for your bullshit." Bobbi pointed a finger at Max, and he looked to Becca and his dad, who both suddenly seemed occupied by other things.

"I have a meeting to get back to, so let me be clear. You signed a contract. And this is not only about you now, you hear me? I've known you since you were knee-high to a grasshopper, and I know you are not the sort to walk away when the going gets real tough. That is not the Brody way."

But wasn't it precisely the Brody way? He had been walking

away when the going got tough for the better part of the past twelve months. Max tried again to explain what had happened at the studio, but Bobbi was having none of it.

"I have two things to discuss with you, Max. One, take a minute and get yourself sorted before you come back to the studio—you can deal with the personal stuff later, but right now your focus needs to be on the work. Cruz is rumbling about Johnny King being ready to go if the two of you can't figure this out." Bobbi raised her eyebrows. "And none of us want to see Johnny King onstage at the Grand Ole Opry, do we?"

Max pressed his lips together, knowing what it would mean if that happened—that he had failed everyone. Along with everything else, he didn't want to be responsible for voiding Sadie's contract along with his own.

"Good. We're on the same page, then," Bobbie said. "After tomorrow night's performance you are done with *Starmaker* and I promise you, we'll figure out what's next for Max Brody, alright? Secondly, Sadie fired Cruz. I just talked with Amalia."

Max's mouth fell open.

"Apparently Mr. McNeil felt he was entitled to more than a great song from Sadie, if you get what I'm saying."

"Is she okay?" He started to pace, clenching and unclenching his fists. "That goddamn snake. If I ever see him again, I'm gonna knock out his teeth and then—"

"Max, take a breath," Bobbi started, putting a hand on his arm. "There will be time to deal with all that later, but right now the only job you have—*the only thing you have to do*—is get that song finished with Sadie."

Max took a deep breath in through his nose, remembering Landon's advice. He then let it out slowly and nodded.

―――――

After Bobbi left, Max went back to pacing—trying to pull it together like he said he would, without much luck.

"Maxy, stop. I'm sure Sadie is fine—"

"*I left her there*, Becks. I left her. I thought she was kissing him back! I'm a damn, damn fool. I wouldn't be surprised if she never speaks to me again."

Becks let him pace a few moments longer before she asked, "How did it not occur to you that maybe Cruz was being predatory?"

"Did I mention I'm a damn fool?" Max sighed, hating himself. "I know his reputation, Becks, obviously. But with that photo, then seeing them like that, well, the pieces fit together."

"Look, it's not entirely your fault. There are some things you don't know about Cruz, and I should have told you this years ago." Becca held Max's gaze. "Remember when Dad fired him, in the middle of his Whiskey and Pearls Tour?"

"Yeah." Max glanced at Holden, who couldn't look him in the eye.

"Do you know *why* Dad fired him?"

Max shrugged.

"He fired Cruz because he caught him feeding me shots and getting a little too close. I was sixteen. I thought I was so mature, and, I'll admit it, I liked his attention. At first." Becca gave a sad smile.

"But then Cruz tried to kiss me, and I didn't know what to do. Dad walked in, and, well, let's just say Cruz was lucky to get out of there in one piece."

"Why is this the first time I'm hearing this?" Max's hands curled into fists of rage.

He remembered that night well. He and his mother had been backstage watching Holden on a monitor. Becca had said she was going to the washroom. And all twelve-year-old Max had been thinking about was getting an ice cream sundae once his dad's set was finished.

"I'm so sorry, Becks," Max said. "I'm sorry you went through that."

Becca gave him a hug, and he held her tight. "I'm okay, Max. And I think Sadie will be, too."

"Dad, I hope you hit him hard."

Holden nodded his confirmation.

"I wish I could do something now, to give him what he deserves," Max said.

"Oh, don't you worry about that," Becca replied. "I've taken care of it."

Max glanced at Becca, then at Holden, who now sported a Cheshire cat grin. "How?"

"Let's just say my story about that night on Dad's tour was of great interest to a certain journalist who is doing a gig at *Rolling Stone*. The story is set to run right after Christmas, and Cruz won't be able to slither away this time."

"He's finished," Holden added, giving Max a serious look. "Mark my word, son."

Max tried Sadie again, but again it went to voicemail. He hadn't left a message because he wasn't sure what to say. *Sorry* seemed too little, too late. So he was getting ready to head back to the studio when Holden knocked on his bedroom door. "I thought you might want to talk about Sadie."

"I'm glad you helped out with the Cruz thing, and I appreciate the effort here, but we don't do *this*, okay? I don't expect fatherly advice from you. Nor do I need it."

"I'd say you sure as hell do," Holden replied with a guffaw.

"As if I'd take relationship advice from my philandering father," Max said, almost instantly regretting it.

"When it comes to my relationship with your mother, you don't know what the hell you're talking about, son."

"Oh, I don't? *I was here, Dad.* After Becca left, it was just me and the two of you. I saw everything. I heard everything."

"You're barking up the wrong tree, Maximillian. That's always been your greatest downfall—believing too much in your own horseshit."

Max gave a sharp laugh. "You really are unbelievable, you know that?"

"I've never said anything to you about this because I wasn't sure *how* to say anything that you wouldn't bite my head off for. I know you have this idea that I destroyed my marriage. That I made your mother unhappy and was responsible for how things turned out. But you couldn't be more wrong."

Max sighed wearily. "Fine. I'm wrong. Can I go now?"

"Please, Max. I know you need to get to the studio, so I'll make it brief. But there are some things you need to know." Holden gestured to the chair nearest to him.

Max glanced at his watch, but sat down. "You have five minutes."

"Maren was my best friend. The love of my life. Damn, I adored that woman."

"You sure had a special way of showing it."

Holden ignored his son's jab. "I'm not innocent, and Lord knows I've made mistakes. But your mother was my best friend. And I miss her every damn day. Truth is, we fell out of love somewhere between the first day we met and the day she died, but it wasn't some 'big thing' that happened between us. And you should know, it was your momma who wanted out of the marriage. She was brave enough to admit it wasn't working long before I did."

Max looked up at his dad then.

"Good Lord, she was smart, Max. Like, plumb brilliant. And that voice . . . honey on a hot summer's day. Reminds me a lot of your girl, Sadie."

She could have been my girl, Max thought, *if I hadn't blown it.*

"Your momma and I loved each other, son, but we were no longer *in love* with one another. But, bless her, she stuck around. She chose this family, and our history, over getting a divorce and her freedom. Raised you kids. Supported me the way I always had, with so much love in her heart. But in those last few years we led different lives. The both of us."

At that Max frowned at his father. "You're lying."

"I swear to you, it's the truth. Maren and I had a partnership—both for the music and our family—but she was as free as I was to explore other options, if you know what I mean."

"You really are something." Max shook his head. "Why would you make this up now? For what purpose? You *wrecked* Mom, Dad. You took her career from her, then kept all the spotlight for yourself, then shit on your vows by flaunting all those other women on your tours. *I saw you.* I heard things."

"I sure did all of that, Maxy, and I am not proud. But it was nothing she didn't know about," Holden replied. "There was no animosity between me and your mother—never was. Like I said, we were best friends. Right up to the end."

Max stared at his father. A wave of sadness engulfed him, hearing all of this about his mom. He desperately wanted to believe his mother had been happy, doing precisely what she wanted to with her one precious life.

"I told you Miss Sadie reminds me of Maren. But when I see you two together, I also see a lot of me in you, Max."

"That is not the compliment you think it is, Dad."

Holden chuckled. "Son, you work so hard to prove to the world you're nothing like your old man, but you truly aren't anything like me, outside of how we look. You never were. You're so much better than I ever was, Maximillian."

Max's breath caught as he worked to hold himself together.

"Now, here comes the advice. Take it or leave it, but I'm gonna give it," Holden said. "You can love someone who isn't perfect, and be deeply loved despite your own imperfections. You and Sadie may not always go together like peas and carrots, but that doesn't mean y'all don't have something worth fighting for."

Max sighed deeply. "What am I supposed to do? I don't know how to fix this, Dad. It's too late."

"Ah, it's never too late, Maxy. All you gotta do is write her the best damn love song you can."

Holden handed Max his notebook and pencil. "I know you need to get back to the studio, but why not sit a spell and write down what you're feelin'?"

After Holden left, Max set the notebook to the side and

pulled out his phone. First, he texted Bobbi, saying he was heading back to the studio shortly, and that she could count on him to see this through. Then he scrolled back through Bobbi's many texts until he got to the video she had sent a few weeks before while he was at the cabin. Of Sadie and Max performing "All I Want for Christmas." He pressed play.

26

Sadie

Nashville, Tennessee
December 23

As Sadie got out of the town car *Starmaker* had sent, she saw a few of those rare Nashville snowflakes swirl above her head. The Grand Ole Opry was even more lit up than usual, with hundreds of strings of Christmas lights crisscrossing its façade, and a massive Christmas tree out front shining and shimmering with festive baubles on every branch. She felt hopeful for some Christmas magic—but when she saw Amalia and Bobbi standing at the entrance of the building, underneath the thickest cedar garland she had ever seen, Sadie knew from the tense expressions that Max wasn't there yet. "He'll be here," was all Bobbi said before hurrying off.

Sadie's heart sank all the way down to the toes of the soft suede cowboy boots she was wearing. Still, she reached up to touch the tiny gold shamrock nose stud her gran had given her as a Christmas gift the year before and forced herself to keep on believing a little luck and Christmas magic would come her way.

"Come on," Amalia said, grabbing Sadie by the hand. "Now, listen to me, this sounds bad but we are going to take care of it." Sadie's heart sank even further, down to the Grand Ole Opry basement now, but she took a deep breath and listened to Amalia's news. "Cruz is saying you came onto him and he turned you down—so you fired him."

"*What?!*"

"I know. It's gross. But Cruz can't hurt you, okay? Right now, he's insisting Johnny King is ready to go with what Cruz says is going to be *the* next holiday classic—something called 'Christmas Train'?" Sadie just rolled her eyes. "But I've already met with the rest of the producers. We have a contract—and no matter what Cruz says, the network's top brass know the world wants to see Saxie and decide for themselves if what's between you is real or not. The ratings are projected to be massive—and it has nothing to do with Johnny King."

"Yes, but Max isn't here."

"He will be."

"How can you be so sure?"

For a moment, Sadie was sure she saw Amalia's confident expression falter—but then she patted Sadie on the back. "Don't be worrying about things you can't control, Sadie," was all she said. And Sadie couldn't help but smile because this was just the kind of advice Gran would have given her right then.

When they reached her dressing room, they both stopped short. "Drink that in," Amalia said. Sadie's name was on a plaque, surrounded by lights. Her breath caught as she looked up.

"*Wow.*"

"That's all you, Sadie. You did this. Never forget it. Your voice. *You.*" Amalia handed Sadie a slim package wrapped in shiny red paper. "A little Christmas gift for you," she said. "No one else needs to know what a big softie I am."

"I'm sorry I didn't get anything for you. I didn't do any Christmas shopping this year. Except for . . ."

Max. She and her mother had gone out to a Christmas market in SoBro the night before, and she had seen the perfect gift for Max. Sadie had had no idea if she would ever be able to give it to him—but she had bought it anyway. *Come on, Max, please, get here*, Sadie willed.

"Nonsense, you've been busy," Amalia said. "Come. Sit. This is nothing, really. Just a small token, something to remember tonight by."

Sadie sat in the chair in front of the mirror and ripped open the festive wrapping paper. These past few years had been a blur, but Sadie loved Christmas, loved giving and receiving gifts. She vowed that the following Christmas, no matter where she ended up, things would be different. She would never again get so wrapped up in her work that she didn't even go Christmas shopping for the people she cared about.

Inside the slim box was a tiny replica of the nameplate they had just been admiring on the door of her dressing room. "Now you'll never forget this night," Amalia said. Sadie had worked with Amalia for a long time, but had never felt truly close to her. Not until tonight, when Amalia suddenly felt like a safe port in a storm.

There was a tap on the dressing room door. Sadie's heart lifted for just a moment—but it wasn't Max.

It *was* a friendly face, though.

"Hugo!"

"Merry almost Christmas, my darling!" He had two garment bags over his arm, and he held them up one by one: a deep red jumpsuit with a plunging neckline and a green one with a high neck and a plunging back.

"The red," Amalia said. "Definitely the red. Sadie Hunter needs to show the world she is not messing around."

"She's right," Sadie said with a smile. "Let's go with the red."

"That's what I was hoping for," Hugo said with a grin. "Okay, I think you're due for sound check now, and by the time you get back, I'll be all set up with accessories. Lucia is doing your makeup and Neil is doing your hair. We are going to make you look like the star you are. So no nerves, okay? You've got this."

He handed Sadie a tissue, and she wiped her eyes and blew her nose.

"Thanks, Hugo."

"Any time at all, and I mean it."

Amalia was checking her watch. "Okay, time to get out there for sound check," she said.

She linked arms with Sadie and they headed back down the hall.

"Now, remember," Amalia said, just before they entered the hallowed auditorium. "No matter what happens, I've got your back. You're not alone. And trust me, I can handle Cruz."

Sadie stepped into the Great Hall—and was dismayed to see Cruz and Johnny King sitting on the stage together. Johnny was singing the sickly, familiar bars of the "Christmas Love Train" song she and Cruz had been working on together at the studio the day before. If nothing else, Sadie felt grateful she was never going to have to sing that terrible song again.

As Sadie made her way to the front of the room to take her rightful place on the stage, Amalia was right behind her.

"Cruz," she said in a firm, cold voice. "My client is here, and the stage is hers at the moment."

Cruz straightened up and checked his watch. "Actually, according to me, my client has the stage for another ten minutes. And then your client is welcome to it." He looked around theatrically. "Only, it won't be much use to her if her partner doesn't show up." As he said the word *partner* he caught Sadie's eye and for a moment her bones felt like they were turning to jelly. She could almost feel his grip again, how helpless she had felt as he forced himself on her.

Amalia stepped closer to Cruz. She wasn't a tall woman, but suddenly, she seemed it.

"Cruz, get the hell out of here," she said in the most venomous voice Sadie had ever heard her use. "You're making assumptions you should not be making about who will end up performing tonight, and you need to back off or face consequences. You are *a* producer of *Starmaker*, not *the* producer. Should I call Penny?"

For a moment, Cruz looked like he was going to argue with

Amalia—but then he backed off. He looked a bit scared, actually. It was incredibly satisfying to Sadie. He said something indecipherable to Johnny and the two of them stalked away.

When Cruz and Johnny were gone, Sadie sat down at the piano—and forced herself to try to settle down. She could feel stage fright and panic beginning to circle around her, looking for an opening.

"Amalia," she said in a whisper. "He's still not here. What if he doesn't come?"

"You just sit tight, okay? Act like you warming up alone is exactly how you two planned it. Let them mic you up when they need to and check the levels on your voice. I'll go find Bobbi."

When Amalia was gone, Sadie surveyed the auditorium. Crew members and tech bustled to and fro. No one was paying attention to her yet. She played a few bars of the song she had written for Max, then started to sing it with her eyes closed. When she opened her eyes, she didn't find the face she was looking for.

Instead, her mother was sitting in the front row.

Sadie jumped up. "Mom! What are you doing here? I thought you were coming later?"

She raced to her mom to hug her—the way she hadn't allowed herself to for so many years. She hadn't realized how much she needed her mom until she showed up.

"You often leave things unsaid—you got that from me." Lynn smiled. "But that doesn't mean the people who care about you most don't know exactly what you need. Now, as Gran would say, go on up there and make us proud," she said.

It was almost enough to bolster her and get her back up on

that stage to rehearse. But the spotlights had been turned on and were shining down on the empty stool where Max was supposed to sit. "I don't think he's coming tonight, Mom. I don't think my dream of singing at the Grand Ole Opry is going to come true after all."

"Look around you, Sadie. Where are you right now?"

"At the Grand Ole Opry."

"And what is that, up there on the stage?"

"A piano. Where are you going with this, Mom?"

"Who is that piano for? Is it for Johnny King? Because I don't think Johnny King actually knows how to play a piano. He can barely play a ukulele."

Sadie couldn't help but laugh. It was true. Johnny had persona and stage presence to spare, but his technical musical talents left something to be desired—which was probably why he was such a showboat. It was a distraction tactic.

"So, if you go up on that stage right now, and you play me your song, what does that mean?" Lynn asked Sadie. "What it means is that you, Sadie Jane Hunter, will have officially performed for an audience at the Grand Ole Opry. Isn't that right? Take it from me, life doesn't always play out the way you imagine it will. But that doesn't mean that what you do instead isn't worth anything."

Sadie glanced at the stage, at the piano up there waiting for *her*, then back at her mom. Could she really be happy with nothing but a rehearsal up on that hallowed stage?

"Sadie, I think it's time for you to start being proud of your-*self*. Now, get up there and do your thing. Don't let anyone—not Cruz, not Johnny, not even Max—take this moment away from you. It doesn't matter if it's not how you imagined it. What matters is that it's happening. It's real. You just have to work with what you have."

"You sound like Gran," Sadie said.

Lynn smiled. "Since she's been gone, I've noticed that more and more. Like she's with me—the way she promised she always would be."

"She promised me that, too," Sadie said softly. Then she and her mother looked around the huge room, and Sadie knew they both felt the same thing. It was hard to fully understand but it was there no less: the presence of a loved one they both needed very much.

"Off you go, Sadie. Make her proud."

Sadie went back up on the stage and sat down in front of the piano again.

She closed her eyes and she started to sing her song for Max again. But she also sang it for her mom. Maybe this *was* all she was going to get, a chance to perform for her mom at the Grand Ole Opry. But it suddenly felt like enough.

Halfway through the song, Sadie felt something. A shift in the air, like an electrical current. It made all the hairs on her arms stand on end.

All at once, she smelled cologne and cinnamon gum. She opened her eyes.

Max.

He was standing in front of her, his head tilted to one side, the way she knew he looked when he was really listening. There was so much to say, but it was all in her song—so she gazed into his eyes and kept right on singing. *"I loved you since the day we met. It was just I didn't know it yet. In this perfect world of me and you, baby, please won't you make my dreams of Christmas love come true?"*

Max joined her on the piano bench. He had his guitar with him and started to strum it. He wasn't playing along with her song, not quite. He was weaving a different song into hers, she realized, a song all his own and yet somehow it fit into hers perfectly. As Sadie sang and played she made space for him in her music the way she should have made space for him in her life. *"Baby, you're hot chocolate running through my veins,"* he sang. *"You're a runaway Christmas sleigh ride and I just can't hold the reins. Come on back, come to me, make my yuletide dreams come true—because, my love, the best Christmas gift is you."*

She felt breathless and elated when it was over—not just her song, but *their* song.

"We did it," she whispered. "We wrote a song."

Max leaned his guitar against the bench and reached for her. "We sure did, sweetheart." She leaned her head against his shoulder, then looked up at him. "I'm so sorry," he said. "I've been an absolute fool, not able to see past my own damn nose. I know you would never, ever have something going on with Cruz, and I swear, if that man comes near you again, I will—"

"It's okay, Max. I'm going to handle Cruz. Amalia and Bobbi are going to help me. It might not be easy, and I may need your help in the future." She reached up and touched his cheek. "Not by getting angry," she said with a sad smile. "Just by being there for me as I try to deal with the fallout of this. Just by never, ever letting me blame myself."

"I can do that, Sadie. Of course I can. Whatever you need."

"Cruz doesn't deserve one more moment of our time or energy, not today. But we'll keep dealing with it. Together, when that makes sense. And I accept your apology, Max. I understand why you would have made judgments about me that weren't always accurate. I never fully let you in, so you didn't *really* know me—not until now. And I judged you harshly, too. I'm sorry for that. I hope you can forgive me. And . . ."

What Sadie wanted to say next was going to take a lot of courage. While she hoped the lyrics of her song had made her feelings clear, she knew she had to stop leaving things unsaid. "I love you, Max. That's the truth. What we have has always been real to me. I want us to be together." As she spoke the words she saw his expression change—and was deeply relieved to see in his eyes that he felt the same.

"Sadie, I love you, too. More than you can possibly imagine." Max had never looked happier, and as he leaned in, he whispered, "I loved you since the moment I first laid eyes on you. I was just too dense to accept it." Then he kissed her passionately, his hands tangled in her hair, their lips speaking a private language only the two of them knew. For a magical moment, the rest of the world fell away. It was almost as if they were standing in the snow, in the middle of the Banff wilderness, just the two of them, their bodies pressed together.

"I have something for you," Sadie said, finally pulling away from the kiss and reaching into the pocket of her sweater. She'd been carrying the tiny tissue-wrapped package around with her like a talisman. Max unwrapped it: inside was a white gold Christmas ornament shaped like snowshoes.

"We were so happy there, together in Banff," Sadie whispered.

"We'll go back. We can be happy there again. We'll go as

soon as we've done everything we need to do here in Nashville."

"But we'll come back here, too?"

"Of course," Max said. "It never has to be all or nothing. Never again." He smiled down at the tiny pair of snowshoes, then tucked them in his pocket.

"Hey, is that your mom, sitting in the front row, there? She looks pretty happy."

Sadie smiled and waved at Lynn. "She *is* happy," Sadie said. "Because she's finally starting to understand—with my gran's help, I think—that I'm exactly where I need to be, right here, chasing my dreams. But I know it isn't going to be easy. And I won't take her for granted anymore. I know how much you wish your mom could be here to see you."

The sound techs had spotted Max and descended on them now. Their private moment was over, for now. But Sadie smiled, thinking about what was to come.

A s they strode out onto the stage, hand in hand, Sadie scanned the audience. She found many familiar faces: Lynn, flanked by Amalia and Bobbi, right in the front row. Tasha, sitting in the same row as her mother, mouthing, *Break a leg, songbird!* Tasha had popped into Sadie's dressing room earlier and Sadie had told her about the happy reunion. Her friend and mentor was thrilled—and had also alluded to the fact that Cruz McNeil was in the process of getting exactly what he deserved.

There was Holden, too, winking at Sadie like the shameless flirt he was, then saluting his son with a smile. Becca was sitting beside her father with her hands clasped over her belly, and Stan, Becca's partner, was in town for the holidays, too. Hugo was sitting near the front, his hand to his heart, mouthing, *You look absolutely gorgeous,* to Sadie. Claire was there, from the Song Sparrow, without whom Sadie's song would not have come to be.

Sadie found her mother's face once more. She touched the side of her nose and smiled.

Sadie took a deep breath and drank it all in. Max squeezed her hand and whispered, "Ready for this, sweetheart?"

"I've been ready for this my whole life, *sweetheart*," Sadie said, giving him a kiss that made the already excited crowd go wild.

They stepped forward and took their places. Sadie on the piano bench, Max on a stool beside her.

The crowd fell silent as Sadie and Max looked into each other's eyes. Sadie began to play the piano, and then Max joined in with his guitar. There were thousands of people in the audience, millions of people watching at home—but as Sadie and Max sang their song to one another, it felt like they were the only two people in the world. They traded lines back and forth, the words intertwining as if they had been written side by side.

When it was over, the audience stayed silent and Sadie experienced a beat of worry that maybe it hadn't gone over the way she and Max had wanted it to. Maybe the crowd just hadn't liked it. Maybe it was really just for them. But the sudden roar of applause was deafening. Most of the audience jumped to their feet to give Saxie a standing ovation. A jubilant Max pulled her from her piano bench and spun her around, then kissed her deeply as the crowd hooted and hollered for an encore.

"We did it!" Sadie said, throwing her arms around Max's neck. "I only wish we had something we could do for an encore."

Max smiled and said, "Darling, all the audience wants for an encore is *this*. I love you, Sadie Hunter," he said as he stared into her eyes.

"And I love you, Max Brody. All I want for Christmas is you."

At that, Max kissed her again, as their adoring fans—and the people who loved them most—cheered them on.

HotStarGossip.com

BREAKING #SAXIE NEWS: Happily Ever After!!!

Nashville's favorite duo has convinced us their love is real, just in time for Christmas!

All we wanted for Christmas this year was for Max Brody and Sadie Hunter to get back together and for Sadie to not really be secretly seeing the catfishing creep Cruz McNeil, but it's a cruel world out there and you don't always get what you want, right? Well, unless you recently moved to Mars (and even then, you probably saw the *Starmaker* holiday extravaganza) you know there has been Christmas romance and magic afoot in Nashville tonight!

Recent rumors of cheating hearts and an acrimonious breakup had us doubting the veracity of what we had all longed to believe was the feel-good romance of the year. But watching #Saxie sing the "The Best Christmas Gift" to each other live onstage at the Grand Ole Opry was enough to make even the most jaded among us believe in true love again. We were scared, though. Was it for real, or were we going to get our hearts broken again?

Maybe #Saxie understood we were feeling vulnerable, after all the uncertainty of recent days. Maybe the most captivating and impossibly good-looking couple in town knew we needed a grand gesture to make us truly believe they weren't just toying with our emotions.

Or maybe Christmas really *is* the most wonderful time of the year, when every wish can come true.

Here's how it went down: the final notes of #Saxie's spectacular Christmas love song faded out, and the two stars stared longingly into each other's eyes for a long moment. Then they shared a kiss that left us all feeling light-headed. If they were faking their emotions, they both deserve an Academy Award. Since it's Christmas Eve, we've decided to hell with it, we're going to choose to believe in this magical duo. Love is in the air, and it really is the most wonderful time of the year!

Next

Christmas . . .

Max & Sadie

Banff, Canada
December 21

C ould you pass me that bowl?" Sadie, holding a needle and thread in one hand, gestured with her other toward the cabin's kitchen, where a large ceramic bowl sat on the counter-top beside two cooling Kringle pastries.

Max brought it over to her, setting it on the coffee table. Then he grabbed a handful of the popcorn that filled the bowl and tossed it into his mouth.

"Hey! How am I going to make the popcorn chain for the tree if you keep eating it?"

He leaned down and kissed her, mumbling a "Sorry, love" around the popcorn in his mouth.

Patsy perked up when she saw the new bowl of popcorn. Sadie took two fluffy white kernels and set them in her palm, holding it out to the little dog—smiling all the while at Max, who tried his best to give her, and Patsy, a stern look.

"It's gluten free," Sadie reminded Max, still smiling as she tucked her gran's hand-knit throw blanket around her shoulders and began threading the popcorn again. The chain was growing in length—it stretched across Sadie's lap and coiled on the floor at her feet. She had been at it for about an hour while Max put up the decorations and Christmas lights on the outside of the cabin, the effect of which was festive against the crystal-like snow.

They were getting ready to host Christmas for their families—Lynn was flying from Milwaukee to Nashville later today to meet up with the Brody family, and then traveling along with Holden, Becca, her husband, Stanley, and Max's almost eight-month-old niece, Hattie, on Holden's private jet on Christmas Eve day.

The cabin had undergone some renovations during the summer months, to add a new section that could comfortably accommodate guests. But Max had made sure the main portion of the cabin remained the same—there were some things that should never change, and the memories of this cabin that Maren had loved so much were important to preserve.

"Did you see the new batch of Christmas cards? They came today," Sadie said.

"I did." Max had strung them on a piece of string along the kitchen island cabinet. One from Tasha, who had taken over as head judge on *Starmaker*, and had just wrapped up this season, and another from Landon, whom Max had helped to secure a job on Tasha's team, as her lead assistant. "Bobbi and Amalia sent baskets, too. Full of some Nashville treats they thought we might be missing this year."

"Already broke into those," Sadie said with a chuckle. But Max didn't respond. He was pacing the cabin's main room, checking and stoking the fire, adjusting the garland that went around the front door, the holly berries bright red against the deeply hued greenery, shifting one glass ball from one side of the tree to the other (for "balance," he said).

"Why don't you come and sit with me? Take a break? You can work on that sweater for Hattie?"

"I'm good," Max replied, giving her a quick smile before crouching in front of the Christmas tree, unnecessarily shifting the mountain of presents around.

Sadie watched all of this, using a thimble so she didn't prick her finger as she threaded the popcorn kernels, and wondered what was up with her boyfriend. They had been at the cabin for almost a week now, and he had become increasingly "busy" as the days counted down to Christmas.

For Max, having their families with them for the holidays meant everything. He had been planning it for months, starting with the cabin renovation and ending with so many decorations. Christmas ornaments hung on every tree branch, fresh garlands on every doorway. Max had knitted stockings for everyone—their names stitched at the top, ready for the candy and clementines and nuts and small gifts that would soon weigh them down. Twinkly lights hung from the ceiling in rows, making it look like stars when they turned off the cabin's lights. It had been a long time since Max had celebrated such a joyful Christmas, and he was determined to make this the best one yet, for all of them.

Sadie hadn't seen her mom in a few months and couldn't wait for her to arrive. It had been another busy year. Sadie and Max had spent the first part of it recording an album together, with a new producer Tasha had helped them secure: her name was Lex Robichaud and she was brilliant, possessed of a creative drive Sadie and Max were in awe of. And she was kind and collaborative—absolutely nothing like Cruz McNeil.

The album—called *Three Cords and the Truth*—was full of the steamy love songs Saxie was known for, plus had some fun, upbeat tracks to round it out. Once it had released, Sadie and Max went on tour to promote it, visiting their favorite cities in North America and a few in Europe. The tour had recently ended, and they were taking a few weeks in Banff to relax before heading back into the studio to record their own solo albums in the new year.

They had assured their legions of fans that this was not a sign they were over, but rather an important step for their relationship. They supported one another and their separate career dreams—but they'd be back in the studio together once more in another year or two. And meanwhile, they had recorded another holiday song. Sadie was delighted at how different it was from "Christmas Love Train," the song she had worked on with Cruz, thanking her lucky stars that all that was far behind her.

Cruz McNeil had threatened to battle Sadie in court for the songs she had recorded at his studio—but on Tasha's advice, Sadie had decided to fight him in a different way, making the decision to rerecord the songs herself, with a new producer. She was considering using Lex, but Dave Cobb and Simon Jennings—who produced Brandi Carlile—were also interested, and all Sadie knew right now was that her future in the music industry was bright. Max's, too: he had been slowly working away on his own collection of solo songs and would be choosing a producer soon.

"So, hey, did you hear back from Allen yet?" Sadie asked Max, putting down her needle and thread and wondering if this was what was behind his apparent sudden case of nerves. Allen Reynolds, Garth Brooks's producer, had taken a meeting with Max before they left for Banff, and Sadie knew how hopeful Max felt about it.

At this, Max grinned. "I was saving that piece of news for later. He listened to my demo and he loves it. Sounds like a sure thing for the new year."

Sadie pushed the popcorn aside and jumped up, crossing the room to give Max a congratulatory kiss. Working with producers like Lex had helped them put all the ugliness of working with Cruz McNeil behind them, and they were looking forward to expanding their horizons even more. It seemed a lot of other artists in Nashville were doing the same. As Holden had predicted, Cruz was finished in Nashville, due to Becca's exposé. Other women had come forward, some of them established musicians and some of them contestants on *Starmaker*. These stories had been the final nails in the producer's professional coffin. No one trusted him anymore, and for good reason.

Sadie took Max's hands in hers. "Come on. A little break."

Max allowed Sadie to pull him to the couch. "You know I'm putty in your hands," he said with a smile, marveling at her and feeling damn lucky to be by her side. Not just on the stage now, but in life, too. It was sometimes hard to believe how much had changed for them in a year. Around this time a year before it seemed that happiness of any sort was out of reach for Max and Sadie. But here they were.

"So, just tell me," Sadie said when they were settled on the couch. "If it's not waiting to hear from Allen, what's got you so hot and bothered?" She lay a hand on Max's cheek. He had a beard again—which, it turned out, Sadie quite liked.

"I just want everything to be perfect," he replied. "For your mom, and my family. I really hope we can make this an annual tradition, you know?"

"Everything *is* perfect," Sadie said, smiling. Then she gestured around the room. "Look at this place! It's a Christmas wonderland."

"More like Christmas threw up in here." Max laughed, noting how not a single surface of the cabin had escaped his decorating frenzy.

"It's *perfect*," Sadie reiterated, holding his gaze. They leaned toward one another, sharing a kiss, and then they broke apart suddenly, staring at each other with wide eyes.

Max grinned. "It's on!" The radio—a twenty-four-hour Christmas music channel—was playing their newly released holiday song.

"Our first time hearing it together," Sadie said.

"When the snow starts a-fallin' . . . " Max's voice rang out from the radio speakers, and Sadie excitedly grabbed his hands.

"And you come a-callin' . . . " Sadie sang her line now, in time with the song, and she and Max continued singing to one another in the cabin, their voices as magical together as they ever had been.

Then the song finished, and the DJ said, "That was Max

Brody and Sadie Hunter's latest Christmas song, 'It's Snowing in Nashville,' and we have to say, this one is destined to be a classic. Those two just keep getting better, don't you all agree?"

"I agree," Max said gruffly. He held Sadie's hands tightly, then cleared his throat—which was locking up on him all of a sudden.

"You okay?" Sadie asked, concerned. "You aren't getting sick, are you?"

"I'm fine," he replied. "But I need to ask you something. And I wanted to do it before everyone got here. So we could, you know, be just the two of us."

"Okay . . ." Sadie replied, looking confused.

Then Max suddenly let go of her hands, and in one swift motion dropped to one knee in front of Sadie.

"Is this really happening?" Sadie whispered.

"Sadie Hunter, damn, I didn't see you comin'," Max started, then cringed when he realized he had cursed. No matter. It was coming from the heart, and Max's heart was bursting with so many things he wanted to say, he wasn't sure he could get them out without fumbling.

"You have pushed me, challenged me, pissed me off on more than one occasion." She laughed then, and so did Max. "But you also have made me a better man, a better person. Everything I am today, everything I have today, is because of you."

Sadie had tears in her eyes now, and her heart beat furiously—she pressed a hand to her chest to try to calm it.

Max reached around to his back pocket and pulled out a ring—a large pear-shaped solitaire resting on a thin gold band. It glittered with the twinkle lights overhead, and Sadie thought it was the most beautiful ring she had ever seen.

"It's a Canadian diamond," Max said, grinning at her. "Conflict free, too."

She nodded but couldn't speak. Sadie could barely catch her breath.

He held out the ring, then took her hand in his free one. Sadie could feel the slight shake of his hand, and squeezed tightly to tell him she was feeling all the same things he was right then.

"Sadie Hunter, we make beautiful music together, but will you do me the honor—and damn, sweetheart, it would be the greatest honor—of becoming my partner in this crazy life of ours?"

"Yes," Sadie breathed out, using every last bit of air she had to do so. Then she took a breath and said, "Yes, yes, yes!"

"So, it's a yes?" Max asked, smiling at her, tears in his eyes.

She threw herself into him, the both of them tumbling to the soft rug. Sadie was on top of Max, and he let out a tiny groan when he hit the ground.

"Are you okay? I'm sorry!" Sadie said, pushing herself up on her hands to take her weight off Max.

"Are you kidding me?" Max replied, chuckling. "I have never—*ever*—been better, darlin'."

Then he reached for her left hand, and she held out her fingers so Max could slide the ring on. "It fits perfectly," he said, his voice soft and low.

"Just like us," Sadie replied. Then something caught her eye out the window. "Hey, it's snowing!"

Max turned to look, and smiled when he saw the fat snowflakes coming down steadily outside the cabin's window. "I arranged that," he said, giving a shrug.

"Did you now?" Sadie replied, grinning at him. "Max Brody, what am I going to do with you?"

"I can think of a few things," Max said.

"I love you," she said.

"I love you more," Max replied, then he took her face in his hands and gently pulled her to him, kissing her.

The popcorn chain would remain unfinished until much later, the cabin sinking into darkness as the daytime light faded, allowing for the glow of holiday lights and the fire embers to be the only thing illuminating the room. But Max and Sadie barely noticed, lost in one another, ready for a future they had only dreamed about.

ACKNOWLEDGMENTS

When we started writing as Maggie Knox, we had one wish: to have fun! Okay, we had two wishes . . . to have fun *and* to create romantic, sweet, and entertaining reads best enjoyed with a glass of holiday nog (Karma) and a decadent square of fudge (Marissa). We wrote these books through the pandemic, through personal struggles, while we were on deadline for our own novels . . . and somehow, we did it. As such, we are grateful for happy endings, and for those listed below, who helped fill our metaphorical stockings with gifts of love and support.

Dear readers, here's our "Nice List":

The Agents, Carolyn Forde and Samantha Haywood, who are our beacons and anchors, along with the rest of the team at Transatlantic Agency.

The Editors, Tara Singh-Carlson, Deborah Sun de la Cruz, Amy Batley. This is a dream team, and we know it.

The Publishers, Putnam, Penguin Random House Canada, Hodder. From cover design (thank you, Sanny Chiu!) to copy editing (our gratitude to the eagle-eyed Lara Robbins) to promotion, we are a lucky pair of authors. We're especially grateful to Ashley Di Dio, Katie McKee, Ellie Schaffer, Emily Mlynek, Samantha Bryant, Ruta Liormonas, Beth Cockeram, and Dan French for all the behind-the-scenes work and enthusiasm.

The Coven, who are always there from the beginning, with pompoms, wisdom, and friendship.

The Writers and others who generously read early drafts, offered kind words, and continuously offer support. Especially to Jaime Sarrio for the Nashville expertise, Lori Boudreau for the travel photos and inspiration, and Amy E. Reichert for her Midwestern tips (Kringle is amazing, friends).

The Readers, who posted amazing photos and reviews, and helped Maggie Knox become a bestseller.

The Pets, Fred and Oscar, for warming our feet and hearts while we wrote.

The Families, who make everything sweeter, and who deserve to get everything on their wish lists for putting up with us when we're on a deadline.

Finally, each other.

Love,

M & K

Photo of Karma Brown by Jenna Davis · Photo of Marissa Stapley by Eugene Choi

MAGGIE KNOX is the pen name for bestselling Canadian writing duo Karma Brown and Marissa Stapley. Brown is an award-winning journalist and bestselling author of five novels, including the #1 national bestseller *Recipe for a Perfect Wife*, as well as the nonfiction bestseller *The 4% Fix: How One Hour Can Change Your Life*. Her writing has appeared in publications such as *Self*, *Redbook*, *Today's Parent*, and *Chatelaine*. She lives just outside Toronto with her family and a labradoodle named Fred. Stapley is a former magazine editor and *New York Times* bestselling author of Reese's Book Club Pick *Lucky*, as well as international bestsellers *Mating for Life*, *Things to Do When It's Raining*, and *The Last Resort*. Many of her novels have been optioned for television. She lives in Toronto with her family and a precocious black cat named Oscar. *The Holiday Swap* was their first novel writing together as Maggie Knox and is a Canadian bestseller.

VISIT MAGGIE KNOX ONLINE

MarissaStapley.com
KarmaKBrown.com
🐦 @MaggieKnoxBooks
📷 @MaggieKnoxAuthor

Bookends

When one book ends, another begins...

Bookends is a vibrant new reading community to help you ensure you're never without a good book.

You'll find exclusive previews of the brilliant new books from your favourite authors as well as exciting debuts and past classics. Read our blog, check out our recommendations for your reading group, enter great competitions and much more!

Visit our website to see which great books we're recommending this month.

Join the Bookends community:
www.welcometobookends.co.uk

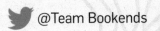 @Team Bookends   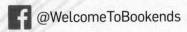 @WelcomeToBookends